THE BODY IN THE BOOKSTORE

ELLIE ALEXANDER

Storm
PUBLISHING

To request permissions, contact the publisher at rights@stormpublishing.co

Ebook ISBN: 978-1-80508-407-5
Paperback ISBN: 978-1-80508-409-9

Cover design: Dawn Adams
Cover images: Dawn Adams

Published by Storm Publishing.
For further information, visit:
www.stormpublishing.co

ALSO BY ELLIE ALEXANDER

A Murder at the Movies

I dedicate this story to bookstores everywhere. Thank you for connecting books and readers, being a safe haven for the bookish, and keeping the magic of reading alive.

ONE

When your best friend is murdered, it can be kind of hard to get over.

At what point does the search for justice, the need to right a wrong, turn into an obsession? I had no idea, but it was a question I had pondered for years, ever since that fateful June afternoon when campus was awash in blooming dogwoods, sherbet-colored roses, and the promise of everything to come. A day that repeated again and again, like the lyrics to an annoying song stuck in your head. The day that Scarlet died.

"Annie, Annie, did you hear me?"

I was staring intently at my laptop screen when I caught movement out of the corner of my eye and my heart leaped into my throat. I let out a small gasp and turned to see Fletcher standing in the doorway to the office.

"Sorry, I didn't mean to startle you." Fletcher stepped closer to the desk, hovering with an apologetic smile, his eyes glancing toward the computer screen.

"It's okay." I shut my laptop, and Scarlet's smiling face vanished from view, just like it had in real life. I wasn't sure what had prompted me to open her file this time, but it was probably a good thing that Fletcher had interrupted my reverie. Reviewing the extensive spreadsheets I used to track every detail and lead I'd ever found on Scarlet's murder wasn't exactly a healthy obsession. I'd spent the better part of a decade squinting at tiny Excel columns, still no closer to the truth. The worst thing was that every time I opened my laptop, it was as if I expected *this* would be the day when something in one of the columns would jump out and the truth would reveal itself.

Of course, today wasn't that day.

"What's up?" I asked, turning toward Fletcher and stuffing the laptop in my bag. Hopefully, he hadn't seen the screen. I didn't want to talk about Scarlet, and Fletcher was just the kind of nice guy who would ask.

My workmate was a few years older than me with a tall, wiry body and a tendency to wear tweed despite our balmy and mild Northern Californian climate. He would have blended in beautifully in Edwardian England. He belonged in a different time, but at least he'd found his calling at the Secret Bookcase. Whenever a customer purchased *The Hound of the Baskervilles* or *A Study in Scarlet*, Fletcher would give them a dissertation on Sir Arthur Conan Doyle's background as a physician, explaining how he'd originally studied medicine and how this expertise worked its way into his novels in the form of Sherlock's sidekick, Dr. Watson. Or he'd detail enthusiastically Conan Doyle's interest in spiritualism and the paranormal, and how his fascination with mediums and seances spilled into his writing. So enthusiastically that I'd have to cheerily intervene to allow the customer to leave the store and get on with the rest of their day. Most of the time, though, Fletcher's extensive knowledge and adoration of Sherlock led customers to return days later for more recommendations. He had an uncanny knack for pairing every novel in the canon with the right reader, an unparalleled skill that I admired hugely.

"Hal's looking for you." Fletcher adjusted his houndstooth

bow tie and pointed to the stairwell. "That author is here for her signing."

"Already?" I glanced at the clock on the wall above a sagging bookshelf crammed with hundreds of dusty advance reader copies, before mentally kicking myself for the millionth time. The battery was as old as the Secret Bookcase and the clock's hands were permanently fixed at nine a.m. "She's not supposed to be here until five."

"It's five fifteen." Fletcher tapped his wrist. "You've been up here for over three hours."

Really? "Shoot." Whenever I revisited Scarlet's murder, hours evaporated like raindrops on a hot July afternoon. How was it already time for the author event? I jumped to my feet. "Sorry, I guess I lost track of time." I smoothed my wrinkled skirt and slid on my clogs, then turned to face the gold-framed mirror hanging above the desk. Strands of my hair frizzed out from my ponytail, the result of a habit of nervous twirling that I'd been trying unsuccessfully to break. I smoothed them down and fixed my short ponytail. My hair is a reddish brown with natural auburn highlights, which usually complements my skin tone, but after hours of staring at a blue screen, my face looked sallow and pale. I pinched my cheeks, hoping to bring back some life beneath my freckles.

"I've got bad news, Annie. There's not a single person down there," Fletcher said, grimacing and propping the door open with his foot. "It's bleak."

I sighed. "What else is new?" When Hal Christie offered me the job of bookseller and event coordinator at the Secret Bookcase eight years ago, I jumped at it. I planned to tuck in with hundreds of detective novels, hide inside their musty, yellowing pages, and try to put the tragedy of my past behind me, which is basically what I'd done. I just never imagined that I'd still be here nearly a decade later. Not that I regretted a minute of my time in the sweet, small town I had come to love so dearly. Redwood Grove had become my home, with its sun-drenched California summers, towering eucalyptus and bay leaf trees, and curiously kind community of friends and neighbors who'd welcomed me with open arms.

Lately, though, I'd wondered what I had to show for these years. And the answer I kept coming back to was not much. I was enthusiastic about author events, but even I had to admit they were dying a slow, painful death, bleeding out by a thousand tiny paper cuts. I'd tried offering snacks and wine, special discounts, and bringing in as many big-name authors as possible, but had to face reality: a boutique Agatha Christie-inspired mystery bookshop in a small town way off the beaten path in Redwood Grove, California, wasn't exactly a draw. Readers had too many other distractions these days, and the days of big-budget book tours were over. And if Fletcher and I couldn't come up with fresh ideas to breathe some new life into the niche bookstore we both loved so dearly, our days were numbered.

The thought made me ill. I felt a duty to Hal, too, who was more than a boss to his staff, and who had created this unique and lovely place. There had to be something—anything—we could do to drum up more business.

"Well, wish me luck," I said to Fletcher, dragging my teeth over my bottom lip and crossing my fingers. "Someone will certainly show up, right?"

Fletcher rocked on his heels and pretended to study me with newfound interest before cracking a smile. "As Sherlock might say, regrettably, my dear Annie, I'm afraid that conclusion is most erroneous."

"I know, I know, don't remind me." I curled my bottom lip and brushed a smudge from my glasses. "I'll think of something. I'll pull people in from the street if I have to."

I took the stairs two at a time. The floorboards creaked as I breezed past the gallery of framed vintage Christie book covers lining the wood-paneled walls. The Secret Bookcase needed an influx of customers. It was a shame that so few book lovers got to experience the bookstore's quirky charm.

Hal had spent decades converting this old manor house into a mystery lovers' paradise. The Study was a quiet, isolated space with a fireplace and antique writing desk typically commandeered by aspiring writers and college students who hung out for hours sipping copious amounts of coffee and pounding away on their keyboards. Cozy books, assorted teas, and candles could be found in the Sitting Room, along with comfortable armchairs and floral wallpaper resembling Miss Marple's home in St. Mary Mead. Poirot fans were known to linger in the Parlor, which captured the Art Deco atmosphere and the famed detective's meticulous eye for detail. There was the Mary Westmacott Nook for romance readers, the Dig Corner with a tent for children's books, and the Library styled after a classic English library. My favorite spot was the Terrace, an outdoor patio with lush potted flowers, sunny benches, and fresh air.

You could spend hours meandering from room to room, getting lost amongst the stacks, discovering rare copies of books long out of print, barely scratching the surface of Hal's extensive collection of mysteries.

I took the stairwell that would have originally been used by servants a century ago and burst out into the foyer. I sprinted past the cash register and raced to meet my author, who was waiting behind the podium in the Conservatory, the space we reserved for events and signings, which had originally been a ballroom. Hal had preserved the parquet floors and mint-green walls with gilded gold-leaf trim and hand-painted murals. Massive arched windows with intricate stained-glass patterns and tiered crystal chandeliers flooded the room with light.

Usually, I loved the elegant room, but all I could focus on was the fifty empty chairs sitting in neat rows, waiting expectantly to be filled. I glanced around, hoping there might be a handful of browsing customers I could encourage to fill seats, but the shop was ghostly quiet.

"Welcome, I'm Annie Murray," I said, extending a sweaty hand in a greeting. "Thank you so much for coming. We are absolutely delighted to have you, and I'm sure this room will be packed in no time." I couldn't believe it wasn't. I had advertised the event for weeks with promotions on social media, fliers posted around town, and articles in our local newspaper, the *Redwood Grove Gazette*. Given the author's extensive backlist, I'd been optimistic that we might have a packed house. I knew it was a stretch, but I never would have anticipated that no one would show.

The author forced a smile.

"Let me run and make an announcement on our speaker system." I could hear my words rushing together, a nervous habit. I had to fix this. "Can I get you anything in the meantime? Water? Coffee? A glass of wine? I know where Hal keeps a bottle of expensive Scotch if you want something a bit stronger before you talk."

She shook her head and swept her hand toward the empty room. "Talk? To whom?"

I gnawed the inside of my cheek, desperately trying to think of ways to salvage the situation and find an audience fast. I refused to accept that no one had come for her signing.

"I'm sure that readers will start to trickle in," I said with a forced cheerfulness. "It's hard on weeknights with people getting off work. I know your publicist mentioned you have a flight to catch later in San Francisco, and we really do appreciate you making a stop. We've been promoting your talk on social, and I have a bunch of pre-orders for you to sign. Plus, I'll set out wine and cookies—that always draws shoppers in."

"No need to go to any extra effort. It's not your fault," she acquiesced, sitting in the front row. "It's not just you. My in-store signings have been sparsely populated this entire tour. You're one of the only mystery bookstores left and, from the looks of things, not long for this world."

She wasn't wrong. Liam Donovan, the owner of the Stag Head down the lane, had been badgering Hal to sell the store so he could relocate his pub and turn it into a full-scale restaurant with guest rooms upstairs. Hal had resisted, but for how much longer could he hold out? He would never admit that he was worried, but it didn't take a seasoned detective to pick up on his long sighs when reviewing the end-of-day sales totals or how his shoulders would sag when the bookstore would be empty for hours on end.

I tried to squash the swirling feeling of nerves in my stomach. I just wished there was something I could do to turn things around.

"Everyone wants a hook these days," the author continued, sounding understandably annoyed. "An immersive experience. Wine pairings with a reading, giveaways, and podcasts. It's endless. Can you believe my publicist suggested trying to attract more readers by offering clues for them to solve? She told me I should write a miniature mystery, print it on special paper, and invite readers to figure out whodunit. Can you imagine? As if I'm supposed to know anything about marketing. I wrote the book. Isn't that enough?"

I wasn't sure it was a rhetorical question.

"It should be," I agreed, trying to give her a sympathetic smile. "There's just so much noise these days; it's hard to break through. Although that is a clever idea." A miniature mystery written by an author sounded like the stuff of my childhood dreams. The hint of an idea began to take hold. What if there was something to that? Could we entice more readers into the store with an interactive mystery they had to solve? Perhaps we could hide clues in different rooms or behind the secret bookcase in the Sitting Room. A thrill went through me as my imagination sparked with possibilities.

"I write books. I don't do gimmicks," she scoffed, putting a decisive end to the conversation.

"Right." I nodded. "Like I said, let me make an announcement and get some readers in the room."

I managed to scrounge up three timid customers to fill seats with the promise of deep discounts on their purchases and complimentary cookies and wine. The event was a bust, but for some reason the author's comment wouldn't leave my head as I listened to her read passages from her latest release and answer questions.

My foot tapped the floor as I imagined what might be possible. If I was going to save the Secret Bookcase, we needed something fresh. Something original.

Chardonnay and shortbread weren't enough anymore.

Once my brain latched on to a puzzle, it had to solve it, for better or worse. It was one of the many reasons I couldn't let Scarlet's murder go. Now I had a new challenge and I was buzzing with ideas on how to unlock it—could I create an event of epic proportions to save the bookstore and celebrate everything I loved about Redwood Grove?

TWO

After we'd put away the chairs and stacked the signed copies in the window, I poured two tiny glasses of the untouched wine and waved Fletcher over.

He gave me a grin as he took the glass from me. "Are we toasting something, Annie? Because I don't think that was an event to celebrate."

I shook my head, acknowledging the abysmal turnout. I was glad Hal wasn't working tonight to see it. "Tonight was a disaster, but it did get me thinking... We love this place. We have to do something to save the bookstore. You agree on that, right?"

"I don't know if I like the sound of *we*." He swirled his wine glass, examining it like he was studying to become a sommelier, and winked. "No, joking aside, I will do whatever is necessary to remain in steady employment. What's your plan?"

"I don't know yet." I tapped my forehead with the tip of my finger, willing myself to come up with something clever. "My brain is working overtime. It has to be something more than this." I swept my hand across the empty ballroom. The Secret Bookcase wasn't a cookie-cutter bookstore. It was equal parts bookshop and living museum. People should see this. Readers should be curled up on the soft benches next to the massive windows, taking in the pastoral views of the open grassy field surrounding the bookstore.

"Are you thinking more cerebral? Lectures on Sherlock or the classics, perhaps? I'd be happy to offer my services for that." Fletcher discovered a discarded paper napkin tucked beneath one of the plush chairs. He picked it up with the tips of his index finger and thumb and tossed it in the trash like it was a biohazard.

"I don't know. It has to be unique and geared toward younger readers, too." I finished the last sips of wine and helped Fletcher stack the unused folding chairs in the storage room. "The author mentioned her publicist had suggested she needs a hook to get readers to show up for signings. That's what we need—a hook."

"I can introduce you to the coat rack in the foyer. It has ample hooks," he replied with a cheeky grin.

I rolled my eyes. "That's bad, even for you."

"What say you, Annie? The night is still young. Shall we continue this brainstorming session? I'd suggest State of Mind Public House, but they're closed tonight, so it will have to be the Stag Head if you're up for it?" Fletcher asked. He tried to sound casual, but his eager eyes were a dead giveaway that he was lonely and hoping for company.

Fletcher was a good friend and I'd come to appreciate his quirks—like his massive collection of Sherlockian memorabilia that took up half of our shared office. However, after a long day in the bookstore, socializing with him wasn't exactly at the top of my list. It wasn't that I didn't enjoy hanging out with Fletcher. It was just that he could spend the better part of an hour offering a lecture on Sir Arthur Conan Doyle's years at the University of Edinburgh Medical School, and I wasn't sure I had the energy for a deep dive into Sherlockian lore.

But I was hardly one to judge when it came to obsessions,

and I felt like the solution to our problems at the bookstore was within my grasp, so I agreed. "Sure, but I only have time for a quick drink. I promised Pri I'd meet her for dinner."

"A drink it is." He circled his hand like he was rolling out a red carpet for me and waited for me to go in front of him.

We locked the bookstore and took the pressed gravel pathway from the manor house to the town square. One of the challenges of getting customers inside the Secret Bookcase was foot traffic. The estate sat at the end of the single-lane drive. Cute, bookish signs posted at the gateway pointed readers our way, but they weren't enough to draw tourists off Cedar Avenue, the main street that ran through town.

In town, the sinking sun illuminated red-tiled roofs and gave the buildings lining the square a fiery hue. As always, the town's prettiness took my breath away and reminded me again how much I loved the place.

I couldn't leave Redwood Grove. Where else would I go?

We had to figure out a way to save the shop.

My mind couldn't let it go as we neared the Stag Head at the edge of the square across from the park. The pub was housed in a single-story brick building painted white and then intentionally distressed to give the building a weathered look. A wooden hand-painted sign depicting a stag's head hung above the door.

Inside, the rustic vibe continued with old, creaky wooden floors and whitewashed wood paneling dotted with cardboard cutouts of stag heads, like a crafter's hunting trophy display. The bar had bare bulbs hanging over the hand-carved wood, casting a mix of shadows and light throughout the room. Historical trivia and board games were stacked on heavy oak shelves. Framed black-and-white photos of Redwood Grove throughout the decades were interspersed amongst the deer heads. The vibe was warm and comfortable; the pub could have been my favorite spot in town, but it was owned and managed by Liam Donovan, my least favorite person in Redwood Grove.

We found a free table in the middle of the busy pub, next to a group playing what appeared to be a very involved World War II board game.

"Shall I get you a drink?" Fletcher offered, waiting with his hands folded together while I studied the menu.

Unfortunately, my eyes landed on Liam, pouring shots behind the bar like he was being filmed for an artsy indie film. He held a stainless-steel shaker above his head and waved it like a tambourine, showing off his muscular frame and the sleeves of tattoos on both his arms.

Liam was a few years older than me with dark wavy hair, matching dark eyes. He could have been attractive if it wasn't for his highly disagreeable personality.

He tilted his head and met my gaze with a slight raise of his eyebrows. Then he poured a shot into a cocktail shaker and twisted it to the rhythm of the country music playing overhead.

My neck felt hot. I put my hand on my chest and concentrated on the menu. "I'll have a glass of the Chardonnay."

"Your wish is my command." Fletcher bowed and strolled up to the bar.

I got us the empty table and tried to avoid Liam's steely eyes while I waited for Fletcher to return. Liam always managed to find a way to get under my skin, usually by making passive-aggressive comments about my love of crime fiction. He was a history buff who exclusively read non-fiction as if that somehow made him superior.

Fletcher came back empty-handed. "Liam offered to deliver our drinks. What a guy." He made a face and rolled his eyes. Fletcher had about as much love for Liam as me, thanks to Liam's unashamed interest in the bookstore as real estate.

I shushed Fletcher as Liam approached.

"There's no mystery in your drink orders." He set a glass of wine with a very generous pour in front of me. "Annie."

"Thanks." I kept my gaze glued to the table.

"And, Fletch, I presume this whisky sour is for you." Liam handed him a chilled glass with a lemon twist and a fresh sprig of rosemary.

"It's Fletcher," Fletcher mumbled through clenched teeth as he took the drink from him.

"Sorry, habit." Liam clapped him on the shoulder. "What brings the bookish crew in tonight?"

Fletcher lifted the drink to his lips and motioned to me. "Annie has a great idea for a new event."

I wanted to kick him under the table. Fletcher might think that he was helping, but he wasn't.

"Really, what kind of an event?" Liam brushed his hands on the black apron tied around his waist and looked at me with newfound interest.

Was he pretending to care? Doubtful. Liam only cared about himself.

"We're brainstorming. Nothing is fleshed out yet." I hoped that would get him to stop asking questions and leave us alone. Whenever Liam was around, I could feel my blood pressure spike.

"*Fleshed out.* You always have to find a way to work in a pun, don't you?" Liam shook his head and smirked.

I couldn't tell if he was trying to be funny or just mean. Either way, I didn't need his input.

"We could partner with you," Fletcher suggested, holding his whisky sour at his lips. "Maybe a books and brews night."

"I think that's probably a better match for State of Mind Public House," Liam said, not even bothering to entertain the idea. "I'll let you two get to the brainstorming. Good luck." He shot me a brief look I couldn't decipher and left.

"Why would you suggest he participate in whatever we

come up with?" I hissed when Liam was out of earshot. "He's so condescending about fiction, especially mysteries."

"I don't know. Keep your enemies close, I guess. I thought maybe if he participated, he'd see how cool the bookstore is, but I'm kidding myself. He's a guy's guy, if you know what I mean?"

"No. What do you mean?" I tried not to look in Liam's direction but could feel his eyes lasered on me.

"He's into history. The man hosts a Roman Empire trivia night; you know his type." Fletcher ran a bony finger along the rim of his glass. "I understand that he's not a hunter, and we live in progressive Northern California, but put Liam in Montana or Wyoming, and those cardboard stags on the wall could easily be his taxidermy trophies. He makes me feel like I need to revisit my masculinity."

I chuckled. "Revisit your masculinity? Oh, no, please don't do that, Fletcher, especially for Liam Donovan. The guy takes pleasure in making everyone around him feel inferior. It's not just you."

"You think?" He grinned and flexed a thin arm. "And miss out on these guns?"

"I'm sure of it." I reached across the table and patted his hand. "Fletcher, you're a good guy. Don't change that."

He cleared his throat and dabbed his chin with a bar napkin. "Thanks, that means a lot coming from you."

"That's what friends are for. Now, let's think about what kind of an event we can host at the bookstore." Hearing Fletcher ask Liam about partnering had given me a new thought. "What about a mystery festival?" I blurted out, almost surprised at the words as I said them.

Fletcher raised an eyebrow. "A festival, hmmm. Tell me more."

I wasn't sure I knew yet, but my brain spun with possibilities. Maybe there was a way we could bring an entirely new tourist to Redwood Grove, not just for the bookstore but for the business community as a whole.

"Okay, let me think this out." I took a long sip of the buttery Chardonnay. If I could get Fletcher to buy in, I knew we could convince Hal. "What if it's a completely immersive Redwood Grove Mystery Fest? Readers from all over the region will come if we brand Redwood Grove as the cutest, coziest mystery town on the entire West Coast. I don't think we'll get any pushback from Hal if we tell him our goal is to make Redwood Grove the St. Mary Mead of the US."

"Annie, how much wine have you consumed?" Fletcher gave me a sideways glance and shifted his glass to his other hand. "That sounds like a huge undertaking. You're talking about getting everyone in town to participate. That could be a lot of work."

"I know. I understand that, but I'm serious that we need something more than your average book signing. Listen, we have to do something to save the bookshop. Hal is the best, but let's face it, he can barely figure out how to turn on his phone. He's content to curl up with his Golden Age biographies and a cup of tea. He's slowing down, Fletcher." I paused, thinking about how recently Hal had been complaining more about his creaky knees and the drafty glass-paned windows keeping him cold at night upstairs in his apartment above the store. "At some point, he's going to retire. If the store isn't making a profit, he will sell the estate. What other choice will he have? A big event could bring some new blood into town."

"New blood. I see what you did there—clever, clever." He laughed and raised his cocktail in a toast.

"What if the Secret Bookcase is the central spot for the festival?" I strummed my fingers on the rim of my glass, feeling my energy pick up. "We can have a variety of author talks and signings. I'm sure the library will help, too. I could craft a puzzle for readers to solve. We could hide clues around the village square. Then, if we could get the shops and restaurants in town involved, they could come up with mysterious food and drink pairings. I'm thinking a pub crawl meets a book festival. Skull lattes at Cryptic Coffee, Hercule's Hops at the Public House, author panels, and pop-ups all over town."

"Okay, okay. I'm feeling you." Fletcher's pale blue eyes shimmered with a hint of excitement. "Tell me more; I'm listening."

"Um." I paused and dragged my teeth over my bottom lip. I hadn't fully formed a vision for what the festival might include yet. "Uh, let's see... maybe we can convince the theater to put on a production of *The Mousetrap*; Hal would love that. If we go all in on Agatha, he'll be on board for sure."

The idea was picking up steam. Yes, this is what we needed. This could breathe new life into the Secret Bookcase. My mind spun with possibilities.

"Yeah. What about a Marple or Poirot film fest?" Fletcher suggested.

"Or both."

"I'll drink to that." He clinked his glass to mine and then polished off the last sip of his whisky. "Can I get you another? I don't think I've had a chance to tell you about the new Dr. Watson documentary I watched last weekend. It was absolutely riveting."

I gave him a regretful smile. "Thanks, but no. As I mentioned, I promised Pri I would swing by after work," I reminded him, setting my empty glass on the table. "I'll keep thinking about the idea. You do the same, and we can pitch the idea to Hal in the morning."

"You know my methods." Fletcher gestured with one hand. "By first light, I'll have stacks of case notes for your consideration and anything else you desire."

He didn't need to go to any extra effort, but I knew it wasn't worth trying to dissuade him. I grabbed my things and headed outside. I couldn't plan an event of this scale and magnitude without help, and I knew that once Fletcher's imagination caught hold of the concept of a mystery festival, he would champion the idea.

I dearly hoped for Fletcher that a fellow Sherlockian would wander into the bookshop one day, and it would be love at first sight. He was a good friend and deserved to be happy. As I headed toward the coffee shop where I was meeting Pri, I thought about my own non-existent romantic life. Love had been elusive for me. Probably because I'd gone out of my way to avoid dating. Swipe-right culture wasn't my thing, and Redwood Grove wasn't exactly a hotbed for singles. After Scarlet's death, dating had seemed frivolous. I could barely function in those early days. I abandoned my dreams of working in forensic psychology or criminal profiling. The FBI was off the table. My criminology degree would go unused, nothing more than a worthless piece of paper stuffed away in a box in my parents' basement. I channeled all my energy and everything I'd learned into trying to solve her murder when the police seemed to get nowhere.

I spent the first six months sleeping on the couch in my parents' house, buried under blankets of notes, old police files, and my Excel spreadsheets. I thought breaking the case might bring me some relief, but now, with distance and time, I doubt it would have mattered. I needed to grieve, to lock myself inside and sink into the sadness. I'd done that well. In fact, I might have holed up in my parents' basement forever if it hadn't been for an ad Hal posted about hiring a bookseller at an off-the-beaten-path mystery bookstore in the small town of Redwood Grove. Books had gotten me through my worst days. They were comfort, escape, and provided closure, which remained elusive in real life. In mysteries, the killer is always brought to justice.

If I couldn't find justice for Scarlet, at least I could surround myself in a world of crime fiction where evidence and clever detectives outsmart villains and restore peace.

A few weeks later, I found myself at the Secret Bookcase, accepting Hal's job offer on the spot. I've never looked back or regretted my decision.

I only had one big regret. I would never forgive myself for pushing Scarlet to help me investigate a cold case we'd been assigned as our final project. Our criminology professor, Dr. Caldwell, had us examine an unsolved murder, tasking us with reviewing the crime scene, suspects, and case notes and extrapolating any new insight. With all the naivety of a twenty-two-year-old student, I had convinced Scarlet that we could crack the case. It was because of me that she was dead. She would still be here today if we had followed the assignment and left it alone. I tried to shake the memory from my head; it didn't do me any good revisiting it.

Lately, I was starting to realize that one of the reasons I'd blocked the possibility of love was that it was too painful to imagine losing someone I cared about again. But where did that leave me?

Alone.

Maybe it was time to reconsider. Maybe it was time to put myself out there more, to break free of the safety of the cocoon I'd created for myself. Maybe being a part of something big was just what I needed.

THREE

My mind drifted away from thoughts of Scarlet and my lonely love life as I breathed the scent of the early spring air. Cryptic Coffee, where my good friend Priya Kapoor worked, was on the east side of the town square. Walking along the quaint sidewalks and taking in the fragrant aromas of the eucalyptus, palm, and bay leaf trees always brought me a moment of respite.

Redwood Grove was nestled beneath the shady trees with a collection of old-world English-inspired estates, Spanish-style buildings with red-tiled roofs, and a few midcentury modern designs mixed in—call it California eclectic or a lack of a cohesive vision by the town's founders. Every shop and restaurant had its own distinctive character and charm. Redwood Grove's uniqueness was what I loved most about the town I called home. That and our proximity to the beach and the mountains. In less than an hour, I could be dipping a toe in the Pacific Ocean or, in double that time, be skiing down a snowy slope in the high Sierras.

Cryptic was situated around the corner from the Stag Head in a renovated auto shop. As was typical during our mild springs, the roll-up garage doors were open, extending the seating area to the outdoor patio. Its color palette of warm earth tones blended seamlessly with the landscape.

"Annie." Pri waved from behind the sleek marble coffee bar, her heart-shaped face glowing with excitement. "Get over here —stat."

I weaved past plush armchairs, wooden benches, and industrial-style stools that matched the contemporary atmosphere. 80s music pulsed on the overhead speakers, meaning Pri had control of the playlist.

"Girl, I've been dying for you to show up. You'll never guess who was just here." Pri's golden-brown eyes brightened with a mischievous delight.

"Who?" I looked around, half expecting to see a celebrity. It wasn't uncommon to have an occasional A-lister in town. Redwood Grove was distinctly not LA or the Bay. Unless you counted trivia night at the Public House, we had no nightlife to speak of. This was the kind of place you could disappear, a concept that appealed to celebrities looking to escape the paparazzi.

"Double Americano with cold foam." Pri grinned, highlighting her dimples. She reached for an earthenware mug and began making my order, deftly navigating the stainless-steel espresso machine.

"No way. Where?" I scanned the coffee shop. A few regulars were enjoying iced drinks on the patio, but otherwise, it was pretty empty, which wasn't a surprise since Pri would be closing soon.

"Already gone." Pri pulled two espresso shots and poured them into the mug. She used a miniature whisk to combine coconut milk, orange bitters, and allspice. "It's tragic. I could barely string together a coherent sentence when Double Americano magically appeared out of thin air and vanished while I mumbled on like a complete idiot."

"I'm sure that's not true." I squinted at her and tapped my fingers on the smooth, cold surface.

"Oh no, I'm sure. She looked at me with a level of concern I'd never seen before. I'm surprised an ambulance didn't arrive to assess my mental acuity. I sounded like I was having a stroke. Seriously, I could not string more than two words together, Annie. It was mortifying." She carefully swirled the milk mixture in the cup and, with a flourish, finished my drink with a foam flower on top.

"There's no way it was that bad."

She handed me my coffee. Then she raised one eyebrow and pressed her glossed lips together in a scowl. "Nope, it was worse. Way worse. I didn't have a chance to begin with, but now, forget it."

I took a sip. Pri's coffees reflected her—warm, bright, and bursting with layers of complex flavors. She had developed a crush on a customer last year. The only problem was that Double Americano wasn't local and made rare, infrequent appearances at Cryptic.

"Sorry." I pouted in solidarity. "It's so unfair, but I know you, and I'm convinced that the interaction was much worse in your head than in reality."

She reached across the smooth, cold counter to squeeze my hand. "That's why I adore you, Annie. Everyone needs a hype friend, and I'm glad you're mine."

I grinned. "I'm glad you're mine, too." An unexpected swell of emotion came over me. I swallowed hard to try and force the lump forming in my throat. I sucked a shaky breath in through my nose and willed tears away.

After Scarlet died, I didn't think I'd ever find another friend like her. I didn't want another friend. She had been like a sister. She knew the best and worst parts of me, and her loss had left an irreparable hole, an ache that never really went away. There were still days when I would start to text her to tell her news about the shop or an idea for a puzzle before the horrific reality set back in.

Scarlet was dead, and it was my fault.

I was glad to have a friend like Pri. She was fun, light, and breezy. And yet, our friendship couldn't erase my guilt. Nothing could. My life continued on. I was free to sip Pri's spicy latte and daydream about hosting a bookish festival while Scarlet's life had been cut short. The guilt of her unsolved murder clung to me like a persistent shadow. Until I tracked down Scarlet's killer and ensured they were behind bars for good, I knew that shadow would never dissipate.

"So tell me, what's new with you?" Pri asked, reaching for her sketchbook and a colored pencil. "I need a distraction after my failed attempt at flirting."

Pri was an artist, while I was more analytical. She doodled to pass the time or settle her nerves, whereas my brain only slowed down when I had a riddle or problem to work through.

"Well, if it makes you feel any better, my author event bombed. But it did give me a new idea." I filled her in on the concept of a Redwood Grove Mystery Fest.

"That's brilliant," Pri exclaimed. "Count us in. We'll devise an entire line of murderous coffee drinks for you."

I held up my palm. "Slow down. I have to pitch the idea to Hal first."

"Hal will do anything you suggest, Annie. Just tell him that you're doing a Mystery Fest, and it's going to be amazing."

My mouth hung open in protest. "That sounds like I steam-roll him."

"I don't mean it like that." Pri lifted her pencil off the page. "Hal adores you. You're like his surrogate granddaughter. I'm sure he'll love the idea."

I appreciated that Pri saw my relationship with Hal the same way I did. He had become like a grandfather to me. "I'll talk to him first thing tomorrow."

"Knock him dead." Pri gave me an evil grin.

After we brainstormed more over dinner, I went home and made copious notes, along with a potential schedule for the weekend and a list of authors. When I finally went to bed, it was hard to sleep; my head was buzzing with ideas. I was determined to make this a success. I owed it to Hal, and the bookstore.

The following day, I got up early to be at work before Hal came downstairs. Sleeping in was futile anyway, with Professor Plum kneading my chest.

"Good morning," I told my tabby cat, running my hand along his silky head. "I've got a big pitch. One that I think would make Scarlet proud."

He purred in response and massaged me with his soft paws.

Professor Plum was Scarlet's cat. She'd adopted him as a kitten the week before graduation. He was going to be our live-in third detective at the private agency we had planned to open together. Instead, he'd become my sole companion.

I gently nudged him off my lap, pulled on a pair of leggings and boots, and layered a pale blue T-shirt with a thin, cream-colored sweater. I tied my hair into two braids and opted for a pair of oversized navy-blue glasses.

"Not bad, Annie," I said to my reflection in the mirror before making my bed.

I absolutely cannot function or start the day without making my bed. I tucked the edges of my pale peach comforter into the bedframe like I'd received military training and fluffed the throw pillows.

A photo of me and Scarlet sat on my bedside table along with a stack of advanced reader copies waiting to be read. In the photo, Scarlet and I were grinning and posing like Charlie's Angels in front of the center fountains on campus with our graduation caps and gowns, ready to take on the world. It was tradition to take graduation pics in front of the fountain the day before the ceremony and then return to splash through the icy waters, tossing caps in the air after we'd turned our tassels and received our diplomas.

Only Scarlet never had the chance to celebrate the milestone. The picture was taken the day before she died.

Sometimes, it still didn't seem possible that she was gone.

I picked up the frame and stared at her black hair and goofy, lopsided grin.

That day was when everything changed.

She told me she had inside information on an informant in the case we were studying. I never imagined that she would set up a meeting with the informant and go alone. If I had known, I would have stopped her. I could have gone with her or at least tried to talk her out of it.

Professor Plum meowed and rubbed his head against my leg.

The familiar pain in the back of my throat swelled. My chest tightened. I set the photo back on my nightstand. "Come on, Professor Plum, let's get you some breakfast."

If I let memories of Scarlet take hold, I knew I wouldn't be able to concentrate on anything else.

"It's salmon for you this morning," I said, scooping the fishy wet food into Professor Plum's dish. "I'll try not to be too late."

I left him with a goodbye pet and headed for the front door.

Outside, the air was still cool. Dew-kissed grass exhaled an earthy perfume, and I caught a whiff of bacon and eggs frying at a cottage nearby. I walked along Woodlawn Terrace until I arrived at Oceanside Park. The town square was quiet at this hour. The only sound was the melodious birdsong that filled the air.

I cut through the park, careful to avoid sprinklers giving the greenery a much-needed dose of hydration. I took the pressed gravel path that led to the manor house, admiring the climbing roses and ivy snaking along the stone wall.

Red and white bunting stretched between the row of ancient oak trees on the lane. When the manor house came into view, I sucked in a breath. I always enjoyed the sight of the stately mansion with its huge ornate carved wooden doors, Dutch gables, limestone, bay box windows, and lush English gardens. The house looked like it belonged in the pages of a Jane Austen novel.

This is what you have to save, Annie.

Hal couldn't sell. Not yet. Not without at least giving my idea a fighting chance.

I approached the front entrance. Everything was dark, which meant that Hal wasn't up yet, or at least not moving. I unlocked the heavy door, flipped on the lights, and began going through our opening procedures. Then I got out the leftover cookies from our author event last night and set them out in the foyer. The area was our first chance to impress book lovers. Not that the house didn't do that on its own, but we made sure to feature new releases and signed author copies in the front of the store, along with bookish trinkets—mystery candles, BOOK CLUB IS MY ALIBI stickers, A DARK AND STORMY NIGHT bookmarks—that were strategically displayed near the cash register. We also served complimentary coffee and tea so that the first thing that greeted customers entering the store was the fragrant aroma of freshly brewed drinks.

After I finished setting up, I checked each of the book rooms to make sure everything was in order. This was my favorite part of the morning, tiptoeing through the hallowed quiet before the world had begun to stir. The faint scent of leather and aged paper hung in the air. Each shelf, laden with the promise of new stories, waited in silent anticipation. I could spend every waking hour of the day reading and barely make a dent. That was a myth of working at a bookstore. Customers assumed that we spent our days with our faces buried in a book. But the opposite was true. I felt like I never had enough time to read.

That was probably why I cherished my early morning sanctuary where my mind wandered free, and for the briefest moment, the Secret Bookcase belonged solely to me.

Fletcher arrived as I finished brewing a pot of coffee and adding water to the kettle for tea.

"Morning, Annie," he said, untying a cashmere scarf and hanging it on the vintage coat rack. He approached the cash register with a stack of papers color-coded with sticky notes. "I took it upon myself to draft some suggestions for the Mystery Fest. Take a look and let me know what you think."

I leafed through the papers, skim-reading his ideas. "Wow, you outdid yourself. This is great." I opened my laptop to show him what I'd come up with. "We're on the same track. Now we just need Hal."

The sound of a throat clearing made us both jump.

"Did someone say my name?" Hal shuffled into the foyer wearing his usual brown corduroy pants, soft leather shoes that easily could have moonlit as slippers, and a well-loved yellow-and-tan-striped cardigan.

"How did you sneak up on us?" I squinted at him with suspicion.

He smiled, his eyes crinkling at the corners as he danced the tips of his fingers along his cardigan and greeted me with a wider grin. "Hey, I still have a few tricks up my sleeve."

"Tea? Leftover treats?" I asked, motioning to the self-serve station near the front window.

Hal rolled up a tattered sleeve and checked his antique gold watch. "It's early. Are we expecting customers already?"

"Actually, Fletcher and I have an idea we want to run by you. If you want to grab a drink, I thought we could chat in the Sitting Room."

Hal's kind face wrinkled in surprise. "This sounds very formal. Should I be concerned?"

"Not at all," I replied with a grin, nudging him toward the tea. "It's a good thing."

He poured steaming water into a handcrafted mug and added a packet of Moroccan mint tea. Then he helped himself to a slice of chocolate-dipped shortbread. "To the Sitting Room?"

"Yes." I bobbed my head. "Let me grab a coffee, and I'll be right there."

Fletcher gathered his papers and followed me as we headed to the west side of the house.

Soft, hushed light filtered through the curved bay windows, highlighting the floral wallpaper and polished wood floors. Furniture upholstered in deep burgundy and gold hues, along with tapestries and paintings procured from Agatha Christie's estate, gave the room a timeless elegance. The room was divided into two parts—with built-in window seating in front of the windows and cozy collections of armchairs for readers who wanted to linger.

Rows of new and used mysteries took up the other half of the room. But the pièce de résistance was a secret bookcase tucked away in the far back corner. Hal had the brilliant idea to convert a linen closet into a hidden room. At first glance, the bookcase appeared like the others, but readers had to sleuth out which spine would release a handle and swing the entire shelving unit open to reveal a narrow hidden room inside.

Hal had aptly named the entire store after his masterpiece.

He sat in a chair next to a collection of book-themed candles. He cradled his mug in his hands and looked from me to Fletcher expectantly. "You have me intrigued."

Fletcher handed Hal his notes and sat down next to him. "You start, Annie. It's your idea."

I took a sip of my coffee and launched into my pitch,

standing in front of the bay windows to soak up the morning sunshine. "As I'm sure you noticed, the author event wasn't well attended last night."

Hal rubbed the back of his neck. "It's such a shame we can't entice more readers into the store."

"That's exactly why we wanted to talk to you. We have some new ideas to remedy that, hopefully," I continued.

Hal cut me off. "Wait, I don't want you to get the wrong idea. It's not your fault. You and Fletcher are both doing a magnificent job. I'm afraid that there might not be a future for a niche mystery bookstore any longer. Readers don't want musty old tomes. They want bite-sized books they can read on their phones." He sighed with resignation, and my heart ached to see him looking so despondent, as if the Secret Bookcase's fate was already sealed.

"It's true that we're competing with online retail giants and the steady stream of consumable media," I agreed. "That's why we think our idea could be a game-changer. We have to think differently. We need a reason to draw readers into the store and encourage them to get off the main highway and take a detour into Redwood Grove."

He bit into his shortbread. "Isn't that what you've tried with author events?"

"Yes, but this is going to be different. Bigger, better, interactive—a mystery festival involving the entire town." I could feel my enthusiasm growing as I explained the concept. "We want to brand Redwood Grove as the coziest mystery village on the West Coast. Redwood Grove could become a real-life version of St. Mary Mead."

Hal's eyebrows raised with interest. "You know my weakness, Annie. If it involves Agatha, count me in."

I grinned and then filled him in on the list of ideas we'd put together. Fletcher jumped in with some of his suggestions, nearly spilling coffee all over his lap. His enthusiasm was contagious. I just hoped that Hal thought so, too.

Hal listened intently, sipping his tea and eating his shortbread. When we finished, Hal pressed his lips together, hung his head, and closed his eyes.

"Does he hate it?" Fletcher mouthed with despair.

I shrugged, waiting for Hal to open his eyes. How could he hate the idea?

After what felt like ages, Hal finally lifted his head and blinked hard. He brushed the side of his eye with the back of his hand.

Was he crying?

"What did I do to deserve you both?" he said, wiping away another tear. "I'm touched. I'm humbled. I love the idea. It's exactly what the bookstore and the town needs. You're miracle workers."

I felt heat rising in my cheeks. Hal was on board with the idea. Now we just needed to convince the rest of Redwood Grove.

FOUR

Surprisingly, the shops and restaurants in Redwood Grove didn't take much convincing when Fletcher and I pitched the concept of a Mystery Fest. Everyone in the village embraced the idea, coming up with ways to get involved and agreeing to promote the event and decorate their windows and storefronts. The library partnered to help us reach out to authors, host panels, and provide the writers with honorariums. As the weeks progressed, the event schedule became more robust with haunted walking tours, mysterious mixology, and secret wine pairings. Fletcher and I had our hands full coordinating the plan. Authors from throughout the region and beyond agreed to participate in panels and do readings around town. I was floored by the level of enthusiasm for the weekend.

There was one exception, though—Liam Donovan. I don't know why I even bothered to try and pitch him. I saved the Stag Head for last, knowing it would likely be easier to get Liam involved if I already had a lengthy list of businesses offering specials for the weekend; also, because the less interaction I had with Liam, the better.

On the day I tried to convince him to participate, I found

him folding a new stag head for the fake trophy wall. It was made of recycled cardboard and appeared to fit together like a 3D puzzle.

"Hey, Annie, did you come to ask me about your Mystery Fest?" Liam asked, not looking up from his project.

"How did you know?" I intentionally ignored his condescending tone. One thing I had learned about Liam was that for some reason I couldn't understand, he seemed to enjoy getting a reaction out of me.

"I live here. Secrets don't last long in Redwood Grove." He tore his moody eyes away from construction just long enough to meet mine in a challenging stare.

"Good. That's going to make my pitch easier, isn't it?" I reached into my book bag for a brochure Fletcher had created for the event. "We'd love to have the Stag Head included on our list of community events. Since you already host trivia night, we thought it might be fun for you to do Sherlock trivia. Fletcher can come up with questions if you can put together some Sherlockian cocktails. Maybe something like an alcoholic London Fog?"

He scoffed and swept a lock of dark hair from his eye. "I do historical trivia nights here. And I don't get the Sherlock connection."

"The stags." I motioned to the wall of taxidermy cardboard. "Sherlock was known for wearing a deerstalker cap." Surely Liam had to know that.

"You realize we're talking about a fictional character, right?" Liam looked at me as if I were speaking in some sort of code. There was the faintest smirk at the corner of his lips as he waited for me to respond.

The muscles around my eyes twitched. I had to remind myself to breathe. Why did Liam have to be so infuriating?

"Yes, because as the name says—it's a *mystery* festival. For book lovers." I tried to keep my face passive. I couldn't let him see that he was getting to me.

"Yeah, I'm not sure that's our scene. It's a bit juvenile."

"That's ironic coming from the guy gluing a paper deer together."

Liam shrugged. "I'll think about it, but no promises."

"Don't kill any brain cells on my account," I said, heading for the door.

"Wait, why are you leaving so fast?" he asked, wiping glue from the edge of the deer with a paper towel.

"Because I think we're done here." I stormed out before he could say anything more. We didn't need Liam's buy-in for the festival, and I certainly wasn't going to let his desire to belittle the books I adored stop me from doing anything. Nor was I going to lose any sleep about him taking his time to consider whether he would stoop so low as to participate in an event that would be extremely beneficial to his business.

Liam's superior attitude only made me want Mystery Fest to be an even bigger success.

The next couple of months blew by in a whirlwind of planning. If I had understood the magnitude of time and effort it would take to coordinate author panels, pop-up appearances, food and drinking pairings, and craft an immersive puzzle for readers to solve, I might have pursued the idea with less enthusiasm. On the upside, absorbing myself in the project reignited my long-buried passions. I felt more like my old self, staying up long past my bedtime, getting lost in clever clues, sketching plot twists, and piecing together what I hoped would become an engaging event that would put the Secret Bookcase back on the map and put the bookstore back in the black.

Despite the long hours and late nights, we'd finally done it. Tomorrow was the official kickoff of Redwood Grove's first-ever

Mystery Fest. Not only had we created a template for the inaugural event, but based on the early interest, I had a feeling that if this first year were a success, the fest would quickly become an annual tradition.

Pri had been an enormous help, brainstorming clever mystery-themed coffee drinks for Cryptic and sharing event details with a couple of her bookish friends with massive social media followings. Their posts went semi-viral, and we sold out tickets the first week the website went live. I owed Fletcher plenty of credit, too. He had taken on the role of getting Redwood Grove's business community on board and designed mystery maps for participants, highlighting each activity and special bonuses throughout town. In addition, he had posted signage throughout the village square, directing festival-goers to the bevy of activities we had lined up for the weekend.

Hal had consulted his old Rolodex and reached out to dozens of his longtime friends in the industry, helping to secure big-name, bestselling authors to headline panels. It had truly been a group effort, but I wouldn't lie—it was also stressful managing what felt like a thousand moving parts.

Author panels would be divided between the bookstore and the library. The head librarian suggested turning one of the small conference spaces into a green room for our guest writers with snacks, water, and drinks, providing them a spot to seek refuge after a day of talking and meeting readers. We had arranged for additional author pop-ups throughout town—books and brews at State of Mind Public House, a vintage-fashion writer doing a special signing with a mini fashion show at Artifacts, and a thriller writer taking readers on an after-dark walking tour.

The kickoff party would be at the Grand Hotel, where readers would be greeted by Sherlock Holmes, aka Fletcher, who was reveling in his official role as arguably the world's most famous detective. He had purchased a houndstooth cape, deerstalker cap, fake pipe, and magnifying glass for the occasion. Guests would mingle in the ballroom with cocktails and small bites and await their first clue. I had pieced together a puzzle that I hoped readers would have to use their "little gray cells" (to borrow a phrase from Hal) to solve, but it wasn't so challenging that it would frustrate them to the point of giving up. Writing an immersive mystery had been more satisfying than I had anticipated. There was something so rewarding about the intellectual challenge of creating a coherent and complex plot, delving into the darker aspects of human nature that motivate crime—greed, jealousy, deception—and crafting a satisfying ending. I couldn't wait to watch readers try to solve the puzzle of the Lost Heirloom. My mystery revolved around the real-life legend of the Wentworths, a wealthy family credited with founding Redwood Grove.

The family was rumored to possess a priceless heirloom—a golden locket with a rare gemstone containing a secret map to their fortune. A fortune that had gone missing since one ominous night nearly a century ago when a fire destroyed the original Wentworth mansion (now the historical society and museum). The family disappeared without a trace, leaving the locket lost for generations. It was a story that fascinated me, and I knew it was the perfect subject for my fictitious mystery.

The clues were designed to lead participants on a scavenger hunt through the town square on their quest to find the Wentworth heirloom. The first clue would be disseminated at the opening reception. Posters with secret messages embedded in the artwork and ciphers that readers would have to solve would be hung throughout the village square.

As I crossed the square toward the Grand Hotel, I hoped the concept wasn't too corny and that the clues wouldn't be too easy to solve. I shook those thoughts away. There was nothing I could do now; in less than twenty-four hours, hundreds of readers would descend upon our little Northern California community, ready to break out their magnifying glasses and channel their inner Nancy Drew. Tonight was our private dress rehearsal before throngs of visitors arrived and my last chance to make sure everything was in order.

Pri was waiting for me by the front doors, looking elegant with her flowing linen pants and a silky tank top that showcased the artisan temporary tattoos on her arms. She reached to hug me. "You ready for this? You look adorable as always, which is really all that matters."

I glanced down at my knee-length skirt and bookish black T-shirt, suddenly feeling underdressed. I chewed the inside of my cheek. "I think so. I don't know. I feel like there are a million details, and I have to be forgetting at least one of them, but at this point, it's too late anyway, right?"

She nudged my waist, grinning. "Come on; you can do better than that."

"I hope so." I crossed my fingers and bit my bottom lip harder, tasting the vanilla-scented lip gloss I had applied earlier.

"Annie, you've got this." Pri held my wrists and stared at me with her perfectly arched brows. "You are the most detail-oriented person I've ever met, to a fault."

"Hey," I protested, laughing at this totally fair assessment.

Pri released my arms and held up her index finger painted with a temporary star tattoo. She dabbled in many forms of artwork. Her latest medium was designing and uploading sketches to a company that printed her creations on transparent film. The inky designs were so real it was hard to believe they would wash off with baby oil. "It's true. We're good. This is going to be awesome. You built it, and they're coming. Now we need to get in there and pump up the businesses like we're at a rave."

"Come on, you know I've never even been to a rave. Look at

me." I pointed to my T-shirt that read: I Closed My Book To
Be Here.

She shook her head in mock disgust and looped her arm
through mine. "We'll talk about that later."

Stepping inside the Parisian Art Deco hotel was like being
transported to another world. Authentic French antiques and
art adorned the walls. Glittery iron chandeliers hung from the
high ceiling. On our way to the ballroom, we passed hand-
carved furniture, a marble fireplace, and stately floral
arrangements.

As we walked into the room, I instinctively pressed my
hand to my stomach, hoping to calm the nerves that rumbled to
life at the sight of nearly every shop owner in town seated and
awaiting my welcome speech. Public speaking isn't really my
thing. I much prefer to watch and observe. That's one of the
many reasons Dr. Caldwell, my former professor, used to call
me her perfect criminology student.

"You got this," Pri whispered, squeezing my arm and
pushing me toward the podium.

I inhaled through my nose, squared my shoulders, and
stepped onto the stage.

"Thanks so much for coming," I said into the mic, giving a
big smile to trick myself into feeling confident. "As most of you
know, I'm Annie Murray from the Secret Bookcase. We're
thrilled to be hosting this event and can't thank you enough for
your help getting it off the ground." I scanned the crowd for
Hal. He was deep in conversation near a grouping of potted
palms in the back of the ballroom, chatting with Caroline Miles,
who owned a local boutique. From Hal's rigid body language
and how Caroline was waving her hands to emphasize her
point, I didn't think now was the best time to call him up to the
stage to say a few words.

"All of us at the Secret Bookcase are delighted with your
enthusiasm and creativity. As I'm sure you've heard, tickets for

Mystery Fest are sold out, and at this time tomorrow night, we'll have over five hundred book lovers here in town to shop, stroll, sip, and dine. The weather forecast is looking good: sunny skies and warm evenings. We're confident that the event will boost our local economy."

A round of applause broke out.

I smiled, feeling the tension in my neck loosening its grip. I became more comfortable as I went through the agenda, the schedule of author panels and signings, and the event lineup. However, I couldn't help but wonder what Hal and Caroline were discussing. Whatever it was, neither of them looked happy.

Was there an issue with the festival already?

Could Caroline be upset that her shop wasn't one of the stops for readers to find a clue to the Wentworth murder?

I tried not to let my anxiety get the best of me as I reviewed the final event schedule and answered questions. When I was finished, I made a beeline for the back of the ballroom. As I approached Hal and Caroline, I did a double take to see a familiar face coming straight at me through the crowd. It wasn't a face I was excited to see.

"Annie? Annie Murphy, is that you?" The woman's heavily lined eyes grew wide. "I thought it was you, and it is you."

Every muscle in my body clenched like a vice, unyielding and unrelenting, as if I was trying to hold on to a lifeboat in the middle of a storm. I was. It was like a flood of long-buried emotions swelling to the surface.

"Kayla." The woman pointed to her chest. "Kayla Mintner. We were at Redwood College together. Remember? My goodness, Annie Murphy, how long has it been? Almost ten years?"

"Eight years, nine days, and fourteen hours." There was no point in correcting her on my last name.

"Wow, good memory." Kayla sounded impressed as she kissed both my cheeks like we were French. The pungent aroma of stale booze emitted from her pores made me wonder if she'd bathed in bourbon.

I didn't tell her that the time of Scarlet's murder was etched in my brain.

"Tell me all about you. I can't believe you ended up here in this tiny little town! I was sure you'd be a detective in LA or San Francisco." Kayla's cloying smile oozed with condescension. "Are you head of the police here? A one-woman show?"

"I'm not in law enforcement. I work at the bookshop." I glanced furiously around the room, hoping to see anyone who could save me.

Kayla's Barbie-pink nails sparkled beneath the ballroom lights as she pressed her hand over her mouth in shock. "A bookshop? That's so cute. How precious, a bookshop. You always were at the library in college. I love that for you. It's perfect. You're so cute and bookish with your red hair and those glasses. Is the red natural?" She reached out to touch my hair.

I pulled away, causing her to swipe the air like she was trying to kill a phantom bug. A burning sensation bubbled up inside me like molten lava threatening to erupt. I fought the urge to lash out and concentrated on taking a long, slow breath. "What brings you to Redwood Grove?"

"There's a mystery festival happening in town, and I thought it was the perfect excuse to come visit Redwood Grove again." She slurred slightly as she spoke.

Kayla was here for the festival? A bookish event was the last place I would have expected to bump into her.

"Oh, actually, you probably know about the festival if you work in the bookshop," she continued, her body swaying like we were on the open ocean. "My cousin Justin is a bartender at the Public House, and I've been assisting Caroline with her social media strategy." She paused and motioned to Caroline and Hal. "I own a marketing company. We specialize in helping local retailers develop an online presence. I've been working to bring her shop, Artifacts, into the twenty-first century. It's a beast of a project. Do you know it?"

I nodded. Redwood Grove had a population of just under five thousand residents. It was impossible not to know everyone and everything happening in town. Caroline's boutique, Artifacts, opened a little over a year ago. Like most other business owners in town, she had renovated a one-story building on the main street, giving it a fresh coat of pastel paint and a modern refresh. Artifacts featured handmade necklaces and earrings crafted from metals and gemstones, scarves, shawls, and hats made from eco-friendly materials, artisanal candles, soaps, bath bombs, local pottery, and one-of-a-kind sculptures and wall hangings.

Kayla fanned her face. "I just can't get over seeing you. We'll have to catch up. A few of us are in town for the weekend. Do you remember my old roommate, Monica Harrison, and my college boyfriend, Seth Turner? They're both here for the festival, too. Apparently, she's some big-name editor who is here with a new author. It will be so fun to reminisce, like our very own mini reunion."

I forced a smile.

"Oh, it looks like Caroline is free." Kayla waved her shimmery fingers and dashed toward Caroline. "I'm going to have a quick word, but let's totally catch up. I can't wait to hear all your news."

I took a minute to compose myself. Kayla Mintner was in Redwood Grove for the Mystery Festival. What were the odds? Kayla and Monica were not the academic types in college. While Scarlet and I had pulled late-nighters in the library researching crime theory and criminal justice systems, Kayla and Monica had partied at the off-campus apartments. I'm not sure Kayla could have located the library on a map. Monica had been an English major, so I guess it wasn't a surprise that she had ended up in publishing.

But what did surprise me was that Kayla was excited about reconnecting with Monica or Seth. They'd all had a huge falling out the last semester of our senior year. Monica and Kayla hadn't been on speaking terms ever since, at least as far as I'd heard. Kayla had broken up with Seth in a very public argument in the middle of the quad. That was a story I wouldn't forget. Kayla had dyed all of Seth's baseball uniforms hot pink. She had trashed them and each of his prized trophies and smashed them in the middle of the quad so that everyone passing by between classes would have no option other than to stare at the mess. Even back then, I was well aware that Kayla wasn't stable. It didn't seem like she'd changed.

I had enough to worry about with the Mystery Fest, and now I would have to dodge old college acquaintances all weekend. I'd never been close with any of them, but seeing Kayla made me feel like I'd been sucked back in time. The weight of memories crushed down on me, making it impossible to breathe. My knees threatened to buckle. I sucked air in giant gulps, searching for the nearest exit. The vividness of my last few days with Scarlet—cramming for finals in the library, drinking cold brew, and eating day-old donuts while laughing for hours and singing along to NYSNC—played like a movie, making it hard to distinguish between the present and the past.

This couldn't be happening.

Not now.

I clenched my hands into tight fists and hurried outside for some fresh air. I needed to pull myself together. Fast. This weekend was my responsibility. It was time to focus on the here and now—launch the festival and keep the past in the past.

FIVE

I didn't get far because Hal grabbed my arm to stop me before I could escape to the Grand Hotel's extensive Parisian gardens.

"Annie, great job up there, kiddo." Hal's kind eyes twinkled with pride. He rubbed the sleeve of his patched cardigan. No matter the weather, Hal wore through his cardigans, literally.

I glanced at Caroline, who was being pulled away toward the bar by Kayla.

Caroline stared at Hal with a pleading look on her face.

The briefest flash of concern crossed Hal's usually kindly face. He had the type of face that belonged on an oil painting in an old English estate, with long jowls, a neatly trimmed white beard, and lines of wisdom etched on his forehead.

I was surprised that Caroline had hired Kayla. They seemed like an odd match. Caroline was in her mid-sixties with a casual, understated elegance. She moved with the grace of a professional ballet dancer. Her long white hair swept behind her back as she stole a final glance at Hal.

"What's up with Caroline?" I asked, watching her and Kayla. It was clear they weren't enjoying each other's company.

Caroline maintained an uncomfortable distance from Kayla like she was trying to keep her at arm's length.

Hal fiddled with a loose thread on his cardigan. "It's nothing for you to worry about. Small business angst. That's all. Don't give it a thought."

"She looks like she's furious," I pressed. "I saw you two deep in conversation while I was up on stage."

"Annie, you have enough on your plate without worrying about Caroline. Don't let her concern you. It's nothing." Hal hesitated as if he wanted to say more, but he folded his hands together and smiled. "It appears that everything is ready for your big day tomorrow. So let me be the first to congratulate you on a job well done."

"It's not just me. This has been a labor of love with the entire town. Fletcher, you, Pri, everyone deserves credit." I couldn't contain my huge grin. His words galvanized me and sent a flush of contented relief through my body. My lungs felt like they expanded to their fullest as I took a deep, satisfied breath. Knowing that Hal thought we had done a good job meant the world to me.

Hal tilted his head and gazed at me with his hazel eyes. "Be that as it may, this is your brainchild, and I'm grateful for your spirit and enthusiasm. Without your creative innovation, this never would have happened. My grandmother would be oh so proud."

I grinned in amusement. "You mean Agatha?"

"The one and only." A half smile tugged at the corner of his mouth, and his eyes sparkled with a hint of mischief. Hal had a naturally calming aura. He was like a grandfather to me and had given me a job at the Secret Bookcase just because of my love of mysteries alone. Although he had never mentioned it, I also wondered if Hal had sensed that I needed a healthy distraction when he hired me. Don't let his penchant for casually sipping tea while deciphering the morning crossword puzzle fool you. There wasn't much that got by Hal. He might have his head buried in a paper or book, but he was always paying attention.

He was a man of many quirks, and by far his quirkiest feature was his insistence that he was the lost descendant of Agatha Christie. Even if the theory was a bit far-fetched, it was impossible not to get caught up in the possibility of it. Hal was convinced he was the reason that she had gone missing in 1926, leaving her home in Sunningdale, abandoning her car near a quarry, and being discovered eleven days later, registered at a hotel in Harrogate under a false name. According to Hal, Agatha had vanished to have a secret baby—his mother, who was given up for adoption.

Hal believed that the great dame of mysteries herself was his long-lost grandmother, and he had made it his life's mission to prove that fact. His office was piled with historical documents, photographs, autobiographies, and letters from Agatha Christie's estate. He attended annual conferences in her hometown and took pilgrimages to interview children and grandchildren of her former neighbors, publishers, and staff.

Was it probable that he was her grandson? No.

Possible? Perhaps.

There were numerous theories about the cause of her mysterious disappearance from amnesia to a publicity stunt or immersive research for a new book, but the exact reason for Agatha Christie's disappearance remains an enigma today. It continues to be a subject of fascination by her fans and, most importantly, Hal.

A commotion at the bar caused us both to turn in that direction. Caroline and Kayla had been joined by two people I also recognized, Seth and Monica, my former college classmates, and it looked like Kayla was causing a scene. When the hotel event staff asked if we wanted to have an open bar for tonight's pre-event gathering, I figured that locals might want a glass of wine or an evening cocktail while we went over the schedule, but I hadn't counted on anyone getting drunk.

Kayla must be drunk. Really drunk.

She staggered with a loose grip on her pink martini glass, causing it to wobble and liquid to spill from the side.

"Pull yourself together, Kayla. You're an embarrassment," I heard Caroline hiss, as she pressed her hair behind her ears, shook her head with disgust, and moved even farther away from Kayla.

It didn't make sense. Kayla had mentioned that Caroline was the reason she was in town. But nothing about Caroline's body language gave me the impression that there was anything but animosity between the women.

"*You're* an embarrassment." Kayla snorted and took a swig of her drink.

"You need to get out of here—now." Caroline lasered her index finger toward the main doors. "You should really go before you do something you're going to regret."

Kayla threw her head back and laughed. She lost her balance and caught herself on the bar's edge at the last minute, spilling more of her martini. "Is that a threat?"

Caroline stood as still as the snowy egrets that frequented the lake nearby. "Don't tempt me."

To my horror, Kayla lunged at her. I wasn't sure if it was intentional or accidental, but her martini glass tipped forward in the process, sending the remaining rose-colored liquid down the front of Caroline's crisp white linen dress.

Caroline looked like she was fuming in silent rage. Then she abruptly spun on her heels, taking quick, forceful strides away from Kayla. Her anger radiated through the ballroom like a wave, causing people to allow her a wide berth as she stormed by.

Seth and Monica tried to drag Kayla away. Kayla resisted, but Seth was twice her size and managed to wrap an arm around her petite frame and escort her outside, with Monica following them like a lost puppy.

An awkward hush fell over the ballroom. It took a few minutes before conversations resumed, and wine began to flow again.

"Well, that was unexpected." Hal cleared his throat and raised a bushy white eyebrow. "One must always have a little drama."

"Uh, what did we just witness?" Pri asked, joining Hal and me with three glasses of white wine balanced deftly in her hands. "Wine?"

"Yes, please." I took a glass from her.

"How thoughtful." Hal smiled thanks and dipped his nose into the glass to smell the wine's bouquet.

"Who was that woman?" Pri's eyebrows shot up as she glanced around us. "Are we on some kind of a hidden camera show? Or is this part of your master plan, Annie?"

I held my left hand up. "I swear that wasn't scripted."

"Although, that's quite a brilliant idea," Hal interjected. "Maybe for the next fest, we host a murder mystery dinner with actors mixed in amongst the guests?"

"Love it." Pri gave him a fist bump.

"I actually know them," I confessed, and I told them about bumping into Kayla and how we had all gone to college together.

"Ewww, I wouldn't want a reunion with her either." Pri shuddered and stuck out her tongue. "There has to be another reason she's in town. She is definitely not the bookish type. Caroline couldn't have gone to school with you, though. She has to be close to seventy."

"Sixty-five," Hal interjected.

Pri shot him a funny look.

"She's sixty-five," Hal repeated.

"No. I mean, obviously, Caroline wasn't at school when we

were there." I glanced in the direction of my former classmates. They were gone. That was a relief. "I met her for the first time when she opened Artifacts, and from what Kayla told me, it sounded like they connected through Kayla's cousin Justin, who works at State of Mind Public House."

"Hmmm. It's quite a coincidence, isn't it?" Pri pondered the thought while sipping her wine.

"You know, in nearly every one of Agatha Christie's mysteries, Poirot and Miss Marple express that same sentiment." Hal paused and waited for us to nudge him to continue. It was one of his idiosyncrasies; it had been unsettling when I started working at the Secret Bookcase. He would often pause, holding his body completely still, like he was lost in his own internal world. The first time it happened during a conversation, I was worried that he had had a stroke, but I had come to learn that Hal took longer than most people to process information. He let it simmer in his brain, like a hearty stew thickening before responding or asking questions. This level of emotional control allowed him to approach issues from a logical and rational lens. Still, it also tended to make people who didn't know him well uncomfortable with prolonged silences.

Pri caved quickly. "What's the sentiment?"

Hal tilted his head to the side, a subtle yet knowing smile on his lips. "There's no such thing as a coincidence."

"Kayla's in town for some other reason," I answered without thinking.

"I think that could perhaps be a fair assumption." Hal's eyes held my gaze briefly before he lifted his wine glass and took a long sip.

As a mystery buff, I had to agree. The signs were all there. Kayla had to have an ulterior motive for her supposed "spontaneous" visit. The question was, what?

And could it have anything to do with me?

I shook the thought away.

"It's going to be a long day tomorrow," Hal said. "I think I'll stroll home and catch some shuteye. You two enjoy the evening, *mes amies.*" He drank the last sip of his wine, winked, and walked away.

Pri studied me with concern. "Are you good? You seem distracted."

"I'll be fine," I lied. "Thanks for the pep talks. I don't know what I'd do without you. You've been like my personal cheerleader this week."

"Annie, Annie, she's our girl. Give this Mystery Fest a twirl." She pretended to mimic a cheerleading rally cry with one arm and then collapsed against me in a fit of laughter. "That was terrible, but hey, at least I tried."

"You stick to coffee, and I'll stick to mysteries," I said with a grin.

We finished our wine and parted ways. Like Hal, I wanted to call it an early night. I had a feeling that tomorrow would be nonstop, and I needed to be fresh and well-rested for the kickoff party. Hopefully, tonight's outburst was an isolated event. However, if Kayla tried to pull similar antics at the Mystery Fest, I might have to take a page from Caroline's book and kindly—or not so kindly—ask her to leave Redwood Grove for good.

SIX

The following day dawned bright and sunny. I woke to the sound of finches, Professor Plum's hungry meows, and the fluttery feeling of nervous anticipation. Today was the day. Within a few hours, readers would be sipping Poirot pour-overs at Cryptic and trying to find the first hidden clue inside the secret bookcase at the Secret Bookcase. Fletcher called the clever metaphor "so meta."

We had decided to hide the first clue to the Wentworth Mystery in the bookshop. That would give the store a much-needed boost in foot traffic, and it seemed only fitting to conceal a hint in our very own hidden bookcase. Anyone attending the kickoff reception would automatically receive their clue, but eager readers could get a head start on cracking the case if they swung by the front register anytime during the day.

I pulled on a pair of capris, my tennis shoes, and another bookish T-shirt. This one read I'M ONLY HERE TO ESTABLISH MY ALIBI.

"Don't worry, but I might be a little late tonight," I told Professor Plum.

He mewed in response and batted a fly that had gotten in

through the window in my dining nook which I'd left open last night.

"I'll try to swing by and feed you, but here's a little extra to tide you over, just in case." I heaped a generous scoop of kibble into his dry food dish. Even the thought of making him eat late made me anxious. Would there ever be an escape from the pervasive guilt I continued to shoulder?

Not until I had closure on Scarlet.

And maybe not then, Annie, the negative voice I tried to silence in my head won out.

I kissed Professor Plum and headed outside before I got sucked down the rabbit hole.

Summer bloomed to life outside. It was like Mother Nature had rolled out the welcome mat for the weekend. Bunches of fresh mint, wild blackberries, and clementines made for a fragrant greeting as I passed through Oceanside Park. Why Redwood Grove had named the park Oceanside was a mystery to me. Technically speaking, we were located east of the Pacific Ocean but a thirty-minute drive away. Emphasis on "side" might have been a stretch, but I loved the park no less. It truly was in the center of the town square with pebble paths for meandering, shady leafy oak trees, a pergola entrenched in old-growth purple wisteria with a grassy seating area for outdoor concerts and movies in the summer, and plenty of sweet little benches tucked between the tree canopy, perfect for transporting myself to faraway places in the pages of a book.

When I arrived at the store, Fletcher had already set out the sandwich board signs and strung forest-green and deep purple bunting with silhouettes of keys and magnifying glasses across the entrance. Mystery Fest posters hanging in the front window were in the same gothic color scheme. The bookshop looked like it was straight from the pages of a Miss Marple novel. Dark walnut trim around the windows gleamed from hours of hand-polishing. Hal had swapped the interior bulbs to a rusty yellow so everything had a vintage, ethereal glow.

Signed copies from each of the authors participating in Mystery Fest filled the front window display, along with parchment, quill pens, and blood-red wax skull stamps.

Inside the shop, collections of notecards, colored pencils, and maps of the London Underground lined the front counter. Raven mugs, bookplates, bookmarks, poison-enameled pins, and tobacco-scented candles awaited readers, as did curated collections of our bestselling mysteries.

Hal greeted me with a beaming grin. "Good morning! Are you ready for the great mystery takeover? I'm wearing a new shirt I had made for the occasion." He unbuttoned his cardigan to reveal a heather gray T-shirt with a famous Agatha Christie quote: VERY FEW OF US ARE WHAT WE SEEM.

"We should sell those." I looked around the store and crossed my fingers. "I hope we're ready. The shop looks amazing, so now I just need to place the letters in the secret bookcase, and then Fletcher and I can set up the Conservatory for the panels and make sure the display cases are stocked with the special mystery merch he ordered. I've been running through the list in my head this morning, and I think we're close."

Merchandising was Fletcher's territory. He had sourced vintage typewriters, quill pens, spy glasses, clock towers, and dozens of other mystery-themed stickers for the front-of-store displays, along with temporary tattoos, bookmarks, journals, and bookish candle sets. We intended to showcase the bookish merch in other sections of the store to add to the mystery aesthetic and encourage impulse purchases.

"Let me know if there's anything this old man can do to help," Hal offered, buttoning his cardigan and motioning to the tea kettle warming on a hot plate near the entrance to the Conservatory. "I'm about to pour myself a strong cup of Earl Grey tea. Would you like one?"

"No thanks." I scooted behind the register and riffled through the junk drawer for tape. "And as far as how you can help—just be your wonderful self and greet everyone who comes in. We could have readers show up at any moment." I felt a surge of affection for my boss. Hal had provided me sanctuary within the walls of the bookstore, and I hoped that this weekend could be my way of paying him back for offering me shelter at a time in my life when everything had fallen apart.

I hurried to the office to get the box of cream-colored letters rolled up in tubes and tied with blood-red ribbons. Once readers discovered them behind the secret bookcase, the letters told the story of the Wentworth family fortune and guided them to their next clue.

I felt proud of the last line I'd come up with, which read: WHERE THE BEAN'S MAGIC MEETS THE MYSTIC'S MIND, YOUR FIRST CLUE YOU'RE SURE TO FIND.

I hoped they would realize the riddle pointed them to Cryptic for their next clue.

The secret bookcase blended in with the dark walnut shelves throughout the room. There was nothing that stood out or flagged it as anything special, with one exception. A black leather hardback edition of Agatha Christie's first novel, *The Mysterious Affair at Styles*, contained a special lever that unlocked the bookcase and rotated open into a secret room. To call it a room was a bit of an exaggeration. The space was eight feet long by four wide, the length of the bookshelf. It still had some original shelving from when it served as a linen closet.

Watching readers try to find the book that opened the shelf was always hilarious. Fletcher suggested installing a hidden camera so that we could spy on readers attempting to figure out how the bookcase worked. We didn't keep anything inside the narrow space. It was more for show and the experience of readers playing out their bookish fantasies in real life.

I grabbed a folding chair and unlocked the hidden room. It

was dark and narrow inside. Typically, small spaces didn't bother me, but there was something about the coffin-like room that made me feel claustrophobic. I used my flashlight app to navigate the dim, musty enclosure and propped the chair against the far edge. Then I set the basket of clues on the chair and ducked out of the space, locking the shelf in place again, glad to be free from the tiny room's clutches.

With the clues in place, I did a final walkthrough of the bookshop and returned to the front. My heart drummed in my chest at the sight of the steady line of customers that formed the moment we opened up. I practically danced in place and beamed with delight as people poured into the store.

I spent the next few hours recommending books for young readers and ringing up copies of our most expensive boxed sets. The bookshop buzzed with happy energy as the first customers rotated through, sipping lattes and iced chais from Cryptic and seeking their first quest of the weekend. The atmosphere was electric. My cheeks hurt from smiling. I found myself constantly grinning and placing my hand over my heart in deep gratitude for everyone who had made the weekend possible. It was a joy chatting with readers dressed in various costumes ranging from iconic trench coats and fedoras to deer-stalkers and Inverness capes. I loved eavesdropping as mystery enthusiasts exchanged theories, discussed their favorite whodunits, and eagerly hunted for their next read. The themed rooms were packed with activity, with guests exploring our carefully curated collections. Laughter and conversation filled the air.

But the best part was the sound of the cash registers ringing continuously, their melodious chimes joining the cacophony of the bustling bookshop. The Secret Bookcase had transformed into a veritable playground for mystery lovers, and I was in my element, sweaty and grateful that I had opted to wear comfort-able shoes as I ran from one end of the store to the other, preparing for author arrivals and using ladders and step stools to reach rare copies for customers.

A little before noon, I ducked into the Parlor to make sure everything was set up for our first author appearance—Eli Ledger. Eli was a much-hyped debut author who had recently signed a large contract with a new publishing house for a collection of noir short stories. His publicist had reached out to ask if we would be interested in a preview reading from his upcoming book. We gladly agreed.

Since Eli was a new author without an established following, the Parlor, with its intimate seating and noir vibe, was the perfect setting. I wasn't expecting a large crowd, and I also wasn't expecting to see Kayla, Monica, and Seth standing near the small podium Fletcher had set up in front of the fake electric fireplace when I breezed into the room, carrying a fresh stack of bookmarks.

Great. The college reunion I couldn't escape was following me.

"Annie, how fun to keep bumping into you," Kayla cooed, swaying as she spoke and nearly toppling over when she turned to Monica and Seth. Monica smoothed her straightened dark hair and held her hands loosely behind her back. Seth's bulky frame shadowed her. He rubbed the back of his sunburned neck and fiddled with his baseball jersey.

"You remember Annie." Kayla's tone was overly enthusiastic. "Annie. It's Annie Murphy from school, can you believe it? We bumped into each other last night."

"It's Murray," I muttered, setting the bookmarks on the podium.

"Oh, no way. Of course. You're in charge of author events for the store. I didn't make the connection with the name when our publicity team sent me the details," Monica said, extending her hand. She was dressed in a well-fitted charcoal gray suit that made it clear she was here for business, not pleasure. I was struck by how different Monica appeared. I remembered her in our college days rolling into class in halter tops and cutoff shorts. She lounged on the quad in a bikini and competed in powder puff football games. Nothing about her had been corporate back then.

"It's great to see you again. Eli is *my* author. We just signed him, and I'm convinced he will be an overnight bestseller. Luckily, you're getting him now while his star is rising."

I wasn't going to debate her, but I also wasn't sure that a collection of short stories, especially noir, would translate into the mainstream book market. Our noir section had a small but devoted fan base, but our bestsellers tended to be big-name mystery authors and swoon-worthy romances.

"It's such a small world that we're all here, isn't it?" Kayla plastered on a cloyingly sweet and suspicious smile. "Seth, did you know our Annie in college?" She pawed at him, but he shifted away from her.

Our Annie?

Gross.

What was her angle?

How had they all ended up in Redwood Grove?

And was she already drunk?

Seth reached out a burly hand and practically crushed me with his grasp. Unlike Monica, Seth looked as if he was trying to intentionally pass as a college student. He chomped on a wad of what I hoped was gum. "Yeah, you were friends with that girl who got killed."

A flush of heat swelled through my cheeks, so hot that it almost burned cold. I wanted to flee. I couldn't do this now. Not here. I swallowed hard and tapped my watch. "Is Eli here? We should get started."

"I just saw him in the room with the teas," Monica said. "I'll go grab him. Oh, wait, here he is now."

We turned to see a man in his late forties wearing black skinny jeans and a black turtleneck approaching us.

A turtleneck in this heat? Could he be any more cliché?

With an air of calculated nonchalance, Eli sauntered into the room. His steps were slow and measured as he passed the smattering of readers awaiting his talk. His entrance was timed to perfection, with a dramatic pause before he stepped behind the podium to allow the anticipation to build.

I took a seat in the front row next to Monica and Seth. Kayla squeezed into the empty seat on my other side. Like last night, she reeked of booze and wiped her clammy hands on her ripped jeans while staring at Eli with a pallid gaze.

Eli skipped any introduction of his work and proceeded to lick his index finger and flip through pages of a loosely bound manuscript. "There is no need for pleasantries. You're here for my words, not me."

Kayla jammed her hands into her armpits and brushed a shaky hand over her brow.

Was she on something stronger?

"Are you okay?" I whispered.

She blinked rapidly like she couldn't speak. What *was* going on?

"I give you *Of Hallows and Hauntings*, a collection of stories that take place deep in the remote Redwood forests which hum with darkness and death." Eli's voice oozed with arrogance as he ran his fingers casually through his wavy hair, ensuring everyone's eyes were drawn to him before he began.

He was about two pages in when Kayla jumped to her feet and interrupted him. "Oh, my God!"

"Shhhh." Monica swiveled her head, pressed her finger to her lips, and glared at her old friend. "You can't troll an author in the middle of their reading. You're a mess."

"No. *He's* the problem." Kayla pointed at Eli. Was she looking for a fight? She started to say more, but Seth stood up, pushing past me and Monica, grabbed Kayla by the waist, and yanked her out of the room. That was the second time in less than twenty-four hours that he had dragged Kayla away before she could cause a scene. First, last night, and now during the middle of an author talk.

What was her problem? And why in the world had she picked this weekend out of all the weekends to come to Redwood Grove?

SEVEN

Eli recovered quickly, addressing the audience with an air of casual dismissal. "Everyone's looking for their five minutes of fame these days. It's easy to judge from the cheap seats, but we artists are in the trenches." He knew how to command his audience; I'd give him that. I loved how the dimly lit sconces we'd set up in the Parlor cast shadows across his face, adding to his mystique.

"I can't believe I was ever friends with Kayla. She's vile," Monica whispered. "She's obviously already drunk. The woman has a serious problem."

Poor Kayla. A heaviness cemented me to my chair. I drew my eyebrows together and leaned closer to Monica. "The scary thing is it's just barely noon. If she's already drunk, that's really worrisome," I replied, glancing at the typewriter clock on the deep purple velvety wall behind the podium. Framed posters of detectives in film and literature flanked either side, none more recognizable than debonair Hercule Poirot with his neatly groomed mustache, monocle, and calculated wisdom.

I wondered what the great detective would deduce about

Kayla's situation. If she was struggling with addiction, connecting her with support and services seemed important.

"Kayla is still stuck in college. It's like she never left. She needs professional help," Monica repeated, raising her eyes to reveal a charcoal-gray shadow that matched her suit jacket. "You should be on high alert if she comes around again. She's on a path of self-destruction, and she doesn't care who she takes out on the way. But I'm not letting her anywhere near Eli. She's not going to ruin his reputation. He's on a path to literary stardom. I refuse to let Kayla get in our way."

A path to literary stardom?

This guy?

Under different circumstances, I might have assumed there was lingering bad blood between the former roommates, but my recent interactions with Kayla told me that Monica probably had a valid point about her needing professional help. They had been close in college. If anyone should suggest an intervention, Monica made the most sense. Though if there was something from our college days still troubling Kayla, then I of all people could understand that.

Thankfully, the rest of Eli's reading was uneventful, although I disagreed with Monica's vision of him becoming a household name. His self-satisfied smile while reading a painfully detailed passage filled with unnecessary gore about a gruesome murder on the rocky California coastline was off-putting, even to a hardened crime reader like me. His short story didn't draw me in. It creeped me out. I suppose that was the point, but I couldn't imagine the uptight man with pinched cheeks who fiddled with his turtleneck the entire time he was speaking going on any of the morning talk shows or even engaging with readers for that matter.

When tepid applause broke out as Eli read the final line in his short story, I ducked out to check in with Hal. I found him behind the cash register in the foyer, placing Signed Copy stickers on a new stack of autographed books. The scent of a woodsy library candle burning on the counter added to the bookish atmosphere.

"Well, how are you feeling about everything so far?" I asked, pointing to a three-foot-tall stack of orders.

He rested his hand on my shoulder. "Annie Murray, you have already surpassed my expectations." His eyes lit up with joy. He held my gaze momentarily. "The cash registers are overflowing, metaphorically speaking." He motioned to the iPad that served as our point-of-sale system. It had taken some convincing for Hal to give up his carbon copy order forms, which he used to always sign with a skull and dagger. "There's a brief lull at the moment since everyone is in the Conservatory, but don't let that fool you. I've been ringing up sales nonstop. The last time we had this many people in the store, the Beatles were still at the top of the charts."

"The Beatles will always have a place at the top of the charts, Hal. They're classic." I winked.

"My point is that the Mystery Fest is already a success, and it has barely gotten started." He stopped himself and held up a wrinkled finger. "Oh, that reminds me. Do you have a minute to swing by State of Mind? They have a couple of questions about the mysterious pub crawl that neither Fletcher nor I could answer."

"Sure. No problem."

Hal smiled kindly, holding back tears. "Annie, I can't thank you enough for this. For all of this." He swept his hand toward the windows where a group of customers admired maps of the English countryside with the locations of every murder in Agatha Christie's novels marked in red ink. Then he pointed behind us toward the Conservatory. Raucous laughter and applause broke out for the thriller writer ending her keynote.

"No thanks is necessary." I squeezed his arm and took off before my emotions got the better of me, too. I didn't know if it was seeing Kayla again or the stress and excitement of the festival, but I felt like I was teetering on the edge of a meltdown and needed to hold it together. It didn't help that having my former college classmates in town had brought Scarlet's murder to the forefront. It was impossible not to think about her. She would have loved this. She would have been my partner in crime with every step of the planning. It wasn't fair that her life had been cut so drastically short.

I closed my eyes tight to try to shut out the memories. When I opened them again, I resolved to push Scarlet to the recess of my head and focus on the rest of the day.

The State of Mind Public House was on the opposite side of the village square from the bookshop. I'd been so busy inside all day that it was a pleasant surprise to step outside into the warm afternoon air and stretch my legs. I couldn't believe how many readers were strolling the sidewalks as I turned off the pressed gravel path. People carried bookish totes and studied the map Fletcher had designed. Redwood Grove glowed underneath the midday sun. Puffy white clouds dotted an otherwise calm blue sky.

I hurried past the Stag Head. There was no chance I was going to risk bumping into Liam Donovan today. I drank in the sound of laughter and conversations and waved happy greetings to readers lined up for ice cream and eating at outdoor patio tables at the pizzeria. It had been one thing to imagine this but another to witness my vision coming true in real life.

When I passed Cryptic, I was tempted to stop in for a coffee and say hi to Pri, but the line stretched from the register to the sidewalk—yet another reason Liam's refusal to participate didn't make sense. Business was booming.

Oh well, his loss.

State of Mind was in a Spanish-style building with a burnt

stucco exterior and red-tile roof. A small enclosed seating area, shaded by large umbrellas, invited people passing by to stop in and enjoy a cold beer on a warm summer afternoon. Music wafted from speakers made to look like rocks artfully placed around the patio. The bistro-style tables were packed with the lunchtime crowd, and the smell of grains, hops, and grilling burgers made my stomach rumble.

My enthusiasm faded as I approached the pub and spotted Kayla arguing with the bartender, Justin. He was a few years younger than us but looked as if he'd seen some rough years.

What was Kayla doing? Was she haunting me?

She was leaning against an oversized terracotta potted palm with a beer in hand.

"You can't take that past the patio," Justin warned.

"What are you going to do? It's beer, Justin. Chill." She lunged at him.

"No, it's the law." Justin responded by physically blocking the exit with his body. "I could get fired if I let you off the premises with an open container."

She ignored him and stumbled forward, holding her beer over the edge of the stucco fence. "It's a freaking pint of beer. This is a mystery festival. What—I can't walk and drink at the same time?"

"No, you can't. You have to finish it here." Justin held his arms out to stop her. He was a good foot taller than her with muscular arms, a goatee, and reflective sunglasses that made him look more like a bouncer at a nightclub than a bartender at an organic taphouse.

"God, you're such a rule follower all of a sudden." Kayla chugged the pint like she was back at a frat party. She set the empty beer glass upside down on one of the outdoor keg tables. "Are you satisfied? Am I free to leave now?"

"Knock yourself out." Justin shrugged and shook his head.

"You wish." Kayla twirled a finger in the air as she tripped over the cobblestones and stumbled away.

I waited until she was out of sight before continuing. I felt sorry for her, but if I didn't see her again for another ten years—or ever—that was fine with me.

Justin watched her go and then picked up the empty glass.

"What was that all about?" I asked, walking inside with him.

"Don't get me started." He rolled his eyes and pushed his sunglasses on the top of his head. His hair was cropped tight in a buzz cut like he'd spent time in the military. "She's at least five or six drinks in. I cut her off, but I'm sure she probably has a stash back at her hotel. She thinks since we're flesh and blood—her words, not mine—I can bend the rules for her. I can't. I had to cut her off."

"That's right. She's your cousin. She mentioned that last night, but it slipped my mind."

"I wish it would slip mine." Justin motioned to the door. "You coming in?"

"Yeah." I followed him inside the pub. An impressive display of taps on the wall showcased the large variety of craft beers brewed on-site. Retro video game consoles like Super Mario Bros. and PAC-MAN, along with shuffleboard and darts, took up half of the interior space. "I take it you and Kayla aren't close." I felt a wave of nostalgia for Scarlet. Being an only child without any extended family living close by made for some lonely times during my formative years. My parents loved me. I had no doubts about that, but they were wrapped up in their own problems and had little time to entertain me. Books became my best friends. I traveled on adventures around the world, curled up in a cozy chair on the third floor of my local library. When I met Scarlet in college, it was like having a real-life sister. Everything I imagined from the stories that shaped me—*Little Women*, The Chronicles of Narnia, and *From the*

Mixed-Up Files of Mrs. Basil E. Frankweiler—were true with Scarlet. She was the cousin and sister I never had, which made losing her sting even more.

"Kayla's only close with herself." Justin walked around to the other side of the bar and deposited the empty glass in the sink. Polaroids of State of Mind's Mug Club members were tacked next to rows of beer steins.

That seemed like a fair assessment.

I swallowed the tightness in my throat and studied the digital display above the tap handles that described each beer in detail. A grapefruit sour brewed with gummy candy and grapefruit rind caught my eye. "It seems weird that she's in town for the Mystery Fest. I wouldn't have picked something bookish as being her scene."

"Is that what she told you?" He sounded incredulous. "Nah. She's not here for the Fest."

That was intriguing; I waited for him to continue but he didn't elaborate.

An awkward silence lingered as he rinsed the glass in the sink and I read the description of the two mystery beers their head brewer had crafted for the weekend. Unlike the Stag Head, the staff at the pub had gone all in for the weekend.

I picked up the special menu they had printed with hop cone skulls.

The first beer was "Everyone's Favorite Belgian Stout." The tasting note read: "Dry and malty, this stout has been aged in German oak barrels, with notes of red wine and tobacco. Wait for a surprising twist at the end."

They also brewed a "Private Rye," a farmhouse ale infused with warming spices and a touch of chili to add extra heat.

I looked at Justin, who was still keeping busy and decided to ask him outright. "So why is Kayla here?" I asked, setting the special beer menu on the bar and glancing around. Most of the tables and booths were empty. Everyone wanted to be outside soaking up the sun. Beer posters and artwork from the region lined the walls. Dried hop strands and tiny lights were strung from the ceiling. Pint glasses waiting to be filled with frothy beer floated on shelves above the taps.

"I don't think that's my story to tell. Kayla's got her reasons, and I'm guessing they all have to do with money." Justin put the glass in the dishwasher and wiped his hands on a logoed towel.

That was an odd response.

"You mean the work she's doing for Artifacts?"

"Yeah. Sure." Justin gave me a noncommittal shrug.

I could tell that he wasn't going to give me anything more, so I shifted gears. "I heard that you had some questions about the pub crawl?"

Justin pulled out his phone and went over the layout of the event schedule. The mysterious pub crawl would have readers stopping at a variety of bars and restaurants for food and drink specials and to search for their next clue. He wanted to make sure our itinerary lined up and needed confirmation about what each of the other participating locations were offering.

I appreciated how invested Justin was in the event. It was the opposite response from insufferable Liam Donovan. I had gone over all these details last night, but Justin couldn't attend the meeting since he was bartending. To be honest, I didn't mind filling him in because if I was going to continue to see Kayla throughout the weekend, it was good to be armed with as much intel on her as possible. After sharing the information I had disseminated last night, we finished our conversation, and I headed back to the bookshop.

We were only a few hours away from the kickoff party at the Grand Hotel. Even though things seemed to be going well already, I wanted to make sure that I hadn't missed any other details or overlooked something important. Between the dozens of authors and hundreds of readers in town for the weekend, my brain was working overtime to keep everything straight.

When I arrived at the Secret Bookcase, Fletcher stopped me at the front door. "Oh, good, Annie, you're back. I'm ringing up everyone in the queue. Would you mind going to help a customer who is on the hunt for some rare vintage titles? She's looking for something similar to a Trixie Belden and Cherry Ames. She's waiting in the Sitting Room."

"Sure. No problem." I walked past the cozy seating area in front of the windows and found the customer in the Sitting Room, delving into the rows of shelves to help the customer find the books she was looking for.

After I sent her on her way with a stack of reads, I decided to check the secret bookcase to see if I needed to restock the clues. A group of readers were huddled together outside it, trying to pose for a selfie in front of the shelves.

"Can I take the photo for you?" I asked.

They squeezed together, holding up their secret letters like trophies.

"Thank you so much," one of the women gushed. "We are so thrilled to be here, and already there are so many authentic touches: a secret bookcase, a dead body. We can't wait for tonight's kickoff party and to find our first clue. We think we know, but don't tell us."

"My lips are sealed." I pressed my finger to my mouth. "Good luck and enjoy." I was about to continue when the words "a dead body" repeated in my head. "I'm sorry, wait, did you say dead body?"

"Yes." The woman bobbed her head and looked at her friends. "For a minute there, we thought it was real. Your actor never flinched. You hired a true professional. They didn't so much as bat an eyelash. And the blood looked so real. When the door spun open, and there was a body slumped on the chair, I nearly had a heart attack." She pounded her chest with her palm to prove her point.

The women giggled and left.

I froze. What body?

We hadn't hired an actor.

Hal would never have okayed fake blood near the rare books.

If someone was playing dead behind the secret bookcase, they definitely were not supposed to be there.

EIGHT

I turned to the bookcase, fully prepared to kick out whoever was pretending to play dead behind the shelves. I didn't have time for pranksters. Not that I didn't appreciate the effort. A body in the bookcase certainly fit the vibe, but since readers had to access the hidden spot to get their first clue, I didn't want to confuse anyone. Or worse, scare them off. That would be a logistical nightmare. I could already picture a line of dozens of angry readers demanding clues to the puzzle I'd worked so hard to put together.

"Can you give me a minute?" I asked another group waiting their turn to locate the lever and swing open the book-filled door. "We have a little bookcase maintenance to take care of. If you can return in about five or ten minutes, that would be great." I didn't want to cause a scene, so I waited for them to clear out.

It was harder than usual to push the bookshelf open. That was probably because whoever had decided to take up residence as a dead body in the secret room was likely crammed in there. It wasn't like the space was big. At most, the person could sit on the chair with their legs stretched out. But who would want to be in the coffin-like space, sitting in the dark for hours?

I shuddered at the thought.

I braced my feet on the floor and forced the door open.

It took a second for my eyes to register what I was seeing. I threw my hand over my mouth and blinked hard as I tried to process it; the clues were scattered across the floor and spattered with blood.

That was blood.

A lot of blood.

And legs and a body.

I realized it was Kayla, slumped in the chair, her head hanging against her chest, and a red stain spread across her stomach.

"Kayla, what are you doing?" I stepped into the stagnant space, overwhelmed by the almost metallic aroma.

Why was she pretending to be dead?

Was she so drunk that she passed out while waiting to scare readers?

She was the last person I expected to play a childish prank. Then again, she had been drinking since long before noon and was volatile, to say the least, so I wouldn't put it past her. Fletcher had ordered fake blood packets and blood splatter, crime scene tape, and plastic cleavers for the noir section. They had been selling well. I guessed Kayla must have stained her shirt with one of the packets.

I had to admit it looked realistic.

"Kayla, get up." I bent over and nudged her shoulder.

Her head flopped to the other side, but she didn't move.

A tightness spread up my neck. I clutched my hands into tight balls.

Something wasn't right.

She was out cold.

"Kayla, are you okay?" I released my grip and nudged her again.

She didn't move.

Was she breathing?

Panic began to build inside me. My throat felt like it was closing up and sweat pooled on my forehead. A mild buzzing sounded in my head. Everything was fuzzy, like I had slipped into an alternative reality.

This couldn't be happening. Could it?

I placed my hand under her nose.

She wasn't breathing. Suddenly, reality hit.

"Get help! Call 911," I yelled, hoping that anyone was within earshot.

The blood was real. She hadn't passed out from drinking. She was bleeding to death.

Then I placed my hands on the wound on Kayla's stomach and tried to stop the bleeding. It was likely futile. There was too much.

Was I applying pressure hard enough?

Should I start CPR?

How long had Kayla been here?

I needed to stop thinking and just act. I wiped my bloody hands on the area rug, lowered Kayla to the floor, and started CPR. Time seemed to move at a surreal pace like everything was moving in slow motion. Five minutes or five hours could have passed.

"Annie, Annie, what's going on?" Fletcher appeared out of nowhere behind me, with wide eyes and sweat beading on his brow.

He broke my momentum.

"Annie, what's going on? Why aren't you answering me? I heard screaming." He took one step closer, peering over me, and then recoiled.

"It's Kayla," I said, continuing chest compressions. "She's not breathing, and she's lost a lot of blood."

Fletcher clasped one hand over his mouth and used the other to steady himself. "I don't do so well with blood."

"How can you have a problem with blood? You watch more BBC mysteries than anyone on the planet," I snapped unintentionally. I didn't want to take my stress out on Fletcher, but I needed help.

"That's different. That's fiction." He shrank backward, clutching his stomach like he was going to throw up. "Annie, your hands are covered in blood."

"I know because I'm trying to save her." I felt like I couldn't get enough oxygen. My chest tightened as I used all my strength to press against Kayla's chest. "Fletcher, you have to help me."

"What do you need me to do?" His voice squeaked as he clenched his fists and came closer.

"Take off your sweatshirt." I kept my rhythmic motions on Kayla's chest. "We have to try and stop the bleeding."

A shudder ripped through Fletcher's body as he tugged off his Sherlock sweatshirt. His breath hitched.

"Put it on her stomach," I commanded.

His eyes widened as he took in the horrifying scene, but he followed my directions, placing his sweatshirt on Kayla's wound with trembling hands.

"Is she dead?" Fletcher's lips curled back slightly like he was trying to get rid of a bitter taste in his mouth.

"I don't know. I think so, but I'm not giving up." I glanced outside the closeted space, feeling like the walls were closing in. "You need to call 911."

He fumbled through his pockets. "I'll be right back. My phone is at the cash register. I'll call for help." Fletcher rushed out to call an ambulance while I continued CPR.

I was vaguely aware of sounds just outside the bookcase. I could hear whispers and nervous chatter, but it was like I was swimming underwater, and my ears had flooded. Nothing sounded clear or crisp.

Kayla wasn't responding.

How long was it going to take for help to arrive?

My fingers were going numb. Tiny zaps spread up the muscles in my arms as I tried to revive Kayla.

Fletcher returned, squeezing back into the room, breathless and flushed. "Okay, they're on the way. What else can I do?"

"I have no idea." My limbs were moving like a puppet being controlled by invisible strings. I couldn't stop, even though I was fairly certain Kayla was gone.

"Does she have a pulse?" He focused on me, refusing to look at Kayla's lifeless body.

I didn't blame him. I wasn't enjoying this either. "No."

"You're holding it together so well, Annie." Fletcher gulped like he was going to be sick. "They should be here any minute."

Everything is going to be okay. Everything has to be okay. The paramedics will be here soon; they will save her.

We had to keep trying until help arrived.

I tried to distract myself, but I kept seeing Scarlet's face instead of Kayla's.

It's just your imagination, Annie.

Was I losing it?

A wobbly sensation came over my body like I was being dropped from the top of a roller coaster. My fingers felt cold.

I wasn't sure how much longer I could do this.

Only seconds later, the paramedics arrived. I got to my feet, stars immediately clouding my vision. Fletcher steadied me as we made room for the professionals. I gladly let them take over.

He braced himself against the closest bookcase, using the shelf for support. "You did great, Annie."

That's when reality sunk in.

Someone brought me a towel to wipe Kayla's blood from my hands.

I stared at my stained fingers like they didn't belong to me. They tingled like they'd gone numb. I felt numb. This couldn't be real.

Fletcher stood next to me, his feet rooted to the floor as if some sort of malevolent force was holding him there. "She's dead, isn't she? I knew it. I knew it the second I saw you. It's too much blood."

A wave of revulsion washed over me. He was right. The blood wasn't coming off of my hands and Kayla wasn't coming back to life.

My knees buckled.

"Annie, are you okay?" Fletcher reached out an arm to help me.

I pressed my back to the bookcase and slid down the stacks until I landed on the floor. Kayla was dead. Dead in our bookshop.

How?

And why?

She couldn't have stabbed herself in the stomach, could she?

Someone must have killed her, but where was the weapon? And how could someone have stabbed her in the middle of the day and not been seen?

Nothing made sense.

"Annie, you don't look so good." Fletcher looked at me with trepidation. "Should I call the paramedics over?"

"No. I'm fine. I just need to sit here and remember how to breathe."

Fletcher chomped the inside of his cheek as he considered this. "I'm going to get you a glass of water. Just keep breathing. You're okay. Don't move."

Where would I go?

I glanced around. The bookshelves that usually brought me so much delight suddenly felt like they were closing in on me.

I had a feeling Fletcher was reminding me I was okay for his own sake as much as mine.

Our roles had quickly reversed.

I've always been good in the moment in an emergency. It's the after where I tend to fall apart. Take Scarlet, for example. I had held it together for her funeral and graduation. I remember everyone praising me for how well I handled my grief. It was just a shaky façade that came crumbling down the minute I was alone.

The same thing was happening now, but it was almost worse because I didn't have the luxury of falling apart for days, weeks, or years. We had hundreds of people arriving for the cocktail party in just a few hours. Even the most macabre mystery fan was unlikely to take any pleasure in hearing about an actual murder.

Redwood Grove was one of the safest places I knew. The closest we came to crime in town was when the high schoolers pulled their annual senior prank and temporarily dyed the lake purple or set up a petting zoo in the village square. It was no secret that Kayla had made a bad first impression, but I never would have imagined that could have led to her brutal and untimely death.

Another thought invaded as I watched the first responders place her body on a gurney. Could we be dealing with a serial killer?

What were the odds that yet another of my college classmates would be killed? Could Kayla's death be somehow connected to Scarlet's? It didn't make sense. I hadn't seen Kayla in nearly a decade. But then again, I couldn't ignore the timing. We bumped into one another last night, and less than twenty-four hours later, she was dead.

Was it me?

Was I some kind of a curse?

NINE

Fletcher returned with a glass of water, and Hal's face went slack with shock when his eyes landed on Kayla's body. He blinked rapidly like he was trying to clear his vision.

"Fletcher told me, but, but I can't believe it," he stammered, pressing his palm against his chest.

I took a timid sip of water. My hands were still so shaky that I didn't trust myself not to spill it everywhere. Logically, I knew Kayla's death wasn't my fault, but I couldn't help feeling responsible. This never would have happened if it wasn't for Mystery Fest. I hated seeing the anguish on Hal's gentle face. This was supposed to be a day of celebration, the start of something great for our beloved bookstore.

"Annie, you found her? Who would have done such a thing?" Hal's bushy white eyebrows shot up. He glanced around the room as if expecting the killer to be standing nearby holding a bloody murder weapon.

"I have no idea," I answered honestly, pressing the cold edge of the glass to my lips.

"How long has she been there?" Hal asked, fiddling with a

string on the hem of his cardigan and staring at the hardwood floor.

I couldn't tell if he was addressing me or the first responders. It was just Fletcher, me, Hal, and the emergency medics in the Sitting Room. From my vantage point on the floor, I could only see the bottom of the bookshelves.

"We've secured the room and informed everyone to stay where they are. A detective is on her way," one of the paramedics replied while silencing a walkie-talkie tethered to his waist. "She'll answer any questions you have."

"How was she killed?" Hal pressed. He yanked the end of the yarn on his sweater as he spoke, wrapping it around his index finger and pacing from one end of the bookstacks to the other. There wasn't far for him to go. It was strange to watch him pause in front of a row of P. D. James novels as our own mystery was playing out in front of us. He looked as lost as I felt. "She was killed in the store? When?"

"Sorry, the police and detective will answer those kinds of questions," the paramedic repeated.

"What do we do about the festival?" Hal asked me.

"I don't know." I glanced to the front of the room where I had helped put out assorted teas and snacks for readers just a short time ago. We had set up a Miss Marple-style self-serve tea for festivalgoers with pretty porcelain teapots and tiered displays with bite-size macarons, petit fours, and chocolate truffles. This couldn't be happening. "What time is it?"

Hal rolled up the sleeve of his cardigan to check his watch. "Nearly five."

"The cocktail party is in less than two hours." I could hear a high pitch creeping into my tone. "Should I call and cancel now? I have no sense of how long this is going to take."

"Is the party here?" one of the paramedics interjected.

"No, it's at the hotel," I said, suddenly realizing I needed to stand.

"The police will likely want to close the bookstore for a while to do their due diligence, but I can't imagine a reason they'd ask you to cancel an event somewhere else." The paramedic turned his torso as he replied to shield my view of the body.

"Is it okay if I move to the front to wait for the detective?" I started to stand, but my legs revolted. My muscles quivered like I'd just completed an intense Pilates session. "I'm feeling a little claustrophobic."

"That's fine. Just don't leave the room."

Hal and Fletcher helped me to my feet, each taking an arm.

"I can walk," I protested, but the truth was my knees felt like soggy oatmeal.

Hal linked his arm tighter and took small steps toward the bay windows.

They walked me to the tea cart.

"Why don't you sit in one of the chairs?" Fletcher suggested, pointing to a soft pale-yellow reading chair beside the bay windows.

I didn't have the energy to refuse. Their kindness made me want to cry.

I sunk into the chair.

Fletcher prepared a cup of tea while Hal shuffled toward the door.

The paramedics had managed to keep everyone out of the Sitting Room, but word must have spread throughout the bookshop because through the open doorway I could see readers pressed together in the hallway, hoping to catch a glimpse of what was happening.

"Let's go ahead and close this," Hal said gently to the paramedic positioned at the entrance to the room.

"Good idea," the paramedic replied, shutting the door.

"Should we have everyone leave?" Hal asked the paramedic, helping himself to a chocolate-covered cherry cookie.

"No one is leaving the premises," an authoritative voice announced.

I looked over just in time to see a woman open the door and push through the group of gawkers. Two uniformed police officers followed her.

Her heels clicked on the floor as she brushed past the cozy sitting area in front of the windows and approached us. "Not until I give you permission to leave."

"I'm not trying to flee a crime scene," Hal protested.

The woman wearing black slacks and a white blouse came closer, giving off an instant air of control. "Be that as it may, this is my investigation, and no one is cleared to leave the building."

I stared at her petite frame, oversized black glasses, and silver-white bob and couldn't believe my eyes. "Dr. Caldwell?"

She inched closer. "Oh, my goodness, Annie Murray, what are you doing here?"

I tried to stand, but my legs refused to obey. "I work here. I found her—"

Dr. Caldwell gasped and placed her hand over her heart. "Annie, it's been years. I'm certainly saddened that we're meeting again under these circumstances, but it's lovely to see my favorite student."

I blushed at her compliment.

"You two know each other?" Hal asked.

"Dr. Caldwell was my criminology professor in college," I answered. Then I looked up at my former mentor. "Are you still teaching?"

"I do an occasional class now and then, but I left not long after you to pursue a career in the field. After so many years behind a desk, I decided it was time to put my theories and research into practice. I've been a detective for nearly six years, but this is my first month in Redwood Grove. I had no idea you were here, too."

I smiled, feeling a sliver of relief. Dr. Caldwell was my

favorite professor in college. She was a brilliant mind who encouraged me to follow my passion. She had been devastated when I told her at graduation that I didn't think I would continue. I think she knew that I was in the throes of shock over Scarlet because she advised me to give it some time and made me promise to reach out if I changed my mind. She had an abundance of contacts in law enforcement and told me that she would gladly help me make connections and provide a glowing recommendation.

Time hadn't changed my mind. Dr. Caldwell and I lost touch. I had left dreams of starting my own private detective agency—something Scarlet and I always planned to do together —or landing a job as a criminal profiler long, long in the past, until now. I wondered how Dr. Caldwell was going to react when she realized that Kayla was the victim. It was quite a coincidence. Too much of a coincidence, in fact.

Dr. Caldwell's eyes scanned the space with an experienced, practiced gaze. I knew without a doubt that she was taking in the number of occupants, the crime scene, visible exits, and potential escape routes. Nothing about her relaxed posture and neutral expression betrayed the rapid-fire analysis happening behind her eyes.

She stepped forward and addressed a uniformed officer waiting nearby. "Clear the room, please. Except for Ms. Murray."

I waited on the chair, drinking tiny sips of the cinnamon tea Fletcher made for me while Dr. Caldwell got right to work. She surveyed the entire room.

She used her flashlight to scan the ceiling, shelves, and flooring. Then she took in the broader room, surveying everything from the tea and cookies to the large bay windows, checking to make sure they were locked.

We had gone through dozens of simulated crime scenes in college, but watching Dr. Caldwell in action was a sight to behold. She directed her team to place yellow evidence markers, collect materials, and photograph the scene.

When she was satisfied that no stone (or book) had been left unturned, she approached me. "Are you feeling up to showing me exactly how you found the victim?" She motioned to two plush chairs near the tea service.

"Yeah." The shaky feeling had subsided. I got to my feet and followed her.

"Take your time," she encouraged. "Walk me through step by step."

Flashes of Scarlet's face came rushing through my vision like a movie. I blinked, trying to force the images away. Kayla was dead. This wasn't Scarlet.

"Um, I was helping a customer find a title." I pointed in the direction of the bookshelves with my blood-stained finger. An ache grew in the back of my throat. "A group was posing for a selfie in front of the secret bookcase. I offered to take the picture for them," I continued, replaying each scene. If I could concentrate on helping Dr. Caldwell, it might keep my fear from taking over. "They were the ones who said there was a body in the bookcase; they thought it was part of the setup—someone playing dead."

"Did you notice anything unusual or out of place before you discovered the victim?" she asked.

"No." I held my elbows tight against my body as I forced my brain to remember every detail. "I asked the handful of readers who were browsing to give me a few minutes because I thought someone was playing a prank. The door didn't budge at first." I continued relaying everything that had happened until she arrived.

"Excellent. Your perspective is quite helpful." She readjusted her reading glasses. "If you don't mind, please wait here while I finish examining the crime scene."

I watched in awe, taking copious internal notes as she

studied Kayla from every angle. Did she recognize her? Kayla hadn't studied criminology, but I wondered if their paths had ever crossed on campus. The college was a small liberal arts school, so it wasn't out of the realm of possibility that she could have known Kayla.

If she did remember her, she gave no indication during her careful assessment of the crime scene. When she finished, she motioned to the front with the tip of her pencil. "Should we go sit and have a chat?"

"Sure," I replied, moving in that direction. I wanted nothing more than to be as far away as possible from Kayla's body.

"Annie, I'm still gobsmacked to see you. How have you been?" Her cobalt-blue eyes narrowed with a mixture of concern and eagerness.

"Okay, I mean, aside from this." I glanced at my bloody hands as I sat on the window bench.

"Of course."

"You don't think this could be connected to Scarlet, do you?" I blurted out before I could form a coherent thought. Obviously, the idea bothered me more than I realized.

"Why would you ask that?" She tipped her head to the side.

"Kayla was in our class, too. Did you know her?" My voice didn't sound like it was coming from me.

Dr. Caldwell's gaze flashed in the direction of the back briefly. "She was? You knew her?"

"Not well." I shook my head. Then I told her about bumping into Kayla last night and what a mess she'd been as well as the earlier incidents I'd witnessed.

She listened carefully and then jotted down a few more notes. "I can't imagine how the two could be connected, but I'll certainly take this background into consideration as I continue with the investigation."

"Do you think someone stabbed her?"

"It appears that way. What's the next question you would

ask yourself?" Dr. Caldwell pressed her glasses back up the bridge of her nose.

"I'd wonder about the weapon, the angle of the wound, and how much force the killer would have had to use to deliver a fatal blow." My analytic mind took over, thankfully.

"Well done." She nodded. "Could the killer have stabbed her inside this glorified closet?"

"No. There's barely enough room for her, let alone another person." I considered my words, realizing that they were true. Kayla couldn't have been killed inside the closet.

"So, we can assume she was stabbed somewhere else and ended up behind the bookcase, correct?"

I felt like I was back in her lecture hall. I could almost see the flicker of yellow fluorescent lighting and smell the overpowering aroma of the industrial cleaner the janitorial staff used to disinfect the classroom.

"Yes." I nodded, feeling my confidence growing. This is what I had spent my entire collegiate career studying. It was cellular memory reigniting in my body. "There's no blood trail, so it's more likely she was stabbed nearby, but then again, she could have stumbled into the Sitting Room before she lost a lot of blood. Or the killer could have found her inside and stabbed her here."

"How easy is it to find the lever on the bookshelf?" Dr. Caldwell pushed her glasses to the top of her head. "Could you show me?"

"Yeah. It's fairly easy if you know what you're looking for." I got to my feet and pointed out the book that unlocked the secret door.

She took a few photos, careful not to touch the book. Then she called her team waiting by the door over to check that area for fingerprints. "Any theories on what might have led our victim here?" she said to me, returning her glasses to the bridge of her nose.

"I've been thinking about that," I admitted. It had been a long time since I had evaluated a crime scene, but the meticulous process came flooding back. "Could she have been looking for something in the secret bookcase or trying to leave a message about someone who was after her?"

"Continue." Dr. Caldwell waited.

"Let's say the killer stabbed her over there." I pointed to the shelves directly across from the secret bookcase. "We've been busy today. Readers have been in and out of the Sitting Room all day. The killer would have had a tiny window to stab Kayla and make their escape. My first thought was that maybe the killer stashed the murder weapon behind the bookcase, but nothing was found with her, right?"

"Correct." She gave me a curt nod.

"That lends to the second possibility, which is that Kayla was attempting to hide or maybe even retrieve something important in her last moments," I said, hearing the doubt in my tone. "Or, she happened to accidentally bump into the lever as she succumbed to her wounds, the latch opened, and she landed on the floor. But readers have since opened the bookcase, so who closed her inside?"

"Who, indeed?" Dr. Caldwell raised one eyebrow.

"Wait, could the killer have intentionally shut her in the bookcase so she couldn't get help? Would her wound have been fatal?"

A hint of a sad smile of approval tugged on Dr. Caldwell's cheeks. "The medical experts will have to be consulted on that, but it goes without saying that had Kayla received medical attention immediately, her odds of surviving her injury would certainly be higher. It's not a guarantee, but the faster the medical response, the better her chances."

"So the killer could have left her there to die," I said sadly, trying to decide whether it was viable. "It would have been pitch-black inside the secret room, and without knowing where the lock was, Kayla would have struggled to figure out how to get out."

"My assessment, exactly." She flipped through her notes. "We didn't see any evidence of cameras in the room. Could we have missed those?"

I shook my head. "No. Hal is a true Luddite. Fletcher and I have been telling him to install cameras throughout the book-shop to catch shoplifters, but he refuses. I don't think he really cares about theft, to tell you the truth. I think he's just happy to have people reading."

"So where does that leave us?"

"Interviewing witnesses to try and determine whether anyone might have witnessed the incident."

"You always were my top student, Annie." She closed her notebook. "I know it's a lot to ask and an imposition, but if you're up for it, I would love your eyes and input over the next few days. It would be helpful to have someone on the inside, so to speak."

She was asking for *my* help?

I had gone from putting on a mystery festival to solving a real-life murder. Could this day get any more bizarre?

TEN

Dr. Caldwell called Hal and Fletcher back into the Sitting
Room to take their statements. She agreed that the opening
reception could continue as planned. She gave us thorough
instructions on how to proceed. "The store will remain closed
through the remainder of the evening," she explained to Hal,
Fletcher, and me. "My hope is that we'll be able to allow you to
re-open in the morning."

"Should we come up with a backup plan just in case?" I
asked, looking at Hal. "Readers are still slotted to pick up their
first clue in the secret bookcase."

"I don't anticipate any issues," Dr. Caldwell said with a
general calm tone. "I will need a staff member to remain on-site
until we complete our investigation."

Hal practically pushed Fletcher and me toward the door.
"You two go. I'll stay."

"But you don't want to miss a murderous cocktail hour
either," Fletcher replied. He realized what he had said and
pressed his hand over his lips. "Sorry, too soon. That was in bad
taste."

"It's fine to continue with the event," Dr. Caldwell assured him. "It's not in the best interest of my investigation for there to be a furor. Proceeding with festivities as normal will be helpful for my team. We know how important this is for Redwood Grove and all of you, and I will do my best to work swiftly."

I didn't doubt that, but I was torn about continuing. My former college classmate was dead. Connection or not, it was impossible not to let thoughts of Scarlet sneak in. Every worst-case scenario played on a loop. What if a serial killer was stalking my former classmates? What if this was because of me? What if I was next?

My chin trembled. I suddenly had a strong desire to be alone right now, back in the cozy sanctuary of my home with Professor Plum, to process what had happened.

But I couldn't escape the reality that Kayla had been brutally murdered. She had been obnoxious, but clearly troubled too; could something else have been going on with her?

Hal nudged me, bringing me back into the moment. "Go on, Annie. You and Fletcher should hold down the fort at the reception. I'll come find you when we're done here."

"Annie, you have my cell. Call me anytime." Dr. Caldwell gave me a knowing look.

I nodded and made to leave with Fletcher.

"I need to change," I told Fletcher as he held open the door for me, noticing my bloody hands quivering uncontrollably.

"Me too. I'll wait for you in the front." He held a deerstalker cap and patted my shoulder. "It's going to be okay, Annie. I think the cocktail party will be a good distraction for you. For all of us."

I swallowed the lump in my throat and went to the bathroom to scrub my hands and change into a black dress I'd brought along with me for the party.

The party. Kayla is dead, and I am going to a party.

I stared in the mirror, splashing water on my face to try and center myself back in reality. My freckles stood out against my pale skin. I pinched my cheeks to try and revive my color. Then I tied my hair into a ponytail and applied some lip gloss. That was the best I could do. Considering the ordeal I'd just been through, being upright seemed like a major achievement to me.

I let out a long breath and worked up the courage to return to the front of the store. My feet felt like lead. I had a feeling that I was going to be bombarded by questions about Kayla's murder tonight, and I wasn't sure how to handle answering any of them.

"You're going to have to wing it," I said to myself as I shut the bathroom door, giving my appearance one final appraisal. For someone who'd just found a dead body, I didn't look as bad as I expected. I just needed to get through the kickoff reception. Then I could go home and fall apart.

"Annie, you look great," Fletcher said, buttoning the top of his cape. No detail had gone unnoticed in his costume, from his Ulster coat with a cape and sleeves, matching hat, monocle, and calabash pipe.

I managed a small smile. "Thanks, so do you. People are going to mob you for Sherlock selfies."

He held the door open for me, gnawing on the tip of his fake plastic pipe with a wry smile. "The game is afoot, my friend."

The evening air was warm, and the sun hung low on the horizon, casting a peach glow over Redwood Grove. It was almost painful to see the village look so peaceful. What a change from a few hours ago. It felt wrong to go on with the festival, but then again, Dr. Caldwell was right. The event was important for the entire village, and readers were already there. It would feel equally worse to send them all home.

I hoped that news of Kayla's murder wouldn't put a damper on the weekend and scare customers away. The entire goal of the weekend had been to boost sales, not close the store.

"Do you think that the detective was odd?" Fletcher asked, motioning for me to go in front of him.

"Odd, how?" I wrinkled my eyes.

He cleared his throat and shifted his shoulders. "Uh, I simply mean it's odd that she was your professor. That's quite a coincidence, don't you think?"

"Yeah, that was a long time ago." I didn't want to talk about Dr. Caldwell or the past. I had one mission for the night—to get through the cocktail party.

Fletcher must have picked up on my energy because he gave me a worried nod. We fell in stride as we walked past the Stag Head, the pizzeria, and Cryptic on our way toward the Grand Hotel.

"Did she say who she thinks did it? You were talking for a long time." Fletcher sounded almost envious.

"No, I think it's too soon." My voice sounded dull and flat.

"It's not too soon if you ask me." He kicked a pebble out of my way. "I have a theory on who killed her. I tried to share my theory with the police officer who took my statement, but she didn't seem interested. I explained that I've read every one of Sir Arthur Conan Doyle's works multiple times, but that didn't even so much as pique her interest."

I almost laughed but stopped myself. It felt equally nice and completely wrong to feel normal, even for a second. "I'm pretty sure that the fictional tales of Sherlock and Watson don't qualify as prerequisites for murder investigations these days."

"Hey, speak for yourself. Modern methods of investigation have nothing on the deduction skills of Sherlock." He pulled a magnifying glass from beneath his cape and held it over his left eye.

"Tell me your theory, Fletcher. We're almost to the hotel."

"Keep your eye on Caroline." He moved the magnifying glass away from his eye and then back again.

I raised an eyebrow. "Caroline Miles? The owner of Artifacts?"

"Yep." Fletcher put the magnifying glass back in his pocket

and tipped his deerstalker cap to a group of readers passing by. "Did you know she came into the bookstore shortly before Kayla was killed?"

Technically, we didn't know when Kayla had been killed, but I decided it was better to gloss over that for the time being.

"No. When was that?" I slowed my pace to make room for a group of book lovers filing out of the wine bar. Readers packed the sidewalks in party attire as we neared the hotel.

"It was when you were at the pub." Fletcher fixed one of the flaps on his hat. "She stormed into the bookshop demanding to know whether I had seen Kayla."

"Really?"

"Yes. I tried to explain that to the police officer who dismissed me. I don't understand why. There's a killer on the loose. You would think they would want to follow every lead." He stopped to pose for photos with a group of readers, taking out his pipe and the magnifying glass.

I offered to take pictures and was suddenly bombarded with dozens of phones.

"Why was Caroline looking for Kayla?" I asked after his impromptu photo session was done.

"That is the question." He held the pipe to his lips. "She was furious. Absolutely furious and going on and on about how Kayla was out to destroy Artifacts and all of Redwood Grove in the process. I've never seen her like that, and to tell you the truth, she kind of scared me."

"What?" I stopped in mid-stride. I was glad Fletcher's pipe was fake because his face had gone ashen, and his voice sounded jittery like he'd had one too many of Pri's espressos.

"Yeah. She was fuming. Like I could almost see smoke coming out of her ears, her face was bright red, her skin was blotchy, and she was ready for war." Fletcher watched my reaction. "Right? That's not normal, is it? I've always considered

Caroline the village's grandmother, but she was more like the creepy old hag from 'Hansel and Gretel.'"

I laughed at his description then shook my head. "No, that's not at all like Caroline. But do you know why she was looking for Kayla at the store?"

Fletcher positioned the pipe on the side of his mouth and chewed on the tip. "She said that Kayla had just been at Artifacts. She kicked her out and followed her to the bookstore. When I told her I hadn't seen Kayla, which I hadn't, she freaked out even more. She took off toward the Conservatory on her own. I didn't see her again after that, but then Kayla ended up dead in the secret bookcase. It's more than a little odd."

"I agree. She's usually so easygoing. Did she give a reason why she was so upset with Kayla? I mean, I understand that Kayla didn't exactly endear herself to anyone in town, and from what Kaya told me last night, she had been working with Caroline to get her online store set up, but it was clear there was a lot of tension between them last night. I wonder if something happened between them?"

Fletcher pushed his houndstooth deerstalker cap off his eyes. "She didn't say much. She was on a mission to find Kayla, and nothing was going to stop her."

I thought back to the conversation between the two women last night. There had been palpable tension between them. Caroline hadn't tried to conceal her anger with Kayla. She had threatened Kayla in front of dozens of witnesses. Was that the behavior of a killer? If so, she'd been pretty obvious. But then again, maybe Kayla's murder looked like it had been a crime of passion. Perhaps Caroline had confronted Kayla and stabbed her in a flash of uncontrolled anger.

It was a stretch. Caroline didn't seem like the killing type, but I knew from my studies that it was too soon to rule anyone out as a suspect.

"What makes you think she killed Kayla?" I asked as we

approached the hotel, where a long line of guests was queued, waiting for the doors to open and the festivities to begin.

"Annie, when I say that Caroline was angry, I mean she was on fire. I could feel the heat coming off her body. She was in a rage. A rage that must have led her to track down Kayla, stab her, and take off before anyone had a chance to realize what she had done."

"That's a big accusation, Fletcher."

He nodded solemnly. "I'm aware of that fact. We need to keep a close eye on Caroline at the party tonight. That is if she shows."

"Okay," I said, humoring him. We squeezed past the line to the front doors.

Fletcher grabbed my arm before we went inside. "Annie, I'm deadly serious. If Caroline is the killer, we could be in danger."

"What? Why would we be in danger?" Caroline hosted wine and paint nights and knitting sessions with tea and pastries at Artifacts. She was also old enough to be my grandmother. I wasn't worried about her waiting to attack us down a dark alleyway.

"Because we work at the bookstore." Fletcher waved the pipe as he became more animated. "You've read enough mysteries. We could have seen too much. That puts us in harm's way. Caroline knows that we could have seen something. She probably knows that we were both interrogated by the police. I'm guessing that she's going to have an eye on us, so we should do the same."

Was he being paranoid?

Definitely.

Caroline sat on the library board and did sunrise yoga in the park. It was hard to imagine her turning violent. But again, I had to remind myself these weren't normal circumstances.

Kayla was dead, and if there was even a sliver of a chance that Fletcher had a valid point, I couldn't dismiss it.

"I always told my parents that countless weekends spent with my nose stuffed into a Sherlock Holmes novel was going to pay off at some point. This is our chance to shine, Annie. We both know the inner workings of the genre better than anyone. You studied criminology in college, and I'm a Sherlock scholar. The Universe is practically begging us to investigate. We just have to be super smart and careful."

I considered bringing up the fact that Fletcher was a self-proclaimed Sherlock scholar but decided against that, too. After my conversation with Dr. Caldwell, I would do whatever I could to bring Kayla's killer to justice.

If Caroline were the killer, that would mean there was no connection between Kayla's death and Scarlet's murder. I didn't believe she was capable of it, but part of me hoped I was wrong.

"I'll be on high alert," I said to Fletcher.

"And watch your back," he cautioned. "Remember, this isn't the plot of a novel. We're dealing with a criminal."

ELEVEN

Fletcher and I parted ways, his warning ringing in my head.

I went to check with the hotel staff to make sure everything was ready for the official opening event. It had taken a small army to prepare Redwood Grove for the influx of bookish tourists. Thanks to Hal's suggestion, we formed a planning committee to divide tasks. A group of volunteers focused on decking out the town square and storefronts with Mystery Fest banners, posters, and directional signs to make sure readers knew how to get from spot to spot. Another crew had concentrated on the pub crawl, assembling a map complete with a QR code and a digital phone app. I was humbled every time I thought about how much work our community had invested in my idea. I almost wanted to pinch myself because it didn't seem real. If it weren't for Kayla's murder, I might have been able to enjoy myself.

I needed to make sure that the rest of the event schedule went smoothly for the sake of my friends and colleagues in Redwood Grove and for my own sanity.

"Are you ready to see the ballroom?" a hotel staffer asked, pulling me out of my head.

"I can't wait." I followed her and let out a small gasp as she opened the doors.

The team at Grand Hotel had outdone themselves. The ballroom had been transformed. Gothic candelabras with flickering, tapered black candles adorned tables draped with matching black lace tablecloths. Antique typewriters held court as the centerpiece at each table. Bundles of burgundy roses added a pop of color. Although the sight of the deep red color made me immediately check my hands to make sure there was no trace of Kayla's blood.

A trio of high school jazz band members played Hitchcockian themes near the food and drink tables. The soft jazz music set the mood. Mournful saxophone notes weaved a melody of suspense. Servers in crisp white jackets were positioned around the room with trays of champagne spotted with bloody cherry syrup and cocktails served in poison bottles.

At the far end of the room, a stage with backlit silhouettes of magnifying glasses, vintage typewriters, and open books. A soft spotlight was poised to highlight the speakers. The mayor would give a speech, followed by the owner of the Grand Hotel, and then Fletcher, dressed as Sherlock, would offer readers their next clue in their quest.

"This is amazing," I told the staff member, who excused herself to check on the servers.

I felt relieved that at least everything in the ballroom was set for the night. The moody atmosphere was exactly what I had pictured when we first began plotting out the festival.

Of course, I never would have imagined that Redwood Grove would have a real murder.

Don't go there, Annie.

Focus on the party—one thing at a time. You just need to get through tonight.

Everyone would be allowed inside in a few minutes, so I

took the opportunity to get a glass of wine before things got busy. Maybe that would help take the edge off.

I felt like I had stepped into the pages of a golden age mystery as I passed the food and drink tables adorned with a carefully curated menu. Silver trays brimmed with hors d'oeuvres of smoked salmon canapés, mini quiches, and tea sandwiches. Spicy meat pasties and standard British fare like bangers and mash, shepherd's pie, beef Wellington, and fish and chips made my mouth water. But the desserts were the absolute stunner of the show. I had to resist sneaking an éclair, fruit tart, or dipping a marshmallow into the chocolate fountain.

Not to be outdone, the drink table was equally dazzling with bottles of red and white wine and champagne. Beside the wine selection, a mixologist stood ready to craft signature cocktails like the Hercule Highball and Marple Martini. Artisanal sodas and sparkling water garnished with berries and fresh herbs rounded out the drink options.

I was so engrossed in surveying the scene I startled when I first saw Caroline standing at the end of the wine table, guzzling a glass of Merlot. She was dressed in a flowy aqua-blue Bohemian dress. A matching blue-and-white scarf tied back her white hair in a style straight from the set of a BBC production of Poirot.

I took a deep breath and approached her, determined to be as normal as possible. "How nice to see you. I wasn't expecting so many business owners to arrive this early," I said, unable to get Fletcher's theory about her out of my head. He couldn't really think that regal, elegant Caroline was a killer, could he?

She studied me with newfound interest. "You didn't?"

"I was worried that no one would show." I tried not to stare at her face, hoping that I might be able to pick up a subtle shift in her facial expression or body language.

"Every business owner in Redwood Grove was invited to come

early. You've really surpassed expectations with this event, Annie. The entire town is buzzing with excitement. I'm surprised that you're surprised. You are Redwood Grove's savior. Don't you know that? No one wants to miss tonight. Not a single person in town."

I glanced around the ballroom. It was true; almost every small business owner had already arrived. I couldn't help feeling proud and grateful for her warm words. "I'm in no way a savior. This has been a group effort. I'm just so glad that everyone is enthusiastic about the weekend."

"Enthusiastic is an understatement. Well done." She raised her glass and chugged her wine.

I asked a waiter passing by us for a glass of Chardonnay. "I'm guessing you've heard about the murder?"

She finished her glass and asked for a refill. "Who hasn't? The entire town is talking about it."

We moved away from the wine table.

Keeping a close eye on Caroline, I said, "I heard that Kayla had been helping you with marketing and social media. How did the two of you connect?" My stomach grumbled as a waiter passed by with a tray of savory quiches.

Caroline held the stem of her wine glass with a death grip. "Is that what you heard?"

"Yeah. Was she not working with you?" Her reaction surprised me. I didn't think it was a secret that Kayla had been helping her at the store.

"Working is one way of putting it." Caroline's gaze drifted to the delicate chandeliers hanging from the ornate ceiling. "I have some other words that I could use to describe our relationship."

This was intriguing. "It sounds like there might have been some challenges between the two of you?"

"Challenges, ha!" She threw her head back, causing the scarf to slip toward her forehead. She fixed it and stared at me before smoothing her long white hair and trying to recover. "That's being extremely generous."

"I noticed that you didn't appear to be on great terms last night. Do you mind me asking why? I went to college with Kayla, so I have—had—my own issues with her." I hoped that if I was open about my relationship with Kayla, she might open up more.

It seemed to work. Caroline's expression changed. Her face softened. "I'm so sorry for you. That must have been a terrible experience."

"Fortunately, we didn't spend much time together in college, and I haven't seen her since. That is until last night. She mentioned that she was in town to do work for you."

"That's a lie." Caroline's entire body tensed. "I made it crystal clear that she was not welcome in Redwood Grove or my shop, but that didn't stop her. She should have listened to my advice, but Kayla didn't care about anyone or anything other than herself. She had one agenda—do whatever it took to get ahead without caring about the people she left ruined in her wake."

"Ruined in her wake? I'm not sure I'm following." I swirled my wine. "Why wasn't she welcome in Redwood Grove?"

"Because she stole my business." Her voice was like ice. "Kayla deserved everything she had coming. I'm glad that she's dead."

TWELVE

Caroline's face hardened again as she took a painfully slow sip of her wine, staring at me as if daring me to ask her more.

I couldn't help myself. "Kayla stole your business?" Artifacts was a local boutique shop in Redwood Grove, California. Sure, Caroline's meticulous collection of housewares, jewelry, and clothing was lovely. It made for an enjoyable afternoon of browsing, but it was hardly as if Artifacts was a recognizable brand name. Why and how could Kayla have "stolen" the business? It didn't make sense.

"Yes, although I didn't realize her true agenda initially. She approached me under the guise of building a robust website with online shopping. She did exactly what she pitched, with one small problem—she stole my entire business plan." Her tone was sharp with a hard edge.

"How did you connect with her, to begin with?" I looked around the ballroom as more familiar faces began to stream in.

"She was in town visiting her cousin Justin."

I nodded. I'd already heard that from Kayla, but I wanted Caroline's perspective.

"I was in the pub for lunch one day and happened to

mention that I was looking for someone to design an e-commerce site. Artifacts is doing well with local foot traffic and tourist dollars, but it's always good to have multiple revenue streams. When I first opened the shop, I had planned to launch a website, but things got busy. I'm a one-woman show with a couple of part-time high school students who help in the summer. The project has felt so daunting that it kept slipping onto the back burner."

"That's understandable."

Caroline gulped her wine. "In any event, I mentioned that I was looking for web help, and Justin suggested that I work with Kayla. She professed to be a web and social media expert and told me she would cut me a good deal since I knew her cousin. She claimed she was giving me the friends and family rate." She tossed her head back and let out a piercing laugh. "What a joke."

I nodded as I listened. It was all making sense. My initial instinct about Kayla and her reasons for coming to the Mystery Fest had been spot-on.

"At first, things seemed to be going fine," Caroline continued. "I will admit that I should have taken a more active role and done a better job of managing the project. Hal and I were talking about that last night. It's one of the many reasons he raves about you. Everyone needs someone young and dynamic on their team. We're both too old for TikTok." Caroline's hand drifted up to her scarf. She brushed her fingertips over her forehead. "I love owning a storefront and working in retail, but I don't have much interest in social media. I don't even have personal social media accounts. I understand that it's a necessary evil in today's world, but I'm too old to learn something new. That's why I was glad to have Kayla on board."

I didn't think age had anything to do with it. I knew plenty of their peers who were active and engaged online. Not Hal, though. He was a self-professed Luddite. It sounded like Caroline was, too.

"Since Kayla was in town visiting Justin for a few days, she came by the store and took inventory. We reviewed my pricing guidelines and all of my wholesale vendor contacts and discussed how best to style photos of each product. She was impressed with the store's physical layout and took some initial photos to launch my social media channels, or so I thought."

"What did she do?"

Caroline looked at the glimmering chandeliers hanging from the ceiling and shook her head. "She copied my business plan and created her own online store. She used my vendors, my pricing, everything—word for word."

"I don't understand. Weren't you paying her? Did you have a contract?"

"No, that was a big mistake on my part." Caroline pressed her lips together in disgust and finished her second glass of wine. She set it on the table with such force that I thought the stem might break off. "I realize in hindsight that I should have, but I never considered Kayla would do something like this. She copied Artifacts online. Item for item. She even called her online store—Artifactual. She wasn't even trying to hide what she was doing."

"Did you have any kind of recourse?" My stomach rumbled as another waiter scooted around us with a tray of crab cakes with zesty sauces and lemon wedges. When had I eaten last? The day was such a blur.

"I threatened to sue her. I demanded that she take her site down, and I refused to pay her a dime, but she didn't care. The damage was already done."

The hostility in Caroline's tone made me stand up straighter. "I don't understand. Why would she pretend to offer her services to build a web presence for you and then just copy your idea? She could have started her own online shop."

"Oh, she built a website and started social media pages for me. They're terrible." Caroline reached for her smooth leather purse. She removed her phone and proceeded to show me the website Kayla built.

She wasn't exaggerating. The site was poorly designed. It wasn't scaled correctly for mobile usage, and the product shots were dark and out of focus.

"I think that was her end goal. She wanted the site to fail. She was double-dipping—charging me while at the same time cherry-picking my best vendors. She didn't have to do any legwork to find the best wholesalers for gorgeous scented candles or cashmere blankets. She simply stole all of mine. Her website is beautiful and lush. Mine is grainy and dark, with blurry photos and the slowest load time ever. That's why I told her she was not getting one red cent from me."

As Caroline spoke, the veins in her neck throbbed. It was obvious that she was still furious. I didn't blame her. I would have been too if Kayla had done the same thing to Hal. But surely Caroline wasn't angry enough to want Kayla dead? She had been in the bookshop right before I found the body, so she certainly had an opportunity, but surely being upset about her business couldn't drive her to commit murder.

"Who killed her? Have you heard?" Caroline changed the subject. Had she read my mind?

Was it my imagination, or did her voice have a threatening quality?

"The police don't know yet," I replied cautiously.

She stared directly at me. Her blue eyes lacked any hint of warmth. "I can name about ten people who could have done it, and part of me wants to congratulate the killer."

A shudder ran down my spine. I understood that Caroline was upset (rightfully so), and even I wasn't Kayla's number one fan, but I didn't take any pleasure in the fact that she was dead.

"If you'll excuse me, I see a friend." Caroline took her empty glass, and I watched as she headed toward the stage.

Why the abrupt departure? I stood in the center of the ballroom, unsure what to do next. Could Fletcher's theory be correct? Had I just had a conversation with a killer?

I needed to approach this rationally. What would Dr. Caldwell ask me to do next?

Methodically observe.

That was one of the first principles we'd learned in her class.

Instead of jumping to conclusions, she instructed us to treat the process like solving a complex mathematical equation. There was a need for diligence and patience. Professional detectives applied their vast knowledge of criminology, human behavior, and forensics while seeking patterns and connections within a chaotic mix of data. Each piece of evidence, every witness statement, was a different variable within that equation.

I remembered her saying that just as a mathematical problem demands logical reasoning and systematic procedures, investigative work requires rational thought and a systemic approach to draw accurate conclusions. I felt a thrill as the detail of what I'd learned came back to me.

I was trained for this.

I could do this.

It felt good to get back to my roots. I was surprised by how quickly my knowledge resurfaced after all these years. It was like I was tapping into the deepest recesses of my brain to access information I had intentionally locked away. I had forgotten the rush that came with the thrill of the chase. I had forgotten how much I liked it.

I rolled my shoulders back and took another sip of wine for courage.

The lights flashed, signaling it was time to open the front doors. The mood shifted almost immediately as a sea of guests in colorful costumes and cocktail dresses came in, oohing and aahing over the atmospheric décor. The band played a welcome march as squeals and laughter from the guests made me smile for the first time since I'd found Kayla's body.

It's all going to be okay, Annie.

I approached a high-top table near the stage and texted Pri to let her know where to meet me. There wasn't much for me to do other than watch the eager faces of happy readers mingling over drinks and appetizers. Some readers had dressed for the occasion in sequined flapper dresses and three-piece suits with Panama hats, while others had embraced the mystery theme, wearing Nancy Drew, Columbo, Professor Plum, and Carmen Sandiego costumes. I loved seeing the effort everyone had gone to.

Pri arrived wearing a flowing burnt orange dress and strappy sandals. After greeting me with a hug, she held out her arms for me to admire her latest temporary tattoo. "What do you think? I went with a skull for the occasion. I ordered dozens of these to sell at Cryptic, but then I heard about Kayla, and now it seems a little macabre. Is it true? Did you find the body, Annie?"

I nodded. "It's true."

"Holy everything. How?" Pri's mouth hung open.

"How much have you heard?"

"Not enough." She stole a glance at Fletcher, who was standing near the stage with a long line of readers waiting to pose with him. "There are so many rumors swirling. Cryptic was on fire this afternoon. It's all everyone was talking about. I heard that Fletcher passed out. And then I heard that he ran the killer down on the sidewalks and tackled them." She raised an eyebrow. "Okay, I know that part isn't true, so tell me everything. Someone else claimed he did it."

"Who?" I asked louder than intended.

Pri pointed to Fletcher. "Sherlock. Can you imagine Fletcher killing anyone? He's afraid of his own shadow."

I glanced at the stage. Fletcher was in his element. His gleeful smile was broad as he tilted his deerstalker cap and held up his pipe, motioning for the next group of readers to come forward for their photo op. "That's quite the rumor. I wondered how that started?"

"You live here, right?" Pri scowled and scrunched her face. "It takes less than ten seconds for rumors to swirl in Redwood Grove."

"True." I filled her in, including the details of my conversation with Dr. Caldwell and Caroline. She listened with rapt attention. When I finished, she squeezed my hand so tight I thought she might crack a knuckle.

"Oh, Annie, I'm so sorry. That had to be terrible."

"It wasn't great," I admitted, gripping her hand in return.

"Is there anything I can do?"

"Thanks, but no, I'm doing okay. I'm glad that the event is going on as planned. It will help to feel normal. I want to pay close attention to Caroline and some other attendees tonight."

"Count me in. How can I help?" Pri reached for her purse. "I don't have a pipe or any murderous props, but I have mints and chocolate. I don't know how either of those help us, but I'm seriously here for anything you need, Annie."

I laughed. "Chocolate always helps."

"Exactly." Pri unzipped her rust-colored purse, which matched her outfit perfectly, and pressed a square of chocolate in my hand.

"Let's mingle," I suggested, nodding subtly toward Eli and Monica and unwrapping the chocolate. "I want to talk to Monica. She and Kayla were close in college but had a huge fight that basically ended their friendship our senior year. I'm curious to hear her perspective."

Priya linked her arm through mine. "Let's go."

Monica and Eli Ledger were chatting near the food tables. Monica had changed into a red flapper-style dress, but Eli wore the same turtleneck from his earlier reading.

"The author is wearing a black turtleneck. That's too much," Pri whispered. "Talk about on the nose."

"This is why I love you. I almost died when I met him earlier," I said through a mouthful of dark chocolate.

I introduced Pri as we approached their table. "Thanks for doing the reading at the shop," I said to Eli. "When does the book officially release?"

He turned to Monica, ignoring me and burying his face in his phone screen.

Monica waited for a minute before letting out a breathless chuckle and answering for him. "We're finalizing the pub schedule as we speak. Signing Eli is a huge win for us, and I've been advocating to bump up the pub date because, as you saw from today's reading, the buzz around this book is huge."

That was a stretch. I would describe the response to Eli's reading as pretty average. However, some (if not most) of that could be due to his attitude. Over the years, I'd met dozens and dozens of authors. Nearly everyone who came to the store for a signing was lovely, kind, humble, and gracious. Eli was none of those things. He exuded self-importance, which made no sense. He was yet to be published. It wasn't as if he had a massive fan base. So why the absurd ego?

"How long have you been in publishing?" I asked Monica.

"Since we graduated. I started as an assistant editor and worked my way up. Eli is my biggest signing to date." She beamed at her star author and smoothed the fringe on her skirt.

He looked smug and bored with her effusive praise as he continued to scroll on his phone.

"That was a strange response by Kayla earlier," I said to Eli, hoping to gauge his reaction. "It must have been shocking to learn that she was killed shortly after your reading."

He looked up from his phone at last and folded his arms against his stomach. "Why would it be a shock? I didn't know the woman."

Again, Monica jumped in and rescued him. Was he contractually obligated to have her as his permanent PR spokesperson? "What Eli means is that Kayla's reaction to his reading was because of me." Monica made a face. "You'll likely remember that Kayla and I were close in college. We were like you and Scarlet. You couldn't separate us back in the day. Kayla was my partner in crime. We did everything together."

I nodded, trying not to tense the muscles in my face too tight.

Pri patted my hip in a show of solidarity.

Eli muttered something I couldn't decipher under his breath. He caught my eye, shrugged, and returned to scrolling.

"Well, that changed our senior year. I don't know if you recall, but we got into a wicked fight and hadn't spoken since." She ran her fingers along her gold-and-silver braided necklace.

"But you were here together last night."

"No, no, no, you're mistaken. We weren't together. Kayla was trying to loop me into her drama, and I was having no part in that. I know that's the reason she interrupted Eli's reading this afternoon. She wanted to get back at me. I'm sure she figured that if she could rattle Eli, it would reflect poorly on me, but what she didn't take into account is that Eli is a pure professional. Kayla could sputter and spew as much as she wanted, but I wasn't going to play into her game. I learned my lesson years ago. She wasn't to be trusted, and I wanted no part of being associated with her. I guess that's not a problem now. Her behavior finally caught up with her—it's called natural consequences." Monica shrugged and attempted to conceal what appeared to be a hint of a smile.

I frowned. I wasn't sure that murder was a natural consequence of bad behavior.

"We don't have to deal with her any longer," Monica said to Eli in a coddling tone. "You have nothing to worry about now that Kayla is dead."

Nothing to worry about? What did that mean? And why was Monica gushing over Eli? The guy was an arrogant ass. He barely acknowledged us. Was his writing that good? It was the only logical explanation. Monica must believe that Eli's work had a lot of promise.

And, if she was so desperate to make him a bestseller, could Kayla have threatened his future success and caused Monica to take matters into her own hands?

THIRTEEN

I tried to remain as neutral as possible as our conversation shifted to Eli's upcoming book tour. Monica's reaction to Kayla's death was unsettling at best. She was obviously invested in making his book launch a success. If she perceived Kayla as a threat to that, could she have done something so drastic? It wasn't out of the realm of possibility, especially given their history.

I was struck by the fact that no one seemed remorseful about Kayla's death. Not Caroline, not Monica, not Eli. I wasn't a fan of her abrasive personality either, but that didn't deplete my empathy for her. It was hard to believe that everyone could be so callous in light of such a tragedy.

Seth sauntered over to join our conversation. He looked out of place amongst the mystery-loving guests in a pair of jeans, a T-shirt, and a baseball hat. I didn't trust him in college and wasn't about to start trusting him now. Seth was the kind of guy who used "Hey, bra" to address his friends and used to always have a wad of chewing tobacco under his bottom lip. A memory of him sitting outside the library with his baseball team, spitting tobacco into used Pringles cans, made me shudder.

"Hey, guys, what's up with the huddle?" Seth clapped Monica on the back like she'd just scored a home run and inserted himself into our little circle. "I'm not interrupting, am I?"

Monica positioned her body away from Seth and crossed her arms defensively. "You're always interrupting. Read the room, Seth."

He didn't look like he'd changed much since college. He reminded me of someone still clinging desperately to the "good old days" when he'd been a collegiate baseball star. At least now he didn't have a wad of tobacco stuffed under his lip.

Seth flipped his hat forward and scanned the ballroom like he had interpreted Monica's words literally. "Are you guys talking about Kayla? I can't believe she's dead. Like, she's really dead?"

"That's what happens when you piss off everyone you come in contact with." Monica avoided eye contact, staring past Seth toward the stage.

I watched them carefully. What was their dynamic? Monica didn't seem pleased to have him butt in.

"I know that Kayla was rough around the edges, but doesn't it seem crazy that someone killed her?" Seth was either oblivious to Monica's body language, which screamed that she didn't want to continue this conversation, or he knew exactly what he was doing and was trying to get a reaction from her.

"You might say she got what she deserved," Monica muttered.

Pri kicked me.

I didn't trust myself to make eye contact with her, so I focused on Seth. This wasn't the first time I'd heard that same sentiment regarding Kayla's murder. "Did you keep in contact?" I asked Seth, hoping to keep the conversation going.

"Kind of." He paused like he was trying to find the right words. Then he smiled politely as if this was a job interview, not a casual conversation between old college classmates. "We bumped into each other occasionally, but I wouldn't say we kept in close contact."

"Except you're leaving out one critical detail: Kayla didn't want you anywhere near her since the breakup." Monica's voice was curt and flat. Her inflection indicated that she wasn't interested in encouraging a discussion.

"That was a long time ago," Seth replied. He shot Monica a pained look like she had injured him physically. "We were kids. We were young and stupid. We both grew up and realized our mistakes."

"Were you dating again?" I couldn't tell if that was what he was hinting at.

"Nope. Those days were long gone. We weren't a good match, but we shared some great memories." He flipped his baseball hat again and stole another glance at Monica.

Was the hat-flipping a nervous habit?

"But you know Kayla wasn't happy to see you here in Redwood Grove?" Monica challenged.

"*You* know that was years ago," Seth said pointedly to Monica. "We've both moved on. It's not like I was thrilled to see her, but it wasn't a big deal." He looked at his watch like he suddenly had somewhere he needed to be.

I got the impression that he was trying to sound casual.

Was Seth that out of touch? I couldn't imagine many people who would be thrilled to bump into an ex, especially in a small town like Redwood Grove.

"It's not like we hated each other," Seth said, studying Monica's face like he was trying to figure out her angle.

"Yeah, well, that's not what it looked like to me last night." She tightened her arms.

"I don't get what you're doing, Monica. What are you even talking about?" Seth asked.

There was something going on between them, but I couldn't

figure out what. Monica's icy gaze made me shiver. I decided it was time to change the subject. "What brought you to Redwood Grove?" I asked Seth.

The question threw him. He ran his fingers on the rim of his hat and stared at the floor to buy time. "Uh, I don't know. I guess I heard about the festival and I was looking for an adventure, something to do. This sounded good."

Where had he heard about the festival? Our advertising for the weekend had been targeted at book and mystery lovers. Seth didn't fit either of those demographics. I was finding it hard to believe that my former classmates had all magically happened upon the Mystery Fest. There had to be a connection with Kayla. And perhaps even me. I needed to keep my guard up.

"Or you were stalking your ex-girlfriend." Monica didn't hold back. She firmed her stance and glared at Seth.

"No. I'm telling you it wasn't like that." Seth's cheeks blotched with color. "I didn't follow her here. It was random that Kayla was in town, too, but when I bumped into her, I thought maybe we were going to have a reunion. Talk about the good old days over beers, but I guess not."

Monica didn't respond.

"What's going on with you?" Seth sighed and gave her a pleading look. "I need a drink or ten."

Monica watched him head toward the bar and waited for him to be out of earshot. "Listen, Annie, Eli and I have some business to discuss, but I want to warn you, friend-to-friend, to stay away from Seth."

"Why?" Her friend-to-friend approach didn't endear her any more to me. I knew her about as well as I knew Seth.

"He has a history of stalking women. I used to think that he was trustworthy, but I was wrong. The only conclusion I keep coming to is that Kayla was the reason he's here." Monica's voice lacked clarity or strength.

Stalking was a serious allegation. Maybe that explained

why Monica had tried to put distance between them. I made a mental note to do the same. "You think he was stalking her after all these years?"

"It looks that way. If you had asked me that yesterday, I would have said no way. But now..." She trailed off. "Anyway, I don't know what to think. They had an on-again, off-again relationship after they broke up in college. I thought it was over a long time ago, but I guess I was wrong."

"Noted. Thanks for the heads-up."

"Don't mention it." She motioned to Eli, who had been silent for the duration of our conversation, so much so that I almost forgot he was standing next to Pri. "Shall we get a glass of wine and have you mingle with your adoring mystery fans?"

"If I have to," Eli said, breaking his silence and sounding like he was as eager to chat with readers as he was to have a root canal.

They left, and Pri collapsed onto the table with her head in her hands. "What did we just witness? That was like something out of a bad movie, and I'm not sure who would win the award for best actor."

"I couldn't agree more." I watched Monica push Eli toward a group of readers who clearly had no idea who he was. "Why would Seth show up for a book festival? He's a baseball bro. I don't think I ever saw him out of uniform or the gym when we were in college."

"*Could* he have been stalking Kayla?" Pri asked. "Monica sounded very sure of that fact, but something about her is off-putting. She treats Eli like he's a toddler. I don't get that relationship at all. And even if you had a falling out with an old friend, wouldn't you step in to help them if you thought they were seriously in danger?"

A wave of sadness threatened to consume me. What if Kayla had been terrified to see Seth? What if he had followed her here with one thought in mind—to kill her? I gulped. "I don't like the stalking part at all. That could explain why she was so over the top and drinking heavily, and seeing Seth might have put her on edge. But you're right. I'm not sure I trust Monica either. She mentioned that she and Kayla haven't kept in touch. How would she know that Seth had been stalking Kayla or that they had gotten back together after their breakup in college?"

"Ooohhh, that's a good point." Pri pressed her finger to her chin and whistled. "You mean like she intentionally slipped up?"

"Maybe." I nodded, trying to will everything we had heard to memory. I knew that later, I was going to want to review my conversation with each suspect and make notes for Dr. Caldwell. "I don't trust Seth, but I don't trust her either."

"We shouldn't trust anyone at this point," Pri agreed, flagging down a waiter and piling mini quiche and salmon canapés onto a plate.

"That's true." I took a meat pasty.

"Do you have a theory? You look like you're deep in thought." She popped a canapé into her mouth and finished her drink.

"Not yet." I shook my head, cutting into the meat pie with a fork. Steam and the fragrant aroma of spicy chicken and herbs wafted out of the hot pastry. "I'm trying to remember everything I learned in school about how to approach an investigation. It's too easy to react with gut feelings, but being in the middle of a real criminal investigation makes me realize how challenging it is to set my personal biases aside."

"I'm sure that even the professionals struggle with that." Pri bit into a sundried tomato and pesto quiche.

"We need to speak with everyone who knew Kayla to get a big-picture view of who she was and what she was really doing here." I blew on the meat pie to cool it down. "The other person

I want to talk to is Justin. He's her cousin, so he probably knew her better than anyone else."

"No time like the present." Pri polished off another bite-sized quiche. "Hurry up, and let's finish. Then we can go straight to the source." She pointed to the wine table where Justin was talking to my least favorite person in town—Liam Donovan.

I savored the herbaceous buttery pastry. It was filled with chunks of chicken and perfectly tender sweet potatoes. My stomach swirled with thanks. I inhaled the rest of it and let Pri drag me over to talk to Justin.

"Hey, Annie, nice little reception you have here," Liam said in his typical condescending tone. He skimmed his strong jawline with his fingertip and made steady eye contact.

Why did his eyes have to look like they were flecked with gold in this lighting? Did his hair have a natural wave, or was it just the way it fell on his forehead?

Stop it, Annie. What are you doing?

I scolded myself and gave my head a little shake in an attempt to brush off any unwanted thoughts.

"I'm surprised to see you here." I crossed my arms over my chest. "I thought Mystery Fest was way below your reading standards."

"As one of Redwood Grove's longstanding business owners, I'm merely doing my duty." He flashed me a toothy smile. "But otherwise, you're right, I would never stoop so low as to pick up a mystery novel."

I stopped myself from rolling my eyes and gave a polite smile instead. "Sorry you have to spend time with the riffraff."

Liam shrugged. "Don't worry. I'm not."

Pri caught my eye and gave me a look I couldn't quite decipher. "Anyway, what are you two bar buddies chatting about?"

Justin flinched. "We weren't talking about bars. Why would we be talking about bars?"

"Because you both work for bars," Pri said with a touch of annoyance. "I figured you were comparing notes. That's what we do in the coffee world."

"Oh, yeah. Sure." Justin shuffled his feet and massaged his sleeve of tattoos.

"I'm so sorry about your cousin," I said.

He made circles on the floor with the sole of his high-top tennis shoe. "I can't believe it. I can't believe she's dead."

"Did you see her again after she left State of Mind?" I asked.

Justin shook his head. "No. I feel terrible. The last thing I said to her was that she needed to sober up and get out of town before she did something she was going to regret, and now she's... she's gone."

"Were the two of you close?" Pri asked. "By the way, I love your art. I dabble in tattoo design on the side." She tapped the skull artwork on her wrist.

"Cool. Thanks." Justin forced a smile and then twisted his head from side to side like he was trying to decide how to answer her question. "I don't know. We kept in touch. She was here on business, and I guess it was nice to have family in town. I've been on my own for a while, but Kayla's hard to get to know. She was six years older than me, so we didn't really grow up together. She was already at college and stuff by the time I was old enough to remember much. We'd see each other at our grandparents' house for holidays, but that was about it."

"What made her come to see you in Redwood Grove?" I asked.

"She never said, other than business." Justin gave me a blank look. "She just showed up at the pub one day and said she wanted to reconnect, but I don't think that was true. I think there was another reason she was here."

"What?" Pri and I asked in unison.

"No idea." Justin shrugged. "She never said. She told me

that she had started her marketing agency and was looking for new clients, so I hooked her up with Caroline, and she ended up staying for a few days. Then she showed up out of the blue again yesterday. She didn't tell me she was coming back or anything."

"Do you know where she was staying?" I asked, smoothing my dress to make sure the hem was in place. Did I have food in my teeth? Why was Liam staring at me? His lips parted in a half smile as he ran his finger along the zipper of his puffy vest.

Justin shook his head. "Nope. I don't know anything. That's what I told the detective. She asked me many questions about Kayla, but to be honest, even though we're family, I don't know her that well."

I believed that much was true, but from the way Justin fidgeted as he spoke, I wondered what he wasn't telling us.

"I heard she was killed at the bookstore," Liam added, keeping his eyes locked on me. "That's too bad. Is that going to put a damper on your weekend?"

"What kind of a question is that?" I scowled and rolled my eyes. My nerves felt like they all fired in unison whenever Liam was around. "Of course. It's going to put more than a damper on the events."

"I don't know." He shrugged and glanced around the busy ballroom, absently toying with the zipper. His gaze turned inward for a minute before he raised one eyebrow. "It seems to be having the opposite effect. These are ferocious mystery fans, after all. They appear to be eating it up." He turned that intense gaze on me. "It's almost like you staged it on purpose."

Was he accusing me of murder?

Pri ran interference. "The Stag Head must really be benefiting from this influx of tourists that Annie has brought into Redwood Grove. Have you changed your mind and decided to embrace the Mystery Fest like the rest of us?"

"Not a chance." Liam cleared his throat. "We're doing just

fine without a bunch of wannabe armchair detectives crowding up our space."

It took every ounce of self-restraint not to punch him.

Pri must have picked up on my tension because she kept talking in a breezy tone. "What have you guys heard about the murder? There are so many rumors I can't keep up."

Justin looked like he wanted to be anywhere but here at the moment. Was it because he was upset about his cousin's death, or could it be because he knew something he wasn't saying and was worried that he might accidentally let it slip?

"I don't know," he replied with a shaky voice. "She mentioned that she was concerned about an ex-boyfriend. Seth, have you met him?"

I nodded.

"I feel bad because now I'm worried that the real reason she showed up in Redwood Grove was because of him. I think she might have been trying to get away from him, and now she's dead. If she had opened up to me, I could have stopped him." Justin hung his head. He looked like he was going to break down. "I can't talk about this anymore, sorry."

Pri caught my eye. I knew what she was thinking. First Monica. Now Justin. It was becoming more and more plausible that Seth could be the killer.

FOURTEEN

"I don't want to keep you from your Sherlockian games," Liam said, rubbing his palm over his heart and waving. "Good luck with the festival, Annie."

I watched him walk away, then turned to Pri. "He's the worst. The absolute worst." I could feel heat spreading across my neck. I hated that my skin blotched, heightening my freckles whenever I was angry.

"I love seeing how fired up you get around him, though. Our sweet, bookish Annie becomes beastly whenever Mr. Donovan is near."

"It's justified. He says stuff like that just to get under my skin." I forced my teeth to unclench. "Why does he do that?"

"Uh, probably because it works." Pri grinned.

"What do you expect me to do?" I wrinkled my nose and then bared my teeth. "Am I just supposed to take it and say nothing?"

She laughed. "Certainly not. I love watching the flirty banter between you two."

"Flirty? Are you drunk? Liam and I loathe each other."

"Yeah, I get that." Her eyes twinkled with mischievous delight.

"Priya Kapoor, do not look at me like that. Liam is a pompous jerk. In fact, I should introduce him to Eli. They probably would hit it off immediately. They could sit around and discuss how cerebral and important they are."

"Do it." She playfully pushed me forward.

"I wasn't flirting with him, understood?"

"We're spending a lot of time talking about Liam, though." She winked. "You may not have been flirting, but he's definitely into you."

"Liam is a walking red flag."

"Yeah, but the guy has a backstory." She stared in his direction.

"He hates me," I protested. "He thinks mysteries are fluffy escapes. He basically said those words verbatim when I told him about the event and asked if the Stag Head wanted to host an event. He thinks mysteries are trashy mind candy. There is no chance that he's into me."

"Okay. Let's go with that. But let me say one thing about Mr. Donovan. That man is your kindred spirit. He's been through some stuff. Heavy stuff. You may not see it, but I do. Behind the banter is a tortured soul. Those long periods of stillness and quiet, his sarcasm, it's all protection to guard his heart." She leaned in, placing one hand on her chin. "I think you might recognize some of his pain."

My breath caught in my lungs. Heat crept up my neck. What did she mean? I wanted to ask but didn't want to look too interested.

"Anyway, enough of that." Pri wrapped an arm around my shoulder. "We should mingle more. I want to see what else we can learn about Seth. He keeps coming up, which I don't think we should discount, especially if he was stalking Kayla."

"Agreed." I was glad that she dropped the subject of Liam

Donovan, but her perspective left me slightly rattled. Could there be a reason for Liam's gruff behavior? Or was it just that Pri was a giant flirt herself and loved the idea of love? She was probably projecting, right? Liam made my skin crawl. He intentionally went out of his way to make me feel small. That wasn't flirting. That was complete disinterest. I had no idea why Pri interpreted our mutual dislike of one another as witty banter, but she was wrong. Really wrong.

I watched as Liam leaned on the edge of the bar like he owned the ballroom, sipping a glass of whisky. He caught me staring at him and raised his glass in a triumphant toast.

The splotchy feeling returned. I looked away and tried to pretend like I was studying the crowd.

People appeared to be enjoying themselves. A handful of couples twirled in front of the stage, creating an impromptu dance floor between the high-top tables. Readers and authors mingled, and appetizers and drinks continued to be circulated by the wait staff. How could Liam possibly find any fault in the event?

"There you are." A friendly voice brought me back into the moment. I looked up to see Hal heading straight toward us. He had forgone his cardigan for a black-and-white plaid shirt, slacks, and a matching bow tie.

"You made it, and you look so dapper." I hugged him. "How did it go? Where do things stand with the store?"

"Why, thank you." He placed a hand on his chest and closed his eyes. Then he inhaled slowly and deeply. "I hope I never have to go through an experience like that again. Owning a mystery bookshop did not prepare me for murder."

"How could it?" Pri patted his arm in a show of solidarity.

"I should have stayed with you," I said. Seeing the worry lines etched on Hal's forehead made my chest ache.

"No, you've been through enough, Annie." He dismissed

the idea with a wave. "I would have sent you away if you tried to stay."

I gave him a grateful smile. "What did Dr. Caldwell say?"

"Not a lot. They were all extremely organized and professional. I mainly tried to stay out of their way. I wish I had installed cameras like you and Fletcher suggested months ago. We wouldn't be in this position. We would have seen the killer in action, and this would be an open-and-shut case."

"It's not your fault, Hal." I felt terrible that he was taking even a hint of responsibility for what happened. It was my fault. If it hadn't been for the festival, Kayla Mintner never would have been in town and would be alive and well right now.

"But I'm an old stodgy. I think this is the first time in years that I've left the house without a cardigan." He tugged at his bow tie like it was cutting off circulation. "I should have listened to you. You and Fletcher have my best interest at heart, and I know you're always trying to get me to modernize the shop. After today, I am changing my ways. Cameras will be ordered tomorrow and installed the minute they arrive."

"We have no idea if cameras would have hindered the killer," Pri interjected. "It sounds like it was a brutal stabbing. The killer might not have cared that they were being seen. They could have disguised themselves—so many possibilities."

"Pri is right," I agreed.

"Nonetheless, Kayla's death has given me new resolve." Hal swept his hand across the room. "Look at this. What a success. This is what happens when I take my younger staff's advice."

I smiled. "The turnout is phenomenal, even with the murder."

"Maybe because of the murder." Pri raised an eyebrow.

"What did Dr. Caldwell say about the store? Can we open tomorrow, or do I need to start enacting plan B?" I had yet to formulate a plan B. It might be a long night.

"She gave us the green light. There's an outside chance that she might drop in and ask further questions, but they've cleared the crime scene, and everything has been put back in order." Hal swallowed at the memory and then quickly regained focus. "Fortunately, the Sitting Room is the only room that was disturbed. She had one of her officers remain with me to help tidy up. However, we'll need to close off that room for tomorrow. She gave me a card for crime scene cleaners. The rugs will need to be steamed and sanitized. We need to make sure that the room is off-limits for the rest of the weekend. We can't have readers disturbing a crime scene."

"Absolutely." Moving the clues to a different part of the bookstore wouldn't be a problem. Given the circumstances, we might lose a touch of intrigue with the secret bookcase, but I was sure readers would understand.

"Dr. Caldwell did mention that they have several leads they'll be following up with over the next few days. She wanted to see our sales logs and look through our customer files. I asked her if she had a sense of whether the killer was local or if she thought it was a stranger who had a personal vendetta with Kayla." He tugged at his tie again.

I wanted to tell him to take it off. He didn't need to dress for the occasion, especially after what he'd been through.

"What did she say?" Pri asked.

"She said it's too soon to make any assumptions." Hal let out a heavy sigh.

I could have told him that.

"Although I am a bit concerned because she was unequivocal that until the killer has been arrested, everyone in town should be aware and on high alert. They don't know who they're dealing with at this point, which means that everyone is a potential suspect or possible victim." The lines on Hal's forehead were etched with worry. "I can't fathom anyone else being hurt. This is most distressing."

"I'm sure that Dr. Caldwell would cancel the entire event if she believed that we're in serious danger," I replied, hoping that I sounded confident.

He nodded but didn't look convinced. "I hope you're right. Still, we must make sure to report anything out of the ordinary."

"Of course." I didn't mention my conversation with Dr. Caldwell. It would be better if Hal were in the dark about my involvement with the investigation. He would worry too much if he knew I was involved.

We circulated the ballroom. I took dozens of photos of readers in costume and of the event. I wanted to document the festival on our social media to help generate future interest. News that a real murder had occurred might spark a different kind of interest. I didn't want to attract the type of crowd that might show up to get a glimpse of a real crime scene. This wasn't *CSI*. A woman's life had been cut short, and I could already imagine throngs of true crime enthusiasts descending on our little town. What was the old saying about any press being good press? That was not true in this case, but it did feel good to take a break from thinking about Kayla and focus on the creative and enthusiastic attendees.

By the time the party began to wind down, I was exhausted and longing for the coziness of my cottage and especially my bed. I couldn't wait to curl up with Professor Plum and a mug of golden milk and tuck into a book. It had been a long day, made even longer by the strange turn of events.

"Come by Cryptic when you have a free minute tomorrow," Pri said as we parted ways. "I'll make something special for you, and we can share notes on anything we hear about Kayla's murder."

"Sounds like a plan." I hugged her and headed for home.

My cottage was only a few blocks from the main town square. It was in a small complex with ten single-level houses surrounding a shared courtyard. I loved that I could walk every-where and that most of my neighbors were retirees who tended to look out for me like I was their granddaughter. I often arrived home to find baskets of freshly baked bread, warm chocolate chip cookies, or a carton of chicken noodle soup waiting for me.

As I headed through town, people were out and about at the pubs and restaurants. Every outdoor table and patio was buzzing with activity. A band played at the pizzeria where the aroma of wood-fired dough and garlic made me almost consider stopping for a late-night snack.

I had never seen Redwood Grove this lively. When I turned off Cedar Avenue, voices and music faded into the background. I could hear my feet on the pavement and the slight breeze rustling through the trees.

I took a shortcut through Oceanside Park, which was dimly lit by solar lampposts lining the pathway.

Typically, it takes a lot to spook me. I don't scare easily.

But tonight, my imagination was getting the best of me.

It sounded like someone was following me.

I could hear their footsteps.

I stopped in mid-stride and spun around.

There was a flash of movement in my peripheral vision.

I froze.

Could the killer be following me?

But why?

Could this be connected to Scarlet's death? What if this was a long game? Maybe the killer was coming after all of us and picking us off one by one.

I hadn't kept in great contact with my other classmates.

For all I knew, there could be a string of deaths that had occurred in the past decade.

My body hummed with nervous energy.

I bolstered my courage and turned around. "Who's there?"

The only answer was a gust of wind that bent the branches of a sturdy oak tree, casting a ghostly shadow on the sidewalk.

"I have mace," I threatened. I didn't, but it was worth a shot.

Again, the only sound was the muffled chatter of festival-goers a few blocks away.

Annie, you're being ridiculous.

There's no one here.

I exhaled and continued.

My cottage was only another block. I could make it.

I needed to get some sleep and start fresh tomorrow. My mind was working overtime, creating fantastical theories of being stalked by an old college serial killer.

I turned onto Woodland Terrace, the street that dead-ended at my cul-de-sac.

I shook off my irrational fears and walked onward with a purpose, but as my cottage came into sight, the sound of footsteps and heavy breathing got closer and louder.

I was definitely being followed.

The question was, could I make it to safety before whoever was behind me caught up?

FIFTEEN

I broke out into a sprint. I wasn't going to take any chances.

My chest tightened.

It felt like I was trying to breathe underwater.

Why was someone after me?

What had I done?

Had I seen something I shouldn't have?

Did the killer think I knew more than I did?

Questions pounded in my brain as I gulped the cool evening air and ran as fast as possible toward my cottage.

The building was dark, and my neighbors were long in bed by now.

I didn't want to stop to dig my keys out of my bag. How was I going to keep ahead of my assailant?

I could scream and hope my neighbor next door hadn't already removed her hearing aids.

Would the person chasing me be so bold as to attack me in front of my cottage?

It was doubtful, but then again, Kayla had been killed in the bookshop during the middle of the day.

I couldn't take any chances.

I had to beat them to my place, unlock the door, and get inside before they caught me.

My lungs burned.

I'd never run so fast in my entire life.

The yellow and mint green cottages of my cul-de-sac came into view and I picked up my pace for the last stretch.

I reached my small front porch and fumbled through my bag for my keys.

Where were they?

My fingers caught a lip gloss container, glasses case, and wallet. No keys.

Oh no. Had I left them at the Secret Bookcase?

I panicked.

There was no way I could outrun my stalker to the bookshop.

I was about to scream when a man's body came into view on the pavement.

I clutched my purse straps. It wasn't much, but I could hit him with my purse if he tried to attack.

My heart thudded against my chest.

Was this it?

No, Annie Murray, knock it off.

You're a strong, confident woman.

Fight back.

I firmed my feet and stood ready for battle as the man came closer.

"Annie, I've been trying to catch up with you. Damn, you're fast." Seth bent over and put both hands on his knees, gasping for air. "Why are you running?"

"I thought you were chasing me." My heart rate slowed, but I kept a tight grasp on my purse. This could be the killer—and I was totally alone with him.

"I was. Well, no, I wasn't chasing you. I was trying to catch up to you, but you wouldn't stop." Seth gulped, clutching his throat.

"What do you want?" I tried to stay calm and stand tall. Monica's statement that Seth had been accused of stalking Kayla rang through my head like a warning siren.

"Geez, that's a nice way to greet an old friend," he huffed, still hunched over.

It didn't seem like he had stayed in the same physical shape from his college baseball days. If he was this winded from the short sprint from the park, I could easily beat him in a footrace. I took some comfort in that.

"We're not old friends, Seth, and you just chased me down dark sidewalks at nearly midnight. How do you expect me to react? Not to mention, *your* old college girlfriend was brutally killed earlier today, so I don't think it should come as a surprise that I'm on edge."

"Yeah, I'm an idiot. When you put it like that..." Seth winced as he stood upright. He massaged the side of his waist. "I cramped up running like that. I haven't run since back in my baseball days."

"You haven't answered my question. Why were you chasing me?"

"Right. Sorry." He yanked off his cap and wiped sweat from his brow. "I wanted to talk to you about Kayla's murder."

"Now?" I pointed to the rising moon. "It's the middle of the night. Why didn't you talk to me at the party?"

"I was trying to get you alone, but you were with your friends all night."

"Why do you need to talk to me alone?" My fingertips were turning white from my death grip on my purse.

"Because I have important information that I need to share." He threw his hands up in surrender. "I swear I'm not going to hurt you. I can't go to the police, and since we were friends— well—since we knew each other in school and you studied criminology, I just thought maybe you would be willing to listen and possibly act as a go-between."

"A go-between?"

He shuffled his feet. "What I'm going to tell you isn't great, but I swear on my life that I did not kill Kayla."

I didn't like the sound of where this was going.

"Could we talk somewhere?" Seth glanced at my cottage.

There was no way I was letting him inside.

"Here's fine." I pointed to a set of white rocking chairs on my porch. They had been a move-in gift from Hal.

"What about your neighbors?" Seth glanced at the dark cottage next door.

"Unless we're about to get in a screaming match, it's fine." Professor Plum was probably starving inside. If we were to do this, I wanted to get it over quickly and out in the open.

Seth hesitated.

I needed to take the lead. "Look, let me be candid. I'm willing to hear you out and listen to whatever you have to say with an open mind, but I don't trust you enough to let you into my house. There's no way that's happening, so if you want to talk, have a seat; otherwise, leave." I pointed toward the park.

"Okay. Okay." He held his arms up again and showed me his hands like he was trying to prove he didn't have a weapon.

I loosened my grasp on my purse and flipped on the porch light. At least if Seth tried anything, he would risk being seen by anyone who happened to be awake at this hour.

"What is so critical that it required chasing after me?" I asked, sitting in one of the rockers. Was this a terrible idea? Kayla had been killed hours ago, and now I was with her ex-boyfriend on a dead-end street with sleeping neighbors.

Seth sat next to me, tossed his hat on the small table between us, and pressed his fingers into his temples. Under the porch light, his receding hairline glowed like it had been polished and shined with a glossy wax. "It's not easy to admit, but Kayla and I had a past."

I already knew that.

"We dated in college. I'm sure you remember. We were like the *it* couple. Everyone had us pegged to get married, but when we broke up our senior year, it got kind of ugly."

My senses perked up. He was admitting that things had gotten ugly.

"I've done a lot of growing up and work on myself the last few years." He ripped off a piece of my potted rosemary and ran it between his finger and thumb. "I'm not proud of some of the choices I made in my early twenties, but we all make mistakes, right?"

"It depends on the mistake." I rocked slowly in the creaky chair.

"I knew Kayla still loved me, and I wanted her back. We dated and broke up a few times and then somehow she interpreted that as stalking her. I can see now why she would think that. I used to drive by her house in hopes that I would bump into her and I'd go to her favorite nightclubs."

That sounded like stalking to me.

"I never hurt her. I didn't touch her. I didn't so much as lay a hand on her. It wasn't like that, but she kind of freaked out and warned me to stay away from her."

"Did you?"

"No." He yanked another piece of blooming rosemary from my potted plant. The calming aroma cut through the chilly night air. "That's my fault. That's why I'm admitting that I'm not proud of some of the choices I made when I was younger. I should have listened to her. I thought we were going to get back together. We did, eventually, but not before things got ugly for a while."

"What do you mean by ugly?" This was the second time he'd used the word.

He leaned his head against the slats on the rocker. "She took out a restraining order against me."

I sat up. "What?"

"We ended up working it out, but, yeah." He tossed the bunch of rosemary on the porch and let out a sigh.

"But she had to take out a restraining order to keep you away from her?" I didn't like this at all.

"Yeah, but you have to remember this was a long time ago, like seven years. That's why I keep saying that I made mistakes. I should have listened when she asked me to give her space. I thought we had a chance at getting back together. The restraining order changed that. It was a wake-up call. I went to therapy. I've changed. Kayla recognized that a few years ago. We briefly got back together again, but I realized that we weren't great together. I felt like I had grown more and done more work than she had. She was still stuck in trying to relive her college glory years."

"Why are you telling me this?" He sounded convincing, but I knew better than to trust him too easily.

"Because the police aren't going to believe me."

"They have access to your records. It's not going to be a secret if Kayla had a restraining order."

"I know." He cracked his jaw. "I'm sure they already know, and they're probably getting ready to arrest me. That's why I had to talk to you tonight."

"Why?"

"You can talk to Dr. Caldwell for me," he pleaded. "You were her favorite student. You were like a miniature version of her. Everyone called you Detective Annie."

"They did?" This was news to me. I was surprised that Seth even remembered me. We had spoken maybe a total of two times in passing in college.

"Yeah. You and Scarlet were always in the library looking at case files and notes."

I flinched at Scarlet's name.

"Dr. Caldwell will listen to you. You're my only hope right now. I know that I'm a suspect. I heard rumors and whispers at the party tonight. People are asking why I'm here. I even over-heard Monica saying that I came to Redwood Grove because of Kayla."

"Did you?" I challenged.

"No." He shook his head so hard it made mine hurt. "I came because of Monica, and now she's throwing me under the bus."

"Because of Monica?" That was an unexpected response.

"She and I have been on and off again. She told me that her new author was doing his first reading at the Mystery Fest, and I thought it would be fun to surprise her and support her. She's been very excited about signing this guy. She thinks his book could be her first *New York Times* bestseller."

"Wait, can you back up? Are you saying that you and Monica are dating?" I must have heard him wrong. He and Monica? That didn't make sense. She had pretty much accused him of killing Kayla at the party.

"Not exactly. We've been dating, but I don't know what was up with her tonight." He pushed his rocker with his feet. "We're not serious yet. I would like to be, but she wants to take it slow. That's fine. I learned my lesson with Kayla, so I've followed Monica's lead."

Surprising her at a work event didn't exactly sound like he'd been very lowkey. If anything, it sounded reminiscent of his behavior with Kayla, but I kept that to myself.

"We were both floored to see Kayla here. What were the odds? I haven't seen her for a few years. I told Monica that Kayla was probably stalking me. She wasn't happy when I broke up with her. I think she liked the idea that I was obsessed with her, and once I went to therapy and evolved a little, she didn't like the new version of me."

It was a lot to take in. "Why wouldn't you have Monica talk

to Dr. Caldwell on your behalf? It seems like she could confirm everything you've told me."

He grew unusually quiet for a moment, pinching the skin between his thumb and forefinger. "I thought so, too, but she's been acting weird since Kayla died. It's like she thinks I did it. I don't know why or what changed. We were fine until this afternoon, and then it was like she's a different person." He smashed his hat between his hands, crushing the bill.

Could that be because Monica had realized that Seth was dangerous? He seemed apprehensive, but was it a ploy to get me to believe him?

"I can't believe this is happening." Seth banged his head against the rocker. "I know that I'm going to get arrested for something I didn't do, and I don't know how I'm going to prove that I'm innocent."

"Dr. Caldwell is extremely reasonable and professional," I said, trying to keep my tone even and steady. If Seth was unhinged, I didn't want to do anything to make him suspect that I didn't believe him. "She doesn't jump to conclusions or make judgments on hearsay alone."

"I hope you're right." Seth sighed. "Will you talk to her tomorrow?"

"I'm not sure what I would say."

"Just tell her everything I've told you. That's all I'm asking. She'll at least listen to you. I don't think she'll listen to me." He stretched out the bill of his hat and put it back on his head.

I wasn't sure I agreed, but Seth sounded so desperate, and I figured the only way to end the conversation was to promise I would talk to Dr. Caldwell.

"I'll do what I can, but the best thing you can do is to speak with her directly. If you tell her everything you've shared with me before she calls you in for questioning, it's going to look much better for you. It's always good to be forthcoming versus trying to hide your past. I'm sure Dr. Caldwell will take that into consideration."

Seth nodded. "You're probably right. I freaked out today when I realized that Kayla had been killed because I knew immediately it was going to look bad for me. It's almost like I'm being set up."

That was a new theory.

Who would want to set up Seth?

I made a mental note to look into that possibility later. Monica was undoubtedly on the top of the list.

Seth sighed and stood up. "Listen, Annie, I know we weren't great friends in college, and I'm sorry I scared you tonight, but I appreciate you taking the time to hear me out."

"Maybe text or call next time."

He chuckled. "Right."

I watched him disappear into the darkness. Then I dug through my purse to discover my keys hiding at the bottom. That was a relief. I didn't think I had the fortitude to make a trip back to the Secret Bookcase.

My conversation with Seth left me more confused. He seemed sincere and remorseful about his past behavior. He had also had the opportunity to hurt me and didn't. That had to count for something.

But I didn't trust him either.

He had dated Kayla and admitted to a nasty breakup, which resulted in her filing for a restraining order. He was also romantically involved with Monica. Was that the reason he had come to Redwood Grove? Or had I just been having a late-night chat with a murderer?

SIXTEEN

I didn't sleep well. For most of the night, I tossed and turned while dreaming of bloody footprints in the bookstore and being chased by faceless strangers. When I finally dragged myself out of bed a little before eight, my body felt like I had run a marathon.

I had to be functional for the day. If yesterday was any indication, the bookshop was going to be slammed, plus I needed to check on how the mystery throughout town was going, greet the guest authors for their panels, and make sure we were set for the pub crawl later. I also needed to restock the clues for the Wentworth murder that readers were solving around town and ensure that the businesses participating in the interactive mystery weren't having any issues with readers deciphering the posters and puzzles. There was so much to do, but my mind just kept being drawn to Kayla's murder and the need to know what happened.

"What do you think, Professor Plum?" I asked, adding his favorite treats to his dish. "Should we make a new spreadsheet? I know Dr. Caldwell doesn't think Kayla's murder is connected to Scarlet's, but what if we missed something?"

I brewed a cup of coffee and pulled up my notes on Scarlet's case. I copied my Excel template and added everything I had learned about Kayla's murder. My top suspects were Caroline, Monica, Justin, and Seth. Who had the most likely motive? Who was at the bookstore when she was killed? Did any of them have an alibi? I had to be methodical. I couldn't let my emotions get in the way, which was easier said than done with Scarlet's case files staring at me.

Taking an analytical approach was the only option. I emailed the spreadsheet to Dr. Caldwell and followed up with a text:

> Here's everything I've gathered so far. Maybe we can chat later?

Three dots appeared on the screen almost instantaneously.

> Nice work, Annie. Meeting with the coroner this morning. Will swing by the bookstore this afternoon. Stay vigilant. Stay safe.

That was interesting. If Dr. Caldwell was meeting with the coroner, I wondered if they knew exactly when Kayla had been killed.

Another text message dinged while I finished a bowl of oatmeal and a breakfast smoothie. It was from Caroline telling me that the book dress I had ordered for the occasion had arrived yesterday. She was already at the store and said I could stop by to pick it up in case I wanted to wear it today.

I did want to wear it, so I finished my breakfast, pulled on a pair of shorts and a T-shirt, said goodbye to Professor Plum, and headed to Artifacts.

It was another gorgeous day and as I walked across town finches flitted between the trees. Leafy palms bent a greeting against a gleaming blue sky. I stopped to breathe in wild jasmine blooming in the park and to center myself for the day.

There was no reason to think that today wouldn't go smoothly. But I couldn't shake the feeling that something else was going to go terribly wrong.

Artifacts was located in a one-story building not far from the library with large bay windows and a sage-green-and-cream-striped awning. Caroline had painted the exterior a creamy pale butter and added touches of green stenciled vines around the door and windows. The door was unlocked, so I let myself in.

The shop's interior was bright and modern, with warm wooden floors. It was divided into sections for jewelry, accessories, home décor, and clothing. Midcentury refurbished couches and wingback chairs provided comfortable seating for customers to relax and admire Caroline's curated artisanal collection. Dressing rooms with long curtains took up part of the far wall. Soft instrumental music played in the background, and a subtle aroma of lavender and sandalwood scented the room.

I had to credit Caroline with creating a peaceful and enchanting atmosphere for shopping.

"Caroline, it's Annie. I'm here to pick up my dress," I called as I approached the cash register.

"One minute. I'm in the back doing inventory," Caroline replied. "Make yourself at home. There's tea and scones."

I looked around and sure enough, a tray with assorted teas and bite-sized scones was set up near the dressing room. I helped myself to a vanilla scone and looked through the racks of flowy bohemian-style dresses and scarves. Caroline had an eye for what sold well in Northern California. Her clothing selection was eclectic and chic.

She emerged from the storage area in the back with a garment bag draped over one arm. Caroline was the epitome of aging gracefully. Her long white hair cascaded down her shoulders. She wore little makeup, just a touch of blush to highlight her cheekbones and lip-gloss to accentuate her lips.

"Here you go, what do you think?" She unzipped a garment bag to reveal an A-line dress made of cotton and spandex with a print of stacks of books intermixed with magnifying glasses. Cap sleeves, a sweetheart neckline, pockets, and a belt to tie around my waist made it the perfect dress for the Mystery Fest.

"It's even cuter in person," I gasped.

She handed me the dress. "It's going to go well with your hair and skin tone. I'm sorry that it took so long to arrive. The vendor had a backlog of orders."

"No problem." I pointed to the dressing rooms. "Do you mind if I change into it here?"

"Not at all." Caroline glanced at my tennis shoes. "Are you going to wear those?"

"Yeah. I'm on my feet all day and will be running back and forth between the store and the library for the author panels."

She shook her head. "Annie, I can't let you leave in those shoes. There are options for functional fashion. Go ahead and change. I'll pull a few sandals for you to try on."

I didn't bother protesting.

I changed into the dress. It accentuated my narrow waist, and the dark navy did complement my freckled skin. I studied my appearance in the mirror. My long red hair fell in loose waves against my shoulders. The color enhanced the golden flecks in my eyes.

Not bad, Annie.

I did a half twirl to fully appreciate how the skirt flared and the bookish pattern on the back.

"You're a stunner." Caroline beamed when I stepped out of the changing area. "Now, you need these and perhaps a pair of earrings to finish the look." She offered a pair of navy-and-cream-striped sandals with a two-inch heel.

"I don't usually wear heels."

"Trust me, you'll love these. They are comfortable and will

look adorable with that dress." Caroline dangled them in front of me like she was trying to tempt me.

I put the sandals on, expecting to hate them, but Caroline was right. They were supportive while giving me a lift.

"Walk around in them," she encouraged. "Aren't they nice?"

"They are," I admitted.

"Great, shall I ring them up, too?" She lifted the edge of her flowing linen pants. "I'm wearing the same shoe. I wear them all day in the shop, and my feet are quite happy. I'll give you a twenty percent discount."

"You don't need to do that."

"I do. I appreciate what you've done for Redwood Grove. Yesterday was our best sales day since our grand opening. It couldn't have come at a better time after everything that happened with Kayla." When she said Kayla's name, her entire body stiffened.

I followed her to the register. "I'm still confused as to why she stole your concept."

Caroline punched numbers into an iPad. "You know, I had a bad feeling about her from the beginning. I'm kicking myself for not trusting my instincts, but Justin was so insistent that Kayla was a pro and that, with her help, I could double or triple my sales."

"You mentioned that Justin recommended her."

"Not merely recommended, he told me I would be an idiot to pass up the chance to work with Kayla. He touted her vast experience in growing online sales for other retailers. I thought it was odd at the time because he pitched me on her services at the pub. Why wasn't she working for State of Mind if she was so good?" Caroline pointed her index finger at me like she expected me to answer that.

"Maybe because they can't sell beer online?" I suggested. Although I agreed with Caroline that it was odd. Last night,

Justin had told me that he and Kayla weren't very close and that her visit to Redwood Grove wasn't planned. What was his motive for convincing Caroline to work with his cousin? Had he been trying to pawn her off on someone else? Or were they working together somehow?

"True, but she could have updated their website, tried to grow their social media accounts, and even set up online sales for their merch. They sell hats, hoodies, frisbees, pint glasses, and posters." Caroline pulled her hair behind one ear and reached for a pair of reading glasses to see the screen.

"When did you realize that she had copied your concept?"

Caroline finished ringing up the sale and flipped the iPad for me to pay. I tapped the screen to finalize my purchase.

"One of my customers brought it to my attention." Caroline carefully placed my T-shirt and tennis shoes into an Artifacts tote. "She had been eying that vase in the front window. She must have come in two or three times to look at it. She measured it to make sure it would fit in her living space and took pictures. But she never went through with the purchase. I figured she had changed her mind. It happens. Retail is often an impulse buy. You must get some of that at the bookstore. Not that your price points are as high as mine, but still."

I nodded. "Oh yeah. For sure. We'll often have readers browse and seem interested in a particular book only to leave. Hal gets frustrated, especially when they take pictures of the books because we know they buy them online."

"I've considered posting signs saying No Photos for that reason." Caroline handed me the tote bag. "My customer returned to the shop to tell me how much she loves the vase and show me photos of it in her living room. That's when we both realized she didn't buy the vase from me." Her eyes drifted to the bay windows. A two-foot ceramic vase with gold-and-silver etching sat on display. It wasn't my taste, but it would easily grace one of the stately rooms at the Secret Bookcase.

"That's the vase?" I asked.

"My customer received a promotional email from what she thought was Artifacts, but it was from Kayla." She paused briefly, her cheeks sucking in with disgust. Then her gaze returned to the vase. She stared at it like she still couldn't believe what Kayla had done. "Not only did she steal my entire product line and misrepresent herself to my vendors. These are vendors that I've spent a year building personal relationships with."

Caroline's dancer-like posture slumped. Her shoulders sagged as she swept a hand toward me. "It's like your dress. When it didn't show up before this weekend, I put in a call to my rep at the wholesaler and explained how important it was that you have it for the Mystery Fest. They overnighted it to me at no additional charge because they know I'm a great partner and will continue to sell for them."

"You didn't need to go to all that trouble," I said. Caroline's commitment to customer service was impressive.

"I do. It's important to me," she insisted. "But what I was going to say was that in addition to lying to vendors about her role at Artifacts, Kayla also stole my customer list. She claimed that she needed access to my email list to build a newsletter and sales funnel, but in reality, she took all that private information and emailed my entire list, pretending to be me. She sent them deep discounts and set up a parallel website. My customers assumed they were shopping at Artifacts, but they were shopping on Kayla's mirrored site."

"That's terrible. And it also has to be illegal. Just stealing your email list alone."

Caroline flipped the iPad around and turned it off. "I'm in contact with a lawyer, but I doubt there will be much I can do now that she's dead."

"Did you confront her?" I knew I had to remain neutral, but I didn't want Caroline to be the killer.

"That was part of our discussion on Thursday evening at the hotel," Caroline said. "I told her that my lawyer would be contacting her about a lawsuit and that I was sending out an email to my customers letting them know that they had been duped."

"How did she react?"

"You saw her, didn't you? She was drunk. She blew me off. I don't think she had an ounce of remorse in her body. Kayla cared about one person—herself. I was so furious that she was in town that I had to remove myself from the event; otherwise, I don't trust what I might have done." Caroline paused like she considered saying more but stopped herself.

"I don't blame you."

She stepped away from the register. "It doesn't matter. She's dead, and part of me is not sad about that. I know it sounds terrible, but it's true."

I tried to put myself in Caroline's position. Kayla had betrayed her and potentially cost her critical revenue. But did that justify feeling okay about her murder? I wasn't sure.

"You probably need to get to the bookshop." Caroline motioned to the front.

Was that a not-so-subtle hint that she had said more than she wanted?

"Thank you again for getting the dress here and the discount." I looped the tote over my arm.

"You're welcome. Good luck with everything today. It's so wonderful to see the town thriving. Yesterday was a boon for business. I can't imagine what today will be like."

"I'm glad to hear that. Let me know if you need anything." I left with a wave.

As I headed off in the direction of the bookstore, I found myself thinking that Caroline didn't seem like a killer, at least not at first glance, but I couldn't dismiss what Kayla had done to her. Caroline had poured her heart, soul, and a lot of cash into

Artifacts. Kayla had nearly destroyed Caroline's entire business. That gave her a clear motive for murder.

As much as I would have loved to eliminate her from my list of suspects, our conversation had had the opposite effect.

In many ways, Caroline had the most compelling reason to want Kayla dead. She had admitted to confronting Kayla and was pursuing legal action, although she didn't sound very convinced that she would recoup anything. But I had witnessed their argument firsthand. The question was, could Caroline have snuck into the Sitting Room, killed Kayla, and left the Secret Bookcase without being seen? Fletcher had mentioned that she had been in the bookshop shortly before I returned from State of Mind. I needed to find out if he could remember exactly when he had seen her. I hated that I needed to look further into her whereabouts, but one key thing I had learned from Dr. Caldwell was not to let my personal feelings impact how I approached an investigation. I hoped that my inquiries would clear Caroline's name, but at the same time, I needed to prepare myself for the possibility that she could be the killer.

SEVENTEEN

As anticipated, the bookstore was packed all morning. I was running on adrenaline and too much coffee after a less-than-restful night of sleep, but the energy of so many readers filling the store was a welcome distraction from getting stuck in my head. I didn't have time to ruminate on Kayla's murder because I was running from room to room, reshelving books, answering questions, and stopping just long enough to snap photos of happy book lovers posing with lovely stacks of new reads.

Fletcher and I reworked the clues for the interactive mystery, hiding new printouts of the ones that had been in the bookcase in a vintage biography of Agatha Christie in the Parlor. The police had blocked the entrance to the Sitting Room with yellow crime scene tape. Explaining that a murder had occurred in the cozy room caused many strange and confused follow-up conversations.

"Annie, I think we need to post a volunteer in front of the Sitting Room," Hal suggested when I passed him with a fresh carafe of coffee for the Conservatory. "I've had to kick out at least a dozen people who have snuck under the caution tape, believing it's merely decoration."

"That's a good idea. Let me finish setting up the first author panel, and then I'll look through the volunteer schedule to see who we can move around. I'm sure it won't be a problem."

"Good. Thank you. For now, I'm going to take up court in front of the Sitting Room and keep readers out." Hal gave me a salute.

I took the coffee to the Conservatory and made sure the donuts and fresh fruit trays I had ordered arrived. One of my volunteers was a greeter and would be moderating the panel, making sure to keep an eye on the time and helping with the Q&A portion of the event. There were six themed panels slotted for the day. Two would take place at the bookshop, and the remaining panels would be hosted at the library. In addition to panels, all the authors in attendance would be doing pop-up appearances around town. I tried to pair authors with businesses similar in theme and tone. For instance, one of my featured authors wrote a long-running cozy coffeehouse series, so I partnered her with Cryptic. Another popular author wrote a hard-boiled detective series that chronicled a retired police chief investigating cold cases in his lakeside fishing village. I paired him with the outdoor store. Piecing together the schedule, panels, and pop-ups had been a brain teaser and gave me a new appreciation for the amount of work that went into large-scale events.

"Is there another volunteer joining you?" I asked, setting the coffee carafe next to the breakfast snacks.

Martha, the volunteer, consulted her clipboard. "There will be two of us."

"Great. Do you feel confident moderating the panel alone?"

Martha checked her notes. "It's two time warnings and directing readers to the microphone for questions, right?"

"Exactly." I glanced at the rows of chairs resting on the polished wooden floorboards. Sunlight streamed in through the large windows, illuminating golden spines.

"No problem." She gave me a little nod.

"Excellent. Thanks so much. Can you do me another favor? When the other volunteer arrives, send them to the Sitting Room. We need someone to be on standby to make sure that readers don't enter the space."

"Count on it."

I appreciated that our helpers took their roles seriously. That was one of the wonderful things about living in a community like Redwood Grove. Everyone wanted this event to thrive and be a success. It was truly a town effort.

I needed to check in with the library and make sure Priya was ready for the pop-up at Cryptic, so I let Hal know that a volunteer would be relieving him soon. Then I made sure Fletcher and our temporary staff were good before I headed to the library.

The library was a short walk southeast of the village square, near Artifacts. It was housed in a grand English estate that offered a peaceful refuge for book lovers and researchers. The library was second only to the Secret Bookcase as my favorite place in town to find a cozy nook and spend an afternoon curled up with a book.

Eli was pacing near the entrance, talking on his cell phone. I wasn't sure if his stiff posture was due to his now-familiar tight skinny jeans and turtleneck or the conversation he was having.

I waved hello as I passed him. He ignored me.

The building radiated timeless elegance and a quiet, studious charm. A harmonious blend of honey-hued stones and dark wooden beams echoed a classical Tudor aesthetic. When I stepped inside the double oak doors, I was greeted with the smell of aging paper and polished wood. High vaulted ceilings were adorned with delicate plasterwork. Shelves carved from dark mahogany wood lined the walls, their surfaces groaning under the weight of so many books.

In the heart of the room, large oak tables with wingback

chairs provided a space for studying or reading. Arched windows flooded the room with light and offered views of the manicured gardens outside.

It was impossible not to be captured by the library's charm. Every time I stepped inside, it felt like traveling to a fairytale world.

A grand spiral staircase to my left led to the second floor. I felt the watchful gaze of eyes in the historical portraits hanging next to the staircase. I loved the sounds of creaking floorboards, rustling pages, and whispered conversations. Despite its regal grandeur, the library was more than an old estate filled with books. It was a sanctuary and a monument to Redwood Grove's literary heritage.

The library staff buzzed with eager energy.

"Annie, the first panel isn't for nearly an hour, and readers are already arriving," the head librarian said, motioning to the far end of the library. Rows of chairs sat in front of a long table, and at least a third of them were already occupied.

"I hope that's a good thing," I said, stealing a glance in that direction.

"It's wonderful. It's such a delight to see this kind of enthusiasm for reading." She beamed with pride. "Your dress is amazing, by the way. Are those all books?"

"Thanks. I just bought it from Artifacts this morning." I held the edge of the flared skirt for her to see the design close up. "I just stopped by to check you're all set for the panels and if you need anything?"

"Our library staff is on top of it," she responded, then scrunched her lips together and glanced behind me. "There is one small thing."

"Sure, anything."

"Eli Ledger is waiting outside. He isn't on our list of panelists, but apparently, he is under the impression that he's supposed to be doing a special meet and greet here. It's not a problem. We can set him up in one of the private study rooms upstairs. Oddly, that was his preference." She considered this for a minute. "I would think an author would want more visibility, but in any event, did we miss something on our schedule?"

This was strange. I frowned and tried to think if, in all the craziness of planning the event, I'd forgotten we'd set up something like this. I was sure we hadn't. "No. Eli had a reading at the bookshop yesterday, but he's not on today's schedule," I replied, second-guessing myself.

Have I made a mistake?

No.

I have gone over the schedule dozens of times. Eli doesn't even have a book out yet. Many authors attending the festival have canons of work to share with readers.

"Okay, that's what I thought. He's outside calling his editor now. As I said, we're happy to accommodate him and his fans. We don't have his title, *Of Hallows and Hauntings*. I looked it up, and it hasn't even been released yet. I can have one of our staff make some signage directing readers upstairs if he wants to read a selection from his upcoming work. We already have the posters you provided for the panels." She nodded to the easels on either side of the circulation desk.

"That's so thoughtful of you. As long as it's not too much trouble." It was weird that Eli was demanding additional appearances, but then again, after his reading yesterday, it shouldn't surprise me. He had an exceptionally inflated ego for an author who had yet to release a single title. Maybe that was Monica's doing.

The head librarian shrugged and smiled. "It's absolutely fine. The more authors, the merrier."

"I'll talk to Eli on my way out. Text if you need anything else, and thanks for your help." I hugged her and left.

Eli was still standing on the front lawn, but for once, he wasn't on his phone. It had to be nearing eighty degrees, but he was dressed in another turtleneck and skinny jeans.

"I hear you're going to do a bonus appearance," I said, hoping my tone sounded professional.

"You're mistaken," he snapped, flexing his long, bony fingers. "I was guaranteed a minimum of three appearances for my time and travel this weekend."

Guaranteed?

My jaw tightened. I could feel my lips turning white from pressing them together so tightly to keep from saying something I might regret. Who was this guy?

I cleared my throat and changed my stance before responding.

"I'm curious. Who guaranteed that? I only ask because I put the event schedule together, and no one told me that any of the authors in attendance were being given a specific number of appearances." I pulled out my phone, ready to show him the schedule I had poured hours into creating.

"Do you realize that I'm not getting paid to be here?" Eli said with a snarl, baring his yellow teeth. "I'm losing valuable writing hours, and in exchange, I'm being put up in a mediocre hotel. There's no food or mileage stipend. I would never have agreed to an appearance this weekend if I knew it was going to be so unprofessional. I can't say that I'll be able to recommend the festival to other authors."

Unprofessional? Did he have any idea how many unpaid hours I had logged, getting support from our local businesses to drum up funds and sponsorship money to provide visiting authors with honorariums and complimentary lodging for their time? If it weren't for the generous community spirit of Redwood Grove, the festival never would have happened.

Talk about entitlement.

I wanted to punch him.

Instead, I clenched my jaw and forced a smile. "I can assure you that the entire town of Redwood Grove has spent countless hours planning and preparing for an event of this scale. We've attracted several bestselling mystery authors, all of whom have been pleased with the events we've been able to put together for this first year."

I watched him flinch at that, but I didn't care. I'd worked hard for this, and I wasn't going to let him ruin it for me or everyone else who had thrown themselves into the spirit of the weekend.

"Most authors are thrilled to have an immersive and innovative festival like this. It gives them the opportunity to really connect with readers on a personal level. It's huge exposure, and book sales have been off the charts." I wasn't going to take any abuse from Eli. Alienating booksellers was one sure way to tank his preorders. Did Eli not understand how connected the independent bookselling community was? We hand-sold so many copies of titles we loved. We promoted books in front of store displays, online, and with our fellow booksellers. We also reported sales to the *New York Times* and *USA Today* and nominated titles for awards. His attitude made no sense. Authors usually had to pay their way to the bigger book festivals. Publishing houses and bookstores didn't front that cost. If anything, Eli should be thanking the library for their support.

Eli scoffed. "That's not my problem. I don't pander to readers."

Good luck selling any books, then, I said to myself.

He cleared his throat. "I've been on a call with Monica, and she's on her way here now to sort this all out."

I suppressed the urge to say something I might regret. "What needs to be sorted?"

"My appearances. I was promised a private signing and

panel in addition to my talk yesterday." He flared his nostrils as he spoke.

The more time I spent with him, the more I couldn't wait to decline any future signings at the Secret Bookcase when his book was finally released.

"It sounds like the library is arranging for you to have a private room upstairs. In terms of panels, there's not anything more that we can do. The panel assignments have been in place for months, and there's simply not space for another author on any of the panels."

"Let's wait and see what Monica says about that." He faced me directly, taking a wide stance like he was trying to intimidate me.

I had news for him—it wasn't working.

I stood tall and said firmly, "Monica isn't in charge. I am."

His intense, dark eyes locked on to me with an unblinking stare. "I would think a struggling bookstore would be grateful to have an author like me bringing readers into your store. I'm quite offended by your treatment of my talent."

Who was this guy?

Monica appeared before I could respond, which was probably a good thing.

"I'm here. I'm here," she called. Her heel caught in the grass. She nearly lost her balance but recovered quickly and hurried over to us.

I'd met my fair share of authors with egos over the years, but no one compared to Eli Ledger. What didn't make sense was where the attitude was coming from. Aside from Monica, he didn't have a following or a single fan, as far as I knew.

His condescending tone made me want to encourage him to take an early leave from the Mystery Fest. Kayla's murder had already put a damper on the festivities, and I didn't need Eli making it worse. I had plenty on my mind, with making the event a success and ensuring that the day went smoothly, without Eli taking up brain space. What I wanted to do was race home, pour myself a steaming mug of golden chai, and delve deep into the potential list of suspects I'd formulated. But my investigation into Kayla's death would have to wait because I was responsible for Mystery Fest, and I wasn't about to let Eli ruin the rest of the weekend.

EIGHTEEN

Monica greeted Eli with a timid smile and me with a shaky hand. "Good morning. I hear that there's a bit of a mix-up?"

Did Eli have something on her?

She seemed skittish around him. Shouldn't it be the other way around? In my experience, new authors were eager to please their editors.

"Excuse me," Eli butted in. "This is more than a mix-up. They don't have me on a panel. I don't have another signing. This is ludicrous. I traveled here for one bookshop talk—I don't think so." A visible tightness spread across Eli's pinched face. He stepped forward, invading Monica's personal space, his expression full of judgment.

"Don't worry. We'll fix this." She looked like she was modeling slow breathing as she gestured placatingly with her hands to try and calm him. "I'm sure it's a simple scheduling error that we can remedy. Isn't that right, Annie?"

Had my conversation with Eli gone differently, I might have been more willing to shift the schedule, but there was no chance I was doing anything extra for him at this point. "As I explained to Eli, the panels are full and not a match for what Eli is writing. The first panel here at the library is all about culinary cozies."

"No. Absolutely not." He flexed his fingers like he was about to draw them into fists. "You realize that I'm giving you literary gold in my collection of noir. I'm not a sellout writing for the masses, and I will not be associated with writers—if you can call them that—peddling cute cats and cakes with their so-called crime." His tone was hostile.

Was he trying to start a fight?

My jaw dropped.

Damn. Who is this guy?

Cozies were some of our most popular titles at the Secret Bookcase, and one could easily argue that Agatha Christie was responsible for creating the genre that not only had withstood the test of time but continued to attract droves of new readers.

I glanced around, hoping that Hal might be nearby. I'd love to see Hal and Eli go head-to-head on the topic. A few years ago, Hal had keynoted a conference in London about the lasting legacy of the genre. Cozies had garnered a substantial and dedicated readership. His talk touched on the intellectual challenges of piecing together the puzzle and how the genre fosters a sense of community and camaraderie with a deep focus on interpersonal relationships. He expounded on clever plot twists, themes of justice, relatable protagonists, and literary craftsmanship.

Come to think of it, I should invite Liam Donovan to the bookstore to have a little cozy chat with Hal.

I addressed Monica, intentionally ignoring Eli. "The library has agreed to set up a room on the second floor and provide signage for any readers who might want a meet and greet, but that's all I can do. I sent the final itinerary and event schedule weeks ago. If there was a problem, you should have reached out then."

"Give us a minute, would you, Eli?" Monica asked her star author, holding up one finger and smiling broadly.

Eli shrugged sarcastically and shuffled over to a bench enveloped by climbing rose bushes bursting with dainty pink blooms.

"I'm so sorry about this, Annie." Monica shifted into PR mode. Her voice was smooth and silky like the gelato served at the ice cream shop. "You must know how it is with high-profile authors. I'm sure you're used to lots of outrageous demands. What's the joke about authors requiring only green candies and dozens of white roses on their book tour?"

I raised my eyebrows. "I've literally never heard of any of that. And he just offended a huge percentage of readers and writers. I happen to love cozies, and they're some of our best-sellers." I was done playing nice.

Monica bristled, wincing and nodding, but recovered quickly by inhaling deeply and pressing her shoulders back. "I know. I'm so sorry. Please accept my apology on Eli's behalf. This weekend is his first official appearance, and I'm sure it's simply nerves."

I begged to differ. Being nervous was one thing. Being a complete ass was another.

"He's on a trajectory to becoming a household name. *Of Hallows and Hauntings* is one of the most compelling short story collections I've ever acquired," Monica continued, twisting a strand of hair around her finger. "If there's any way you can make some extra space for him this weekend, we will return the favor by cementing the Secret Bookcase as his official bookstore. You'll get signed copies, merch, first appearance, you name it."

She spoke fast and seemed desperate.

I shook my head, holding my ground. "Why are you so convinced that his book will hit it big? In my experience, collections of short stories tend to have a more niche readership." Was

Eli blackmailing her? I couldn't wrap my head around their relationship.

"Eli's stories have mass appeal. He's going to be the next Sir Arthur Conan Doyle. I'm talking like Sherlock Holmes kind of appeal. I'm already negotiating foreign rights, movie rights, audio." She licked her bottom lip and pressed her hair back into place. "We're putting big money behind this debut, and that's why I'm eager to partner with you. I understand that Eli can be rough around the edges, but it's part of his author persona. Readers are going to love that his aloof attitude matches his detective's bold style."

I wasn't sure about that either. Readers tended to appreciate authentic, warm, welcoming, and self-deprecating authors. Eli was none of those things.

"Adding an appearance at the library would be great, and if there's anything else you can squeeze him into for the weekend, I will forever be in your debt," Monica pleaded. I half expected her to drop onto her knees and beg.

"I can't make any promises," I said with reluctance.

She stole a glance toward the library. "Listen, can I be honest with you? I really need this, okay? I've jumped around a bit from job to job like you do when you're first starting out. Getting this position was huge, and I'm desperate to keep it. I don't know if I'll get another chance, you know? I'm completely committed to making Eli a bestseller because my career and future depends on his success."

Wow. That was a lot of pressure. I felt bad for her. Although Eli, not so much. "I'll see what I can do. Maybe he can give a brief talk or a short reading at State of Mind Public House during the pub crawl later."

"That would be fantastic. Thank you so much, Annie. You're such a good friend," Monica gushed, reaching out to hug me. "What would I do without you? I lucked out that you're running the festival."

We were hardly friends in college, and I hadn't seen her in almost a decade. Monica's effusive praise felt forced.

"How long have you been working with Eli?" I asked.

She untwisted the thin, patterned scarf around her neck and wrapped it around her arm. "I've been actively growing my list and trying to acquire new authors, especially in mystery and romance. I met Eli at a conference last year. He did a pitch roundtable, and I immediately loved the concept. Short stories are so underrated, and I feel like they're having a moment. Readers have so many distractions these days and shortened attention spans. There's a huge opportunity with short story collections that have been under-represented in genre fiction. I told him to send me a proposal and some sample pages, and I immediately made him an offer."

She did have a valid point about the plethora of entertainment options available to readers. We had to compete with audiobooks, gaming, streaming shows and movies, and screen time at the bookshop. Like the library staff, we were thrilled that readers still enjoyed perusing the stacks in search of an obscure or out-of-print title or stumbling upon a childhood favorite.

"What was that exchange between him and Kayla during his reading?" I asked.

Monica's face flushed. She fidgeted with her scarf and spoke rapidly. "Kayla was drunk. Who knows what that was about? She enjoyed getting under people's skin. It made her feel better about herself to make other people feel belittled and small. She took pleasure in her superiority. I'm guessing that's why she tried to interrupt Eli's reading. She probably couldn't stand not being the center of attention. That's one of the many reasons that she and I are—were—no longer friends."

I watched Monica's body language. She didn't make eye contact with me as she spoke. She focused on the library in the distance and talked fast, seeming almost breathless. Bringing up Kayla had obviously made her uncomfortable.

"I thought I was hallucinating when I saw her at the hotel. I've gone out of my way to avoid her in the years after college." Monica draped the scarf around her neck again. "I'm sure she was hoping to get a rise out of me with her treatment of Eli. I made the mistake of introducing him as my star author. In true Kayla form, she pounced. She held a grudge. I ghosted her after college because I couldn't deal with her drama anymore, and she hated that. She kept trying to text, call, and message me on social, but I blocked her everywhere. That's the worst possible thing I could have done because, like I said, she must be the most important person in the room. I'm sure it drove her bananas to have me go radio silent."

"So the other night was the first time you had seen each other since college?" I was glad that Monica was opening up. I didn't know what it meant in terms of Kayla's murder yet, but the fact that the two former friends had such a contentious relationship could have given her cause to want to kill Kayla. The tiny hairs on the back of my neck stood at attention, watching Monica's feet shift and sink into the dewy grass as she took her time responding. What were the chances the two former roommates had happened to run into each other during the festival? It couldn't be a coincidence.

Guests were beginning to gather for the first panel. I checked my watch. I needed to get back to the store, but I couldn't pass up the chance to hear what else Monica might have to say.

"Uh, well. Technically, no. We had bumped into each other at a few sorority events over the years, but I did my best to avoid her there." Her smile faded quickly. "None of our sorority sisters liked her either. I don't know anyone who did like her, to tell you the truth. Mainly, people put up with her because they didn't want to end up on her bad side. She could turn nasty real quick."

"And you think there's a chance that Kayla was trying to sabotage Eli's reading to get back at you?"

"Yeah." Monica shifted her weight from one foot to the other. "You knew her. That shouldn't surprise you. Don't you remember what a drama queen she was? She was always lying, gossiping, trying to get sympathy for her outlandish stories. She was a nightmare. I wouldn't put anything past her, and I'm convinced she would do anything to destroy my career. She had a personal vendetta against me, and I have no doubt that if she hadn't been killed, she would have spent the remainder of the weekend trying to wreck my career and ruin Eli's reputation."

I considered pointing out that Eli was doing a fine job of that without any interference from Kayla, but Monica's revelations piqued my interest.

"Kayla cared about one person and one person alone—herself." There was a hardness to her voice and a hardness in her eyes. "I don't know what her ulterior motive was in attending the Mystery Festival, but I wouldn't put it past her to have learned that I was coming with my soon-to-be bestseller."

"Wait, you think she came to the festival because of *you?*" This was news.

Monica rubbed the hair at the top of her head and then grabbed a fistful. "It's a strong possibility. She's been trying to undermine me and thwart my career ever since we had our falling out in college."

"Why?"

"Because she was furious that I was the one to end our friendship. She couldn't handle it, and she's been out to impede my success ever since." She tugged on her hair like she was going to yank it out.

"But I thought you two hadn't remained in touch?"

"*I* didn't stay in touch with her, but she was obsessed with my career." Monica flushed slightly. Her voice elevated in pitch like she'd been caught in a lie. She released her hair and exhaled slowly. "I've worked at three publishing houses now, and each time an announcement was posted about my role, she would message the company and say terrible, awful things about me."

"Really?" Did Monica realize she was revealing a solid reason to want Kayla dead?

"It's true. I also had to block her from our professional social media pages."

I tried to take it all in and reserve judgment, but it was hard not to wonder if this routine of stalking Monica had caused her to finally crack. I also couldn't help but wonder if this was also about Seth, especially after our conversation last night. "What caused your fallout in college?"

She tensed her jaw and stepped away from me, putting more distance between us like she was trying to avoid the source of her discomfort. "Everything I already told you. I got fed up with dealing with her, and to top it off, she stole and plagiarized my final English paper. It was a classic Kayla move. She'd gotten in trouble before with a story she'd stolen from someone else. I almost didn't graduate because of her. They thought I was the one who had copied Kayla's paper."

"What?" I hadn't heard anything about that at the time, but then again, I'd been preoccupied with Scarlet's murder.

"I never should have trusted her." Monica's tone was icy. Her phone rang. "Sorry, this is work. I need to take the call. Thanks again for your help with Eli, and let me know about the pub crawl."

"Will do." I had no interest in another conversation with Eli, so I opted to head over to Cryptic for a latte and to check in with Priya.

My conversation with Monica replayed as I wandered through the park. Could Kayla have followed her here? That seemed extreme, but I couldn't rule it out. In some ways, it made more sense than Kayla visiting Justin or returning to check in on Artifacts, especially given what I had learned from

Caroline. It also made my stomach rumble with guilt. If I hadn't suggested the Mystery Fest and promoted it online, Kayla might still be alive. My event listing had drawn everyone to the festival. What if posting about it on social media had sparked the killer's plan?

I tried to work out if there was a connection to our past—if Kayla's and Scarlet's murders were intertwined somehow. I couldn't wrap my head around it, and I knew that Dr. Caldwell had dismissed the idea, but I still couldn't shake the coincidence of my former classmates arriving in Redwood Grove, and within hours, one of them being dead.

But what could Kayla and Scarlet's killer have in common?

It did seem like a long shot.

What I did know was that Monica claimed Kayla had stolen and plagiarized her final paper in college. That matched Caroline's experience. Apparently, Kayla had a habit of taking people's ideas, businesses, and creative identities and passing them off as her own. She had put herself in harm's way through her actions.

Monica still seemed to hold a grudge about what had happened between them in college. It seemed like a long shot, but stranger things had happened. Monica's obsession with Eli's burgeoning career was also clearly an issue.

Caroline and Monica both had motives for wanting Kayla dead, which meant that instead of shrinking, my suspect list was growing.

NINETEEN

I was badly in need of coffee and a chance to talk everything through with Pri. As I walked into Cryptic, I was greeted by the heady aroma of freshly ground beans and hot-from-the-oven cinnamon rolls. Priya was busy pulling espresso shots and chatting with customers waiting for their specialty drinks. "Annie, the Marple Mochas are going fast. I don't think I've ever seen this many people here at once. Should I make you one before we run out of our spicy, dark chocolate syrup?"

"Uh, yes, please. Is that even a question?" I waited for my drink, taking in the buzzing coffee shop. Pri wasn't exaggerating. Readers were huddled at outdoor tables, the comfy couches inside, and people spilled out onto the sidewalk, sipping their morning brews while reviewing their clues and town maps. Festivalgoers traded book totes, pins, and bookish stickers while devouring sugar-coated blackberry scones and egg bagels.

There was such an overwhelming sense of camaraderie that my heart swelled with pride. I've always believed that book people are the best people, and this weekend proved that point. I could tell that friendships were forming and lifelong connections were being made. I never anticipated that the Mystery

Fest would turn into something quite this spectacular and touching. I felt a sense of relief and pride that the weekend was even better than I expected. It meant that Hal might not have to worry about selling the bookstore and that our community was humming with vibrancy and cash flow again.

"One double Marple Mocha on the bar," Pri announced, handing me my drink. "By the way, I love, love, love the dress. It's perfect on you."

"Thanks. Caroline ordered it for me." I ran my tongue over my lip gloss as I breathed in the rich, chocolaty scent of the coffee. Pri had hand-poured a foam skull on the top of the latte that was so cute I didn't want to ruin it by taking a sip. "This looks and smells so delicious."

"Instant hit." Priya pumped her fist in the air. "This one is going to need a permanent spot on the menu. What do you think of the skull?"

"It's incredible. You're a true artist." I took a sip of the creamy coffee. It went down smoothly and finished with a fiery kick. "Wow, this is amazing."

"You think?" Pri's eyes sparkled with delight. "The spice gets you at the end. Just like that sweet Miss Marple, sitting in a cozy chair with her tea and knitting and not missing a single thing with her eagle eyes."

I chuckled. "It's true. Marple is stealth like that."

"And hits you with a punch of the truth, doesn't it?" Pri winked.

"Absolutely." I wiped foam from my lips with the back of my hand. "How are things going so far besides selling lots of Marple Mochas?"

"Great. Your readers are very enthusiastic. It's fun to see." Pri glanced at the line, which had thinned slightly. She lowered her voice. "Any more news on the murder?"

"I had conversations with Caroline and Monica this morning," I said, leaning my elbows on the counter and making sure no one was listening. "Kayla stole both of their intellectual property." I filled her in on everything I knew.

"So either of them could have done it," Pri said. It was incredible to watch her multitask. She deftly tamped down espresso shots and worked through the drink orders while we chatted. Prince played on the overhead speakers. Pri occasionally stopped to review orders and package bloody cherry turnovers and Poirot popovers for customers. She had gone all in on the alliteration, and I was here for it.

"At the very least, they each have motives," I said, wondering if it would be bad to order a second cup. I'd had a cup of coffee earlier at the bookstore, so I probably needed to pace myself.

"We can't rule Eli out either." Pri vented steam from the shiny espresso machine.

I liked that she was using "we." It felt good to have a partner. I hadn't done this since Scarlet. The thought made my chest feel tight. I knew Scarlet would be cheering me on, but it was hard not to feel like I was betraying her at the same time.

"That's interesting. I hadn't thought of him as having a motive, but he's definitely worth considering." I took a drink of the mocha. "I hope to find Dr. Caldwell soon and relay everything we've learned."

"I wonder if she has a suspect in mind," Pri said, drizzling dark chocolate sauce on another drink. "It seems like in the movies, the police always know who did it and just have to do their due diligence to gather enough evidence to prove it."

"I have a feeling that if Dr. Caldwell has someone in mind, she will keep her cards close to her chest. I can't imagine her sharing that with us. I'm supposed to catch up with her sometime this afternoon. Hopefully, if there are any new developments in the investigation, she might tell me." Like with Monica, it was hard for me to wrap my head around the fact that Dr. Caldwell was in charge of the investigation. How was it possible that my college professor and classmates were all in Redwood Grove for the weekend? Dr. Caldwell had seemed fairly confident that there wasn't a connection with Scarlet's murder. However, she was human. What if she was wrong? What if she made a mistake?

"But she did ask you to assist." Pri finished the drink order and slid it to a waiting customer down the bar.

"Assist might be a bit of a stretch." My gaze drifted to the pastry case. The chocolate-coated donuts with pretzel rods stabbed in the center, releasing oozing raspberry jelly, made my mind flash to finding Kayla. I clutched my stomach and forced the image out of my head.

She waved me off and lowered her voice. "I've been doing my own investigating this morning in the form of eavesdropping on every conversation."

I grinned. "I don't remember eavesdropping being in my criminology course catalog."

"You must have missed it," Pri said with the utmost sincerity. "The Art of Eavesdropping 101. I heard there was always a waiting list for the class."

I chuckled. "Did you learn anything new with your stellar listening skills?"

"As a matter of fact, I did. I'm offended that you'd doubt my abilities," she teased and used a stir stick to point outside.

I followed her gaze to a table where Justin and a group of guys I recognized from Public House were gathered, drinking coffee and devouring a plate of pastries.

"This isn't officially confirmed, but one of my sources—" She paused for dramatic effect and wiggled her eyebrows. "That's right, don't look at me like that. I have sources."

"I never doubted otherwise."

She grinned. "In any event, my sources claim that Justin is in deep financial trouble, and the rumor is that Kayla might have been involved."

"Involved in what?" I swiped a taste of chocolate syrup from the bottom of my mug.

"His money struggles. Money, as in a motive for murder," she said with satisfaction.

"Really?"

Pri's eyes were wide as she watched me take in the information.

"But it's just a rumor, right?"

"Yeah." She conceded the point with a noncommittal nod. "Think about it, though. If money was involved, that could give Justin a solid reason for wanting Kayla dead."

"They were cousins." I couldn't imagine harming anyone in my family. Maybe that was due to always longing for cousins or siblings, but nonetheless I couldn't imagine wanting to harm anyone.

"Has blood ever stopped murder?" Pri lifted a single eyebrow and twisted her lips together.

"I guess not, but I can't picture Justin killing his cousin." I wrinkled my nose.

"Can you picture anyone we have on the list as a murderer, though? Having a motive is one thing, or even wishing someone would die, but carrying that out is a whole new level of terrifying." Pri stuck out her tongue, closed her eyes, and shuddered at the thought.

"True." I agreed. "It's hard to imagine how someone could be that brutal." Scarlet's and Kayla's faces flashed in my mind. The idea that anyone could want to end a life was abhorrent to me.

Pri busied herself, wiping down the counter. Suddenly, she stopped and made a slicing motion across her neck. I turned around to see why she was acting so weird all of a sudden and saw that Justin was approaching the bar with an empty coffee cup.

"Hey, can I get a refill?" He handed Pri an empty turquoise earthenware mug and nodded hello to me.

"Sure." Pri wasn't subtle as she took his mug and urged me to do something.

"Justin, can we chat for a minute?" I decided that there was no reason to hold back. "Something has come up about Kayla's murder that involves you."

He flinched and took a step away from me. Then he stole a glance at the table where his friends were laughing and enjoying morning coffee underneath the golden California sun. "Yeah, uh, I guess."

Pri placed a steaming cup of coffee in front of him. "Cream? Sugar?"

"No, just black. Thanks." Justin smiled at her and avoided looking at me.

"Let's go sit over there." I pointed to a table away from the crowd.

Justin followed me without a word.

I waited for him to get comfortable. He crossed and uncrossed his legs twice, removed his stocking hat, and then put it on again. If his fidgeting and buggy eyes were any indication of his comfort level, then maybe Pri's sources had been correct. His hair that was just beginning to grow back reminded me of peach fuzz. He wore a pair of baggy shorts and a State of Mind T-shirt.

"What's going on? Did you hear from the police? Do they know more about what happened to Kayla?" Justin's words smashed together in one jumbled sentence.

"Actually, this is about you."

He took a sip of coffee and spit it on the ground. "Sorry, it's scalding hot. I wasn't expecting that." He fanned his mouth with his hand.

Was it? Or was he freaking out because I was bringing up Kayla's murder?

"What about me?" He flicked his tongue from side to side like he was trying to get feeling back.

Maybe he had burned it after all.

"I've heard that you're having some financial difficulties."

His tongue hung from the side of his mouth in disbelief. He used one hand to fan it. "What? Where did you hear that? How?"

"There are rumors going around town. That's the con of living in Redwood Grove. Rumors have a tendency to spread quickly," I replied in what I hoped sounded like a calm tone. I wanted Justin to open up, so I needed him to see me as an ally.

A look of utter sadness washed across his face. It was the same look I used to give my mom when I was younger, and she would tell me that I had surpassed my reading limit and it was time to turn out the light for bed.

"Everyone knows?" Justin sounded shocked. "Even the police?"

"I don't know about everyone, but certainly, if I'm hearing about your financial problems, then I think it's fairly safe to assume that Dr. Caldwell and her team are also aware."

Justin puffed out his cheeks. "Crap."

"So, are the rumors true?"

He swished air in his cheeks like it was mouthwash. "This is bad. This is really bad. They're going to arrest me, aren't they?"

"Why would they arrest you for having money challenges?"

"Because of Kayla." He gulped.

I almost felt sorry for him. Justin looked even younger in distress.

"What does Kayla have to do with your financial problems?"

He looked at me with wild eyes. "I was in debt. Pretty bad debt, and she loaned me money. The police are going to see that in my bank account. I'm dead. It's over."

TWENTY

Justin looked like he was on the edge of a full-blown panic attack. He shut his eyes tight and backed up against the base of the patio umbrella like he was using it for protection.

"Take a long, slow, deep breath." I breathed with him, letting my lungs fill with air and then releasing it through my mouth.

Justin's fingers shook as he tried to steady his breathing.

He clutched his throat. His knee bounced so hard on the ground it felt like the earth was shaking. "I can't believe everyone knows. I swear I was going to pay her back, every penny. I just needed a little more time, that's all. I told her that. I gave her as much as I could, and I promised that as soon as I got my next paycheck, I would give her more. It's been hard to get on my feet in a new town. I had to pay first and last month's rent and buy furniture for my apartment. Kayla knew that."

"Kayla loaned you money?" I couldn't believe Justin was admitting this to me, or at least that the rumor Pri heard was true. I was also ready to jump beneath the table. The ground continued to tremble as Justin shook both of his feet. We were prone to earthquakes in Northern California, but I could tell the source was from his nerves.

"Yeah. She wasn't happy about it, but when I got her the gig with Artifacts, she agreed to help me out. We're family, after all. It wasn't a huge amount of money. Only twenty grand to pay off some of my debt and help me get into an apartment. Moving to Redwood Grove was a fresh start for me." He paused and put his hands on his knees to stop shaking. "I made some bad choices. I got sucked into gambling, but I've changed my ways. I gave that all up when I moved here. I haven't gambled in months. I've been working steadily at the pub. This is the longest I've ever had a job."

I was still stuck on the fact that Kayla had loaned Justin money. Maybe twenty thousand dollars was a small sum to him, but for me, that was a substantial amount of money. Was it worth killing over?

"Can you start from the beginning?" I asked, still modeling calm breathing for him.

He looked like a fish out of water, gulping for air. His cheeks turned as red as the geraniums dangling from hanging baskets on the Cryptic patio. "Crap. Crap. This can't be happening."

"Maybe it would help if you could explain the situation," I suggested.

He massaged his neck like he was willing his airway to stay open. "Yeah, right. Okay. So it was weird. Like I told you the other day, Kayla showed up in Redwood Grove unannounced. I was surprised to see her, but it was kind of good timing. I got the job at the Public House but didn't have a plan when I moved here. I slept in my car for the first couple of weeks. It was rough, but I could shower out at the fairgrounds, and at least food was free while I was on shift, so I didn't go hungry."

I felt for him; that sounded terrible.

Justin cleared his throat, forcing a low cough. "Then Kayla

showed up out of nowhere, and at first, I thought maybe she was my fairy godmother. She offered to loan me the money I needed to pay off my gambling debts and get into an apartment here."

"Out of the goodness of her heart?" I interrupted.

"No. That would be too good to be true." He ran his hands over his fuzzy head. "Kayla and I were never close growing up, like I told you. I didn't know her well, but I witnessed enough interactions between her and other family members to know how she operated."

"How was that?" I could tell that he was nervous. Was it because he was upset about his cousin's death or involved in killing her?

"A lot of different ways. She told some outrageous stories. You never knew what to believe with her, but her real power was that she traded in secrets. She would learn your weaknesses and then use them against you." Justin blew out another breath. "I never told her about my past, but I think that's why she came. She must have known. She probably heard about my problems from my mom or maybe our grandmother. It wasn't a secret. As part of my gambling addiction therapy, I came clean. That's why I left my childhood hometown. I knew I would be more tempted to get sucked back in with my gambling friends. Coming here was starting over."

I knew something about starting over.

"And you feel like Kayla used this to her advantage?" I couldn't figure out her angle.

"Now I do. But after sleeping in my backseat for three weeks and eating pub fries for days on end, her offer was like a gift. She told me she would loan me the money, but there were some terms." He flicked an ant off the table with his middle finger and thumb.

"Like what?" I gave a group of teen detectives who swooped over to grab the table next to us a thumbs-up for their clever outfit choices. They were dressed as each of the characters from

Scooby-Doo, including Velma with a pumpkin orange sweater and oversized black glasses and Shaggy, who, aside from his lime-green T-shirt and brown pants, didn't look that much different than most of the Redwood Grove high school students with his floppy hair and Birkenstocks. Even though the beach was a bit of a drive from town, the California surfer vibe ran strong. I didn't envy whoever had drawn the short straw to wear the Scooby costume. Fake synthetic fur head-to-toe and the afternoon heat were going to be a sweaty combination.

Justin stretched his fingers together and then cracked his knuckles. "I had to start paying her back in installments immediately with my first paycheck."

That sounded reasonable.

"Did you?"

"Yes, I haven't missed a payment." His face turned as purple as Daphne's costume.

"How long ago was this?" I asked.

Justin looked up and scratched his forehead. "Uh, about four months ago."

"Okay, so you've been paying her steadily. What other stipulations did she have?" I wanted to keep him talking.

"She wanted me to set up a meeting with her and Caroline from Artifacts, but this part is weird. She wanted it to be casual. She made me promise that it would seem like the idea for her to help Caroline was all mine and spontaneous, on the spot."

That was odd. Did that mean that Kayla had targeted Caroline?

"Did she know Caroline?" I asked.

Justin shrugged. "I don't know. She never said. She just said that if I didn't make sure that it was my suggestion for the two of them to work together, our deal was off."

"Did she have any other terms?" Everything he was sharing made it seem more likely that Kayla had singled out Caroline. Could they have had a connection that no one knew about?

He shook his head. "Only that I couldn't tell anyone about our deal. That was fine by me."

"Did she give you a timeframe to pay her back?"

He swallowed hard. "No. She was taking half my paycheck every two weeks. She left me with just enough to cover my rent, utilities, and barely anything for miscellaneous expenses. She knew that I could eat at work and said I didn't need extra cash for groceries."

Half of his paycheck sounded like a lot to me. "But she didn't give you an ultimatum to pay her by a certain date?"

"Not originally." He didn't elaborate.

I waited. One lesson we learned early on in Dr. Caldwell's lectures was that silence could be a motivator when interrogating a potential suspect. It was a deliberate tactic police would employ to build tension and encourage self-incrimination. Using the "silent treatment" created psychological pressure. A prolonged silence could make them feel vulnerable, isolated, and exposed. It also served to demonstrate the detective's authority and control over the conversation.

I had no idea if it would work or not, but it was worth a shot.

I pretended to be listening in to the chat at the Scooby crew's table, hoping that Justin might fill the void with more details.

He must have realized that I was perfectly content waiting because, after a few awkward minutes, he finally shifted in his chair. "This is where the rumors are going to be bad for me. I'm surprised the police aren't surrounding the coffee shop and getting ready to arrest me."

"Why?" My heart rate picked up.

"Because when Kayla showed up on Thursday, she demanded I repay the loan in full by the end of the weekend." He hung his head like his fate was already determined.

"What?"

He scowled and nodded. "Yeah, it was a gut punch.

Someone must have heard our argument at the Public House. She stormed in, already drunk at noon. I guess the addiction gene runs strong in our family. Anyway, she told me her situation had changed, and she needed her money immediately. I told her I didn't have that kind of cash, which she already knew. She knew exactly how much I was making each paycheck, and she knew that I was handing over everything I could."

"How much did you still owe her?" I shifted my tangerine chair to make room for a group of readers looking for an empty table.

"Sixteen thousand dollars," Justin said, blowing the air out of his cheeks.

"And she wanted it all—now?" No wonder he had freaked out. That was a lot of money.

"By the end of the weekend. There was no way I could get that kind of cash in three days. Not unless I robbed a bank. She told me that's what I should do because if I didn't pay back every last cent, she was going to go straight to the police." He pressed his fist to his lips and shook his head.

Justin seemed earnest. But was it an act?

Owing his cousin sixteen thousand dollars, which she demanded he return by the end of the weekend, gave him an apparent motive for murder.

I wanted to believe him but couldn't take his words at face value.

"What did you do?"

"What could I do?" He sounded powerless. "I told her I would work extra hours for tips, but that might give me a few hundred dollars, not the thousands she was demanding."

"Do you know why she had such a change of heart?"

He shook his head and stared at the table. "No idea. I just know that this is going to look really bad for me in the eyes of the police, isn't it?"

I bit my bottom lip. "It's not great, but if I can offer a little advice, I would suggest you find Dr. Caldwell and explain this to her yourself. It will definitely be better if it comes directly from you versus from the rumors going around."

He picked up his empty coffee mug and pushed back his chair. "Yeah. I guess that's true. Thanks for giving me a heads-up about what's going on. I appreciate it."

"Let me know if you think of anything else."

Justin stood. "I guess I'll go to the police headquarters now."

I sat for a minute in order to analyze what I had learned. I pulled up the spreadsheet I'd made earlier and added this new information. Justin owed Kayla a large sum of money that she suddenly wanted to be returned in full. What was her financial situation to begin with? She must have had ample cash in her bank account to loan Justin the money. What was her real motivation for lending him the money and showing up in Redwood Grove?

It seemed to be connected to Caroline, which meant I knew who I needed to talk to next.

TWENTY-ONE

"Well, what did he say?" Pri strummed her fingers on the counter. She had painted her nails to match her sleeve of temporary tattoos. Her sketchbook lay open next to her. I would pay money to frame one of her colored pencil doodles, like the sketch she'd done of Cryptic from her vantage point behind the coffee bar. She captured the whimsical vibe of the bustling coffee shop in soft pencil strokes, the cheerful patio umbrellas, hanging baskets, customers sipping lattes, and the way the late afternoon light streamed through the roll-up garage doors, casting halos on the ground.

"He admitted everything you heard. The rumors are true. Kayla loaned him twenty thousand dollars and gave him an ultimatum to pay it back by the end of the weekend or else she was going to the police."

"I knew it," she exclaimed. "But what will the police do?"

"Good question. I'm thinking that now would be a good time for me to find Dr. Caldwell. I want to give Justin a head start because he's going to talk to her, but I'm not sure I trust him. I'll swing by the bookshop and make sure Fletcher and Hal don't need me, and then I'll head to the police station. I want to fill her in on everything we've learned, make sure that Justin follows through on his promise, and see if there are any other details about the case that she can share."

"Sounds like a plan." Pri motioned to the pastry case. "Do you need a Poirot pasty on your way out?"

"It's tempting." I glanced at the clever hand-calligraphed signs Pri had placed next to each pastry tray. The flaky hand pies were filled with chicken curry and a mystery spice.

"They are delicious and ridiculously addictive. I asked the pastry chef if she put some kind of special ingredient in them." Pri picked up a pencil and absently began shading in red geraniums in her sketch.

"That sounds worrying." I made a face.

"The kind that keeps you coming back for more and more because it's so, so, so buttery and flakey. Seriously, you should take one or, like, the rest of the tray, Annie. I can't be trusted around them. And given my luck, Double Americano will probably stroll in while I'm stuffing my face."

I laughed. "I guess that's a risk you'll have to take."

Pri glared. "Some friend you are."

"Meet you at Public House later for the pub crawl?"

"Yes, only because there's beer, though." Pri winked.

I left before she tried to talk me into more pasties, vanilla bean cupcakes stabbed with candy knives, or Edgar Allan Poe eclairs.

The Secret Bookcase was humming with readers waiting to get a seat at the "How to Tail a Suspect" panel. During our initial brainstorming session for Mystery Fest, we worked hard to come up with clever and interactive panels. The "How to Tail a Suspect" panel was Hal's brainchild. Authors would be paired up with groups of readers and sent around town, trying to dodge being caught. I couldn't wait to see the friendly chase that was sure to ensue.

"Has there been a lull at all?" I asked Fletcher, who used a silk houndstooth scarf to mop his forehead while ringing up sales and directing readers to the Conservatory. He had abandoned his Sherlock costume for a pair of tailored khaki slacks, a white linen button-up shirt, and a scarf. He looked like he belonged on the pages of an Elizabeth Peters novel at a dig site in Egypt.

"They just keep coming." He wafted his scarf toward the line. "The 'How to Stage a Death Scene' panel earlier was standing room only. It was a huge hit."

"I'm sorry I missed it." The problem with hosting and organizing the event meant that there was no possible way I could attend everything. Following leads on Kayla's murder made it even more impossible. I wished I could clone myself. I had been looking forward to the panel. We had invited actors from the local theater company to act out death scenes written by authors. The lineup of afternoon panels was equally compelling. There would be a tarot card panel, complete with a psychic who agreed to do readings on the spot. Fletcher had ordered shiny new card decks ready for purchase so readers could try their hand at fortune telling at home. An author who wrote locked room mysteries would teach readers how to pick locks and free themselves from handcuffs. I wanted to be at all of it.

"It was raucous," Fletcher said, bagging a massive stack of cozies for a customer. "I listened in, and from what I could hear, it sounded hilarious."

"Oh, it was the most fun I've ever had," the customer waiting for her purchase interjected. "I hope you do it every year because I'll be back for sure."

"I'm so glad to hear that," I said to her as I walked around the counter to help Fletcher. "Let me jump in."

He didn't protest.

"Do you want to take a break? I've got this." The long line didn't intimidate me. If anything, it re-energized me. Seeing the store buzzing with happy customers had been my dream all along. I almost wanted to pinch myself. It was too good to be true. But then again, it wasn't. A crowded store and steady sales didn't change the fact that Kayla was dead.

"If you're sure?" He mopped more sweat from his forehead.

"Of course." I looked at him with concern. Was it the pace of keeping up with events and shoppers, or had the reality of Kayla's murder finally caught up with him? "You should have texted me. I would have come back right away."

"No, it's fine. It's just that—" He paused and scooted closer to me so as not to be overheard by the waiting customers. "The police are here again, and they want to ask me some follow-up questions. What do you think that means, Annie?"

"It means they want to ask you some follow-up questions." I placed a set of Mary Higgins Clark novels in an oversized bag and handed it to a customer.

"But why me?" Perspiration stained his collar. He busied himself restacking sticker sets, but his hands were so sweaty they kept slipping out of his hands.

He was really nervous. Why?

"Do you think they saw something?" he asked, wiping his palms on his khakis.

"Like what?"

"Uh, nothing. Never mind. Forget I said anything." He stuffed the damp scarf in his pocket and took off.

I watched him go, with wide eyes. Did Fletcher have something to hide?

It was standard protocol that Dr. Caldwell would follow up with each of us. I pushed the thought aside as I made a dent in the line. When I finally had a minute to tidy up the cash register, I noticed I had missed multiple calls and texts from Monica.

I read the first text.

> Pub crawl is all set. Public House will host Eli.
> Thanks!

She had taken it upon herself to set up the signing for Eli—
what? I had mentioned looking into the idea in passing, but I
hadn't imagined she would take that as a sign to move forward
without checking with me. Part of me wanted to cancel it on the
spot, but I had enough on my plate. At least I didn't have to
spend any more time trying to figure out where else to put the
egocentric author.

I also couldn't imagine Eli being excited about the pub
crawl. Readers strolling between restaurants and pubs for beer
tastings and bloody margaritas while mingling with authors
sounded way too cozy for him.

"Annie, you're just who I was looking for." Dr. Caldwell's
voice pulled me away from my phone screen.

I looked up to see Dr. Caldwell approaching the register.
Her narrow slacks, white blouse, and short heels were fitting for
a detective. She could have been auditioning to play a role with
the way she immediately commanded a room. A black leather
notepad was tucked under her arm. Fletcher was correct—she
must be doing follow-up interviews with witnesses.

"Hi, Dr. Caldwell." I smiled, shutting off my phone. "Great
minds think alike. I was planning to come find you."

"Is now a good time?" She tilted her head to the door.
"Could we step outside for a few minutes?"

The line had vanished, but I couldn't leave the register
unattended. "Give me a minute. I'll track someone down to take
over for me."

"Why don't we meet in the park in twenty minutes?" she
suggested. "I could use a refresher, and I heard that the
lemonade stand has a special raspberry murder mix."

"I'll meet you there."

Was that code for wanting to speak with me away from the store?

I watched as she took notice of every detail as she exited the bookshop, methodically scanning the front-of-store displays, peering into the Conservatory, and pausing to pay careful attention to a collection of books in the front window. She remained composed and still as she leafed through a few pages, returned the book to its spot, and made her exit.

Again, I felt relieved knowing Dr. Caldwell was in charge of the situation. I had no idea why the book had caught her eye, but I did know that she was employing every technique she had taught me in school. Assessing witness accounts from me and Fletcher was likely part of her piecing the puzzle together.

I took comfort in that. Fletcher was probably overreacting.

I found a part-time staff member to manage the cash register and wound my way to the park.

Oceanside Park might not have ocean views, but it did offer a peaceful respite. Towering redwoods flanked the park. There was a children's play area, rose garden, walking paths, and the natural wood pavilion in the center, where dozens of community activities took place. Dr. Caldwell was waiting for me on a bench beneath the ancient wisteria. She offered me a pink raspberry lemonade.

"I wasn't sure if you would prefer regular or raspberry, but how can you resist this color?" She held the blushing pink drink toward the sun to admire the color.

"You can't." I took the drink. "Thanks for this."

"My pleasure." She took off her glasses and rested them on the top of her head. Then she took a long sip of her lemonade and looked at me intently. "I'm sure this experience must be triggering for you, given Scarlet's murder."

I wasn't expecting her frank words, and they caused me to throw one hand over my chest as if to protect my heart.

She patted my forearm. "I'm sorry, Annie. Our shared history has me feeling nostalgic, too."

I wasn't sure nostalgic was the term I would use to describe my state of mind.

"I think of Scarlet often," she said quietly, setting her drink on the park bench.

I didn't trust myself to speak, so I nodded.

"There are some cases that stay with us, and Scarlet... well, I don't have to tell you how much her loss has changed me. She's the reason I'm here now."

"She is?"

"I couldn't keep teaching after what happened." She swirled the ice in her glass. "My way of coping, of trying to abate my guilt, has been to throw myself into my policework."

I frowned. "Your guilt?"

She became unnaturally still for a moment. "I never should have had students looking into an active case."

"You couldn't have known," I said, trying to comfort her. Guilt was my most faithful companion. It was hard to see those same feelings on her face. I spent the better half of my adulthood wishing I could go back and change the past. "You're sure there's no connection with Kayla's murder?"

She cleared her throat. "As sure as I can be in a case like this, yes."

I wasn't sure if that made me feel better, or worse.

"There's no point in living in the past, is there?" A strange look crossed her face. She shook it off and sat up taller. "In any event, what I'm trying to say is that while it certainly is a coincidence that two former classmates were killed, I've reviewed every piece of tangible evidence and conducted initial interviews with suspects, taken witness statements, and spoken with the coroner. There is nothing that meaningfully links the two cases. I hope that puts you at ease, at least to some extent."

"It does." I took a sip of the tangy, cold lemonade, not realizing how much relief her words brought me until this moment. I hoped that she was right. She was an expert at this. She had to be right. Plus, it was an outlandish theory anyway. What were the odds that Scarlet's killer would strike again almost ten years later? Even though it was unlikely, I realized now there had been part of my subconscious that was holding on to the fear that their deaths were related. It was a relief to have it dismissed by someone with authority. "I know it sounds far-fetched, but I was wondering if there was a serial killer coming after all of my classmates. I guess it's good to know I'm not in danger."

"I wouldn't go that far." She held up her index finger in a warning. "Kayla's killer is still at large. Until we are able to make an arrest, I urge you to continue to use caution. Stay aware of your surroundings. Stay vigilant."

"You don't think that I'm personally in danger, do you?" My gaze flitted around the park. It was unnerving to imagine that a killer was among us. I knew Dr. Caldwell would tell me if there was a serious threat. It seemed unlikely, and yet with Kayla's connection to my past, I couldn't shake the fear that I might be missing something.

She pursed her lips. I couldn't tell if it was from the puckery lemonade or because she didn't want to tell me the truth. "It's my responsibility to keep the entire community safe."

That wasn't really an answer.

"Do you have any further leads?" I asked, sensing that she wasn't going to expand on whether or not she thought I was in a precarious position.

She cleared her throat and reached for her drink. "Tell me more about Fletcher Hughes."

"What about him?" I tried to convince myself that she wanted to review our witness statements, but her piercing gaze made me think otherwise.

"Did you see him around the time you found the body?"

Her face remained neutral. Too neutral. I could tell she was holding something back.

I shook my head, glancing at the fountain in the center of the park. Its calming, bubbly waters felt like they were in complete opposition to the nerves assaulting my stomach. She couldn't really think Fletcher was involved, could she?

"No," I said after a minute, making sure that my memory was correct. "It was just me and three women. Fletcher asked me to help a customer locate a title in the Sitting Room. That's when I took a photo for the women and they started talking about how authentic it was that we had an actual body." I had already told her all of this. Why was she asking again?

"How long did it take for Fletcher to appear after you discovered Kayla's body?" She picked up a bag resting next to the bench, took out her leather notebook and pen, and waited for me to respond.

"I don't know. It's kind of fuzzy. A couple of minutes, maybe." I spotted a group of readers tailing the thriller writer who had packed the Conservatory yesterday. The game of cat and mouse was afoot. I wished I had time to pull out my phone and document the chase, but I didn't want to miss anything Dr. Caldwell might have to say.

"Mm-hmm." She sounded noncommittal.

Why all the questions about Fletcher? From the very first day I walked into the Secret Bookcase, Fletcher had taken me under his wing. I'll never forget him greeting me with a hot cup of coffee in one hand and immediately proceeding to take me on a two-hour tour of the store, showing me how to open the secret bookcase and where we shelved rare first edition copies. His enthusiasm was contagious, and his bright-eyed lens about working in the bookstore made me even more confident that I had made the best decision to move to Redwood Grove. We'd been close ever since. I didn't like Dr. Caldwell bringing up his name in association with Kayla's murder. There was no chance that Fletcher was involved. None.

"You don't think Fletcher could be involved, do you?"

Her lips puckered again. "Mr. Hughes neglected to share a critical piece of information. I'm not at liberty to expand on details, but I do have some serious concerns about him withholding information about the case."

"He did?"

She remained tight-lipped. "How long have you known him?"

"Years." I shifted on the bench, crossing my legs and pushing the edge of my dress over my knees. "He was already working at the Secret Bookcase when I was hired. Fletcher is a good friend. He wouldn't hurt a fly."

"Be that as it may, withholding information about murder is a crime of its own." She set down her notebook and swirled the ice melting in the bottom of her glass. "You should remember that from your coursework."

She was right. Obstruction of justice was serious. Withholding information from the police could land Fletcher in jail or force him to testify in court. This was a turn of events I hadn't seen coming.

"I don't know what Fletcher did, and you don't need to tell me, but I can vouch for him. He's quirky and awkward, but he's not a killer," I insisted. I could hear a touch of a sharp edge in my tone. I knew that my personal friendship with Fletcher was coloring my perspective, but she couldn't really believe that Fletcher had killed Kayla.

Dr. Caldwell stirred her ice with her straw. "I'd appreciate it if you could keep an eye on his movements in the store. Please report back if you notice anything odd."

"Okay," I agreed, but I still felt in shock. I refused to believe that Fletcher had a violent bone in his body. "Did Justin speak with you?" Fletcher couldn't be her only suspect. I needed to know if Justin had followed through.

"He did." She nodded curtly.

"What do you think of his financial situation? Could he have killed Kayla because he realized that there was no way he could pay her back in time? Also, what could the police have done if she had come to you and explained that he owed her money? Would they have intervened?"

"Not likely. They would have sent them to mediation to figure out a plan, but if she loaned him the money, especially if there was no paperwork involved, there wouldn't be much we would do. That would be a matter for lawyers, not the police."

"That's what I thought." I sighed.

"I can inform you that Justin has an alibi for the window of time when Kayla was killed."

An alibi likely meant that he would be removed from her suspect list. "Does that mean you have an official timeframe for when Kayla was killed?"

She flipped through her leather notebook and found the page she was looking for. "The coroner believes that time of death occurred between three and four o'clock. Justin was at State of Mind Public House and seen by multiple witnesses."

"So you don't think he could have done it unless he had an accomplice?"

"Unless he had an *accomplice*," she repeated, emphasizing accomplice.

My stomach dropped. She wasn't implying that Fletcher was his accomplice, was she? Could I have read my friend wrong?

No. Fletcher wasn't a killer. He *couldn't* be.

I had always admired and respected Dr. Caldwell, but she was wrong about Fletcher. I refused to believe that he could have had anything to do with Kayla's death, and if necessary, I would do whatever it took to prove that to her.

TWENTY-TWO

Dr. Caldwell returned her glasses to the tip of her nose to review her notes. "Is there anything else you've observed that you can share? I received your email and appreciate your notes. They were quite extensive. Not that I would have expected otherwise. You always were my top student."

"Thank you. You were always my favorite teacher." I couldn't let the conversation about Fletcher end there. I still felt an urge to defend my friend. "I'm sure that Fletcher wasn't involved. He's one of the gentlest people I know," I insisted, noticing that my voice sounded pitchy.

She turned her head from side to side in acknowledgment. "There is some evidence that says otherwise. Some footage posted to social media that's currently under review indicates that Fletcher had an altercation with the victim."

"What?" I wanted to pull out my phone. Fletcher had an altercation with Kayla? When?

"As I said, we're reviewing the authenticity of the video now." She turned a page in the notebook. "Is there anything else you can share?"

I told her about my conversations with Caroline and

Monica. She listened intently, jotting down something in her notebook every so often. I was glad to get everything off my chest, but I couldn't stop thinking about Fletcher. What could he have done to make her question his involvement with Kayla's murder? As soon as I was alone, I would try and find the footage to see what happened.

"Seth was also a student while you were in school," Dr. Caldwell said. "Did you know him well in your college days?"

I shook my head. "Not at all. We didn't have much in common. He spent his time partying and playing baseball. I was focused on my classwork."

"Yes, you were. Let me tell you again how much I appreciate earnest students like yourself. Annie Murrays are few and far between." She pressed her hands together in a show of gratitude. "Have you had any interactions with Seth this weekend?"

"Yeah, he followed me to my cottage last night." I couldn't believe I hadn't started our conversation with this detail. I had too much on my mind to keep everything straight.

"You didn't mention this in your text this morning." Dr. Caldwell's eyes widened. "Did he threaten you?"

"No." I sucked on an ice cube, getting shivers at the memory of Seth following me home. "At first, I was terrified, but I was smart about it. I didn't let him inside."

"Annie, you should have called 911," she interrupted, her voice thick with concern.

"I would have, but he was gassed. He couldn't catch his breath after running to try and keep up with my pace, so I knew I could outrun him if I needed to or pound on one of my neighbors' doors."

She didn't look convinced. "The police should always be your first line of defense."

"Yeah, but he explained that he wasn't chasing me. He just wanted to talk. In fact, he asked if I would speak to you on his behalf." I caught the eye of two readers wearing fedoras and trench coats, trying unsuccessfully to look inconspicuous while hiding behind a redwood tree.

"Interesting." Dr. Caldwell cleaned off a speck of dust from her glasses with the sleeve of her blouse. "Did he mention anything about his past relationship with Kayla?"

I nodded. "He admitted that their breakup wasn't exactly amicable and that she had taken out a restraining order against him many years ago, but he made it sound like she was the one who was clinging to him, not the other way around."

She held her glasses toward the sun to check and see if the spot was gone. "Did Monica come up in your conversation?"

A cloud that had been shrouding the sun floated away, revealing intense afternoon rays. I squinted and placed my hand on my forehead to shield my face. "He mentioned that they've dated on and off, which surprised me because, at the cocktail party, she seemed upset with him, almost accusatory?"

"Did she?" Dr. Caldwell asked.

"He said that things were casual between them." The readers in trench coats must have spotted their mark because they ducked and ran to the next tree.

She put her glasses back on and flipped through her notes. "Hooked up is the terminology my team heard."

I laughed. "That checks out."

"Take this information as you will. If any opportunity arises with Seth to discuss your college days and you can find a way to work the topic into the conversation casually, I'd appreciate hearing your perspective, but only—and I caution *only*—if there's a natural way to bring up the topic. People often have a tendency to shut down when they're speaking with the police or an authority figure. I've found that a chat with an old friend can be much more conducive to gaining valuable insight into a person's character, and since he's already confided in you, perhaps there's a chance that we can leverage that bond. But only if it's safe for you to do so."

I didn't think "bond" was the term I would use.

"I understand." I nodded solemnly. "I can do that."

"Approach him—carefully, very carefully, Annie. Under-stood?" She hesitated for a minute, weighing her words. "We should brainstorm ways to make your encounter appear casual. Maybe it's as simple as having a follow-up conversation from last night, letting him know you've spoken to me. Although I wonder if that will shut him down. Perhaps under the guise of wanting to reminisce about the good old days? Or would that feel too obvious?"

"Sure. I mean, I probably wouldn't refer to the good old days, but we already talked a bit about college, so I don't think he would find it strange if I brought it up. Is there something specific you want me to ask him?"

"Use your discernment." She gathered her things. "I must say, Annie, that although I'm not pleased with the circum-stances that reconnected us, I am glad to have your assistance in this matter. You will tell me if I'm asking too much or pressuring you in any way?"

"Not at all. I'm happy to help. It feels better to do some-thing, you know?" My thoughts drifted to Scarlet.

"Yes, I do." She gave me a serious nod, stood, and picked up her empty cup. "Let's touch base later this evening. I intend to be visible during the pub crawl."

"Okay." I watched her cross the park with a perfectly erect posture. She tossed her cup in the recycling bin and turned toward the library. Using my discernment in a conversation with Seth was very open-ended. I hoped that I could learn something useful.

I returned to the bookshop with a double mission. I needed to find Seth and see what I could learn from him about his rela-tionship—or hookup—with Monica, and I had to find out what on earth was going on with Fletcher.

There was no sign of him at the front register.

"Annie, you're back," Hal said, greeting me with a finger wave. "Could I beg a favor of you? My creaky knees are no match for the cellar stairs. Would you mind heading down to the storage room to see if we have another box of socks? They've been flying off the shelves."

"Of course. I'll be back in a flash." I was relieved that Hal asked for help. The basement stairs were old, rickety, and dimly lit. I didn't particularly enjoy spending any extended amount of time in the creepy basement, but I certainly didn't want Hal to break an ankle or hip navigating the narrow staircase.

A cobweb swept across my face as I opened the basement door and fumbled for the lights. A damp, musty scent permeated the tight passage. The flicking overhead lightbulb emitted a feeble, soft glow that did little to illuminate the stairs.

I readjusted my glasses, hoping that might help, but I still had to squint to see.

Just get down there, grab the socks, and get back upstairs. It's no big deal.

My pep talk was about as effective as the faded lightbulb.

Why was I so skittish?

Probably because there had been an actual murder in the bookstore. Maybe the events of the past few days were finally catching up with me.

I ventured further downward, stuffing my anxiety and the feeling that the walls were closing in on me. The wooden banister, worn smooth over the years, felt cold to the touch.

When I reached the bottom of the stairs, I noticed that the heavy storage room door stood ajar.

Why was it open?

No one was allowed down here other than Fletcher and Hal.

A sour taste spread over my tongue. I gulped hard to force my throat to stay open and took a timid step forward. Dust danced in the feeble light filtering in through a single paned window.

The sound of a scuttle forced me to halt.

Was it a mouse?

Hal had mentioned needing to get mouse traps a while ago.

It had to be a mouse.

I squeezed my thumbs and index fingers together and peered around the door just as someone sprinted straight at me.

I let out a scream and blocked them with my hands.

"Annie, what the hell?"

I lowered my hands in time to see Fletcher drop the box he was holding, sending dust particles flying like confetti.

"Jeez, you nearly gave me a heart attack." Fletcher fanned his face.

"Same. What are you doing?" I exhaled slowly to try to regain control of my breathing. Ever since finding Kayla, my body had been running at high speed, like I was racing in a perpetual marathon. What was it going to take to return to a normal state of calm?

"We ran out of socks." Fletcher bent to pick up the box.

"Hal sent me down to find those." I coughed and licked my lips to get rid of the dry feeling in my mouth.

"You know my methods, dear Annie. I would never allow the socks to run low. They're our best seller." Fletcher hoisted the box and waited for me to lead the way.

A mild sense of relief flooded my body as I retraced my steps upstairs. At least Fletcher was still acting like Fletcher.

"Ah, socks, excellent." Hal rubbed his hands together. "I never anticipated that book socks would sell so well. It's a good thing this old stodgy keeps you young ones around. That's the last box. We're going to need to order more. Who knew?"

"Me." I pointed to my chest and winked.

"And me," Fletcher added.

Hal threw his head back and chuckled. "Well, remind me to always listen to you two."

"You already do," I replied honestly.

"Only because I have the best staff in all of Redwood Grove." Hal patted me on the shoulder and shuffled toward the Conservatory.

Fletcher restocked stickers and the bookish socks in the cozy reading nook near the front of the shop. I was glad that there was a lull in the line. I wanted to talk to him about my conversation with Dr. Caldwell.

"Where did you vanish to before you scared the living daylights out of me? You were gone for a while." He used a pocket tape measure to ensure that the stickers were all level.

"Dr. Caldwell had some questions for me." I studied his body language for any signs of stress.

"You too? That's a relief." His shoulders sagged. "What did she ask you?"

"The usual. She had me go through exactly what happened right before I found Kayla. Which reminds me, where were you when I found her body?"

He cleared his throat. "Huh?"

"You showed up right after I found Kayla, but I thought you were working the register."

"I was. I heard the screams." He patted his chest with both hands.

Were there screams? I didn't remember screaming, but then again, the entire scene felt fuzzy, like a distant dream I couldn't quite recall in detail.

"Who screamed?" I asked. Thankfully, the front of the store was quiet. Authors and readers were still off tailing imaginary suspects around town.

Fletcher measured the space between the stickers. "I don't know. One of the ladies who was in the Sitting Room with you, maybe?"

Had the readers screamed? I searched my memory but drew a blank.

"It was chaos," Fletcher added.

"Was it? My memory is really gummy." I rubbed my temples, wishing that I could will myself to remember every detail.

"Gummy?"

"I don't know how to explain it. I'm sure it's a stress response, but everything from the time I overheard the women talking about the body in the bookcase through discovering Kayla's body is a weird blur."

"That makes sense." Fletcher adjusted a stack of cozy cat stickers. "You were out of it. I thought you were going to pass out."

"Did something happen with you and Kayla?"

The stickers slipped out of his hand and scattered on the floor.

I bent over to help him pick them up. "Fletcher, is there something you're not telling me?" I wanted him to come clean about whatever had happened between him and Kayla.

He blinked rapidly like he was about to have a seizure.

I reached for his arm. "Fletcher, it's me."

He stood up, clutching a handful of stickers, and looked at me, his expression stricken. "Annie, I might be in trouble."

"Why?" I studied his body language again. His fingers had a death grip on the stickers, turning his nails white. He continued to blink as if he was having trouble seeing. This wasn't his typical behavior. Sweat dripped from his forehead down his cheek. His eyes were as wide as the plastic monocles for sale next to the cash register.

"Fletcher, you can trust me," I nudged.

He squeezed the stickers tighter. "Annie, the police think I did it."

"Did what? Killed Kayla?"

He hung his head and nodded, mopping his brow with the back of his arm.

"Fletcher, hold up. Why don't you start from the beginning?"

He loosened his grip on the stickers and let them drop on the bookcase. "They saw me assault her. It's on camera. I'm in big trouble, Annie. Big trouble."

I let out a breath. Thank goodness. If he was telling me, then I knew my instincts about him were correct. But *assault*? "No way, Fletcher. You're not that kind of guy. You wouldn't do that. Tell me what happened."

"But I did." He gnawed on this thumbnail. "I didn't actually hurt her, but it looks bad on camera."

"Can you back up and start from the beginning?"

He picked up a sticker in the shape of a coffee cup with the words READ BOOKS, DRINK COFFEE, AVOID PEOPLE.

"I didn't assault her, but that's not what it looks like on the footage the police showed me." He flipped the sticker like a magician practicing their sleight of hand. "She burst into the store, barely able to stand, slurring her words, yelling at me, yelling at customers. Then, as you. know she caused a scene during Eli's reading. She was furious that she'd been kicked out of the event, and she refused to leave the Foyer. I had to do something. I couldn't stand by and let her destroy the store."

"Do you think she would have destroyed the bookshop?" I asked. That sounded like an exaggeration.

"She tossed merchandise off the shelves; she threw rare books on the floor. She was out of control."

How had I missed this?

"Hal and I had a convo about what to do. He suggested that I kindly ask her to leave, and if she refused to comply, then I needed to escort her out." He gestured to the front doors.

"And did you?"

"I told her she was making a scene and asked her to leave. She refused. She took a swing at me." He massaged his jaw.

"Kayla hit you?"

"She missed because I ducked just in time, but she went wild—swearing, claiming that she was going to sue. I had no choice. The bookshop was packed with customers, so I gently took her by the arm and removed her from the store."

"That doesn't sound like assault to me."

"But someone filmed the entire incident on their phone. They turned the footage over to the police. It's all over social media. There's a hashtag and everything." He ran his fingers through his hair. "It doesn't look good for me, Annie."

"Why?"

He got out his phone and opened it to show me. "Look at this. She is dragging her feet, literally. You can see me yanking her from the store while trying to avoid getting punched by her. I didn't do anything wrong." He tapped the screen to prove his point. "I just held out my arm to defend myself, but from the angle of this video, it looks like I'm hitting her back. I swear on my collection of Sherlock Holmes that I didn't lay a finger on that woman."

"Did you explain this to the police?" I reached for his phone to watch the video again. It was true that from the angle the reader had shot, the footage made it appear that Fletcher had hit Kayla at first glance, but the second time, I could see that he lifted his hand to block her punch.

I handed him back the phone. "I can tell that was a defensive move. I'm sure Dr. Caldwell can see that, too. You did explain that, right?"

He tucked his phone in the top drawer. "Yeah, but they don't believe me. They asked me a dozen questions and told me that I was not allowed to leave Redwood Grove without their permission. It doesn't sound good. I'm waiting for them to show up any minute to arrest me."

"It's standard procedure to ask anyone with information about a crime to check with the lead detective before leaving town," I said, hoping to reassure him. I wasn't going to let on that I'd already had a conversation about him with Dr. Caldwell.

"No, Annie, you don't understand. They think I did it." His voice cracked. "They think they have an open-and-shut case. They have video evidence of me 'assaulting' the victim who ended up dead in my place of employment shortly after."

"That's all circumstantial evidence, Fletcher. What's your motive?"

He threw his hands up. "Does it matter? Do I need a motive if I'm the last person who saw her alive?"

"The last person to see her alive?"

"That's what Dr. Caldwell said. Well, technically she said, 'one of the last' people to see her alive, but I caught her meaning."

So Kayla had been killed right after her interaction with Fletcher. Did that mean that she snuck back into the Secret Bookcase? But I'd seen her at State of Mind after Eli's reading. Could she have gone around through the patio on the Terrace?

"Who shot the video?" I asked.

"An anonymous source came forward," Fletcher said. "That's why she questioned me again. Apparently, she asked everyone who was in or around the bookshop on the day of the murder to send her photos or videos they might have taken. Unlucky for me, a bystander caught me kicking Kayla out of the store."

Or could there be more to the story? What if the "anonymous source" had intentionally set Fletcher up? It seemed odd that this new evidence was emerging now. I also knew that Dr. Caldwell wouldn't use video footage to arrest Fletcher, not without a motive or any other tangible evidence.

"It's going to be okay, Fletcher," I said with a confidence I actually felt. Fletcher was not a killer, and I was more determined than ever to find the person responsible for Kayla's death and see that they were brought to justice.

TWENTY-THREE

I tried to concentrate on the next events in the program, but it was impossible to stop my thoughts from circling back to Kayla's murder. She had managed to have run-ins with nearly everyone in Redwood Grove, including Fletcher. The only thing keeping me focused for the remainder of the day was the constant rush of customers through the store. If sales continued like this, we were going to have to put in new orders with our book distributors to restock the shelves. I wanted to do a backflip. Never in my wildest dreams would I have imagined that book sales would have gone this well. In the last few years, even new releases tended to sit on the shelves for weeks and weeks until we offered deep discounts. I couldn't remember the last time we needed to do a complete restock. I felt relieved for Hal and the store.

I also felt a newfound tinge of pride in myself and my abilities. Scarlet's death had derailed my confidence. Not being able to solve her murder had made me question my skills, but maybe I had something to offer after all. And maybe if I could help Dr. Caldwell close Kayla's case, it would finally lead me to a breakthrough in what happened to Scarlet.

The bookstore was a disaster when we locked up for the evening. Stickers, candles, pens, and bookmarks were scattered in nearly every room. Books were misplaced, which was nothing new. Whether intentional or accidental, the bane of closing the bookstore every night was discovering books and merchandise in all the wrong places. Customers often left them scattered throughout the store. Even well-intended readers would return books to the wrong section. It was always a challenge to find and reorganize items. It was a bit like a scavenger hunt, especially when our inventory listed a book as "in stock," but we couldn't find it anywhere. We worked hard to keep the Secret Bookcase well-organized and the collections pristine.

After a day like today, it was no surprise that cozies mixed in with noirs, and the entire shop needed attention. Fletcher and I spent the next hour returning everything to its intended place.

"Annie, have you seen the sales total?" Hal asked when I returned to the Foyer, pointing to the spreadsheet at the cash register after I finished restocking the shelves. "I've checked it three times. This can't be right."

I looked over his shoulder. "That's more than what we made last month."

He made a motion like his head was exploding and intentionally bugged out his eyes. "You are keeping us afloat, my dear."

"We're all doing it."

"Don't sell yourself short." Hal shifted into his grandfatherly mode. "I'm sure I sound like a broken record, and I realize that you're too young for record players, but, Annie, the Mystery Fest has absolutely surpassed my wildest dreams. We're back in the black with two days of sales, and there's still tomorrow. If we have another day like this, we'll be able to afford the repairs I've been putting off for years."

"It's pretty great." I patted Hal's arm. "You've poured so

much of your heart into the store that I'm happy to be able to be a tiny part of helping it stay open."

His eyes welled with tears. "I don't know how I'm going to be able to repay you, Annie, but I'll find some way."

"You don't need to repay me. I'm serious." I placed my hand over my heart. "I love the Secret Bookcase as much as you, so we're even, okay?"

He nodded but didn't look convinced.

"Listen, I need to head over to State of Mind to get ready for the pub crawl. Do you need anything else before I go?"

"No, you go. Fletcher and I can handle the last of the cleanup." Hal glanced to the Conservatory. "We're keeping the chairs set up for the final panel tomorrow, so I'll do a final sweep, close the lights, and call it a night."

"Okay, everything else should be good. Someone turned an entire shelf of spines backward in the Mary Westmacott Nook. Can you believe that? It took me fifteen minutes to fix them. I bet it was someone trying to make a statement about romance." I rolled my eyes.

Hal scowled. "The nerve. Many scholars contend that my grandmother's romance novels outshone her mysteries and were on par with the likes of Jane Austen. You can't argue that her greatest gift was anything other than her incredible insight into human nature. Her Mary Westmacott books are emotionally profound and some of my personal favorites."

"I agree." I patted his arm in solidarity. "I promise they're all safely returned." The fact that he referenced Agatha's nom de plume when talking about *his* grandmother brought me such delight. I hoped that one day, Hal would unearth a tangible piece of evidence to prove his theory right. It was a long shot, but how cool would it be if Hal actually was a descendent of the grand dame of mysteries?

Hal smiled. "Another reason I don't know what I would do without you."

"Well, on that note, then I guess I'll see you bright and early tomorrow unless you're coming out for pints?"

He held his hands up in protest. "You don't want an old man slowing you youngsters down. Go have fun."

I left the bookstore feeling a touch lighter. At least something had gone right this weekend. We were profitable again. Hal would never want to worry me, but I knew that without the revenue from the Mystery Fest, the Secret Bookcase's days were numbered.

You did that, Annie.

I gave myself a little pep talk on the way to the pub.

Now you need to find Kayla's killer.

That should be easy enough, right?

I laughed out loud. But it wasn't a happy laugh. The nagging voice of guilt returned. After not being able to solve Scarlet's murder or track down her killer, this was my chance at redemption. That failure had followed me like a pervasive shadow. Suddenly, with the festival's success, I felt even more compelled to figure out what happened to Kayla. None of my achievements would matter if a killer continued to walk free.

As I approached the pub, I made a promise to myself to stay vigilant.

There was already a line at State of Mind Public House. I squeezed past customers waiting to get their signature pint glasses, the next clue, and maps of all the stops on the pub crawl.

"We should be ready to kick off in about ten minutes," I said to the queue of people waiting as I ducked inside.

Justin was positioned at the front, acting as a bouncer. "We're not letting anyone inside yet," he said in a firm voice before realizing it was me. "Oh, hey, Annie. Sorry."

"No worries. I wanted to make sure you're all set. There's quite a line out there."

"Yeah, tell me about it. I've been holding people back for

nearly an hour. I'm not exactly the bouncer type. I should have hit the gym." He flexed his arm, revealing rock-solid muscles and dozens of tattoos.

I smiled, but watching him flex made my mind go to Kayla again. Maybe Dr. Caldwell and I had been wrong about the murder. If she had been killed in the secret bookcase, her killer wouldn't have needed to be that strong, but if she had been stabbed first, her killer would have needed muscles like Justin's.

I noted the thought and glanced at two large tables that had been pushed together. There were rows of engraved pint glasses, wristbands, maps, and clues along with a stack of menus with their beer specials and two bonus appetizers for the pub crawl—"Mummy dogs" and "Bones to pick" ribs.

"What can I do?"

He motioned to the table. "Can you hand out glasses? I'm checking IDs. We were supposed to have a volunteer for the table, but I heard they got reassigned."

"No problem."

"Cool, well, if you're here, I guess we can open the doors."

The next thirty minutes were a blur. Justin confirmed that readers were of legal drinking age and secured hot pink bands around their wrists. I passed out tasting glasses and maps and made sure that everyone participating in the mystery had their clues.

"Whew, that was a rush," I said to Justin after the last person in line headed for the bar.

"Yeah. I can handle it now." He re-stacked the menus and maps, placing them in neat piles next to the remaining pint glasses and wristbands. "Thanks for stepping in."

"You bet. I'm going to get a beer for myself, but I'll keep an eye out. If there's a line again, I'll come back."

He gave me a thumbs-up.

"Hey, before I grab a beer. Did you have a chance to speak

with Dr. Caldwell?" I already knew the answer, but I wanted to hear what he had to say.

His face seemed to glisten. Was it the lighting or was he sweating?

"I went to see her after we talked earlier." He counted the wristbands and sorted them in piles.

"How did it go?" Was he avoiding eye contact on purpose?

"Fine, I guess. She's, uh, what's the word? A vault? She doesn't show any emotion. Maybe she's a robot." He stretched a wristband between his index fingers like he was testing its elasticity.

"I don't think she's a robot. I think that's probably her strategy for staying neutral during an investigation. I studied criminology in college, and one of the first things we learned was that you have to remove your personal feelings and biases from a case."

"Makes sense." Justin wrapped a wristband around his index finger. "She took a bunch of notes and thanked me for informing her of my situation, but other than that, she said that financial issues like mine didn't involve the police. She suggested I speak with a lawyer. I don't know who I pay back now, you know?"

"I never thought about that."

"Me either." He tugged on the plastic band. "Dr. Caldwell said my debt would probably transfer to whoever inherits Kayla's estate, but then she told me to find a good lawyer, so I guess that's what I'm going to do tomorrow."

"Kayla's estate?" I said out loud. "Did Kayla have an estate, or was Dr. Caldwell speaking generally?"

Justin made an odd face. His mouth fell open. "Kayla had a huge estate. I thought everyone knew that. She inherited our grandparents' property near Napa. That's why she lent me money. She was loaded, which is why I don't understand her reason for suddenly demanding I pay her back."

My smile went stiff in an effort not to reveal my surprise. Kayla owning a Napa estate was big news.

"Your grandparents left their estate to Kayla? Not to you or any other family members?" I tipped my head to the side and waited for his response. This was new information that Justin had failed to mention earlier. Was that an oversight? Or was it because he knew this fact implicated him further? Could he have held a grudge against her for inheriting their family fortune?

"We don't have any other cousins." He flicked a bracelet against his palm like he was trying to inflict pain. "They said I was too young and irresponsible. I didn't blame them. Like I told you, I made a bunch of mistakes, but I've changed. People don't believe that, but I have."

"I believe you," I said, and I meant it. I'd never bought into the theory that people couldn't change.

Justin crumpled the bracelet in his hand. "Thanks, I appreciate that." He turned his attention to a late-arriving pub crawl participant.

I went to the bar to order a beer. While I waited in line, I reviewed everything I had learned from Justin. According to Dr. Caldwell, he had an alibi at the time of Kayla's murder, but did that mean he was completely off her suspect list?

Kayla being the sole recipient of their grandparents' estate certainly changed things. That could have given Justin an even bigger motive for wanting her dead. Was he next in line? If Kayla was out of the way, could that mean he would inherit the property?

Who else knew about Kayla's wealth?

An estate in Napa had to be worth millions.

Would anyone else, aside from Justin, potentially benefit from her death?

What about Seth?

After my conversation with Dr. Caldwell earlier, I wanted

to speak with him tonight, but now it was imperative that I find him.

The crowd was even bigger than expected. Huge numbers of readers waited in front of me in a neat and patient line for tastings and to get their first stamp of the night. When it was my turn, I ordered State of Mind's classic IPA, fries, and a veggie burger and checked my text messages. Pri had texted to say she was running about thirty minutes late, so I found a table and settled in with my beer to wait for her and my food.

The mood in the pub was lively. People sampled tasting flights and studied their next clue. There were six venues, including State of Mind, participating in the pub crawl. The tasting flight advertised on the specials board behind the wall of taps included six mystery beers. Six tastes would have me feeling tipsy. I had a feeling that some mystery fans might not make it to each of the stops if they didn't pace themselves.

But that wasn't my problem.

Seth was my problem, and my heart thumped against my chest when I saw him wander past my table, balancing a pitcher of beer and two pint glasses.

"Hey, Seth, do you have a second?" I waved at him.

It took him a minute to register who I was. Was he pretending, or had he already been imbibing?

"Oh, yeah, Annie, what's up?" He sat across from me, sloshing the pitcher of beer as he filled his glass. "It's nuts in here."

"It's a good turnout for sure."

He mopped up the spilled beer with a wad of paper napkins. "I can't believe so many book nerds are into beer."

I cringed at his use of "book nerds." It was a term of endearment in my world, but Seth definitely didn't mean it that way.

"Books and beer go hand in hand," I countered.

"I think you mean baseball." He pushed the soggy napkins to the edge of the table.

"Do you still play?"

"Nah, just for fun. Weekend leagues, that sort of thing. Monica teases me all the time that I can't let the college days go. It's not that. It's that I love the sport, the field, the smell of the grass, the grease under your eyes, and the sound of the ball cracking against the bat. There's a reason that baseball is America's favorite pastime."

I wondered who had deemed it our favorite pastime. That sounded like a sentiment from the past. Not to mention, Seth was solidly stuck in college. Since he brought up Monica's name, I decided now was as good of a time as any to follow through on my promise to Dr. Caldwell.

"Do you and Monica spend that much time together? I thought you mentioned last night that things weren't that serious."

Seth recoiled slightly. "No, they're not, but we hang out as friends, yeah."

I was worried that he would shut down if I pushed too hard, so I tried another tactic. "You're lucky. I feel like I lost touch with so many people after college. It's cool that you've stayed connected."

That seemed to relax him. He kicked one foot onto the empty chair next to him and lifted his beer in a half toast. "To the best years of our life. I wish I could go back to those days. I guess that's why I have to stay in touch with people. I miss college. The real world isn't all it was cracked up to be."

I understood that. I loved my college years, at least up until those last days when Scarlet died, but I also hoped that I would continue to evolve. Hal told me once that his favorite year was always the year he was living. That was the kind of philosophy I wanted to embrace as I aged.

"Was it awkward for you when you and Monica started hanging out, since she and Kayla didn't get along?" Cheers erupted at the shuffleboard table.

Seth glanced toward the game and then looked back at me. "Why would it be awkward?"

"Because you dated Kayla..." I watched his face for a reaction. It seemed like a benign and obvious question to me.

Seth looked around us like we were being watched. "Did Monica say something to you?"

I reached for my drink, hoping to buy myself a minute to answer. "No, after you followed me home last night, I've been thinking about it and wondering why she's distancing herself from you if you two are really together," I said after taking a sip of my beer.

"Damn if I know." Seth pounded his fist on the table.

"Does she not want to go public with your relationship?"

Seth's eyes suddenly appeared beady. He tossed off his baseball cap and simmered. "Who told you that? Did she say that?"

"Honestly, no." I had clearly hit a nerve.

He made a fist and punched his palm repeatedly.

Wow. Was this a warning to me, or was this how he dealt with stress?

"God, I knew this was going to happen." He pounded his fist into his hand twice.

"What?" I was confused and not tracking his train of thought.

He kept pounding his fist into his palm. It made my hand sting. "Kayla ruins everything. Everything."

"How?"

He chugged his beer and refilled his glass without answering my question. "You want me to top you off?"

"No, thanks, I'm good." I placed my hand over my glass. "I'm confused. How does dating Monica connect to Kayla? You said you broke up years ago."

"Yep. We broke up our senior year *because* of Monica."

Ah. That made sense.

"I'd had a crush on Monica." A faint blush spread across his cheeks. "Things weren't going well with Kayla. We had been on-again, off-again for months. Then, one night, Monica and I hooked up, and I broke it off with Kayla for good. She didn't take it well."

This wasn't exactly what I had heard.

"She wouldn't let it go. She was obsessed with me." Seth drank his beer like he had just finished a marathon and was severely dehydrated.

His words mirrored what Monica had said about her relationship with Kayla.

"It got bad. Like I told you last night, she claimed I was stalking her. This was after we had been on and off again a couple of times. She went to the police and got a restraining order against me. No one believed me that it was the other way around." He ran his hand over his chest. "Look at me. I'm a big dude. The judge wouldn't even listen when I told her that Kayla was stalking me. She just immediately assumed that since I'm a big, beefy baseball guy, I had the problem. I didn't. By that point in our relationship, I wanted nothing to do with Kayla, but she would call, text, stop by my apartment, and follow me to the field and the batting cages. She would take pictures of me and Monica together, rip them to shreds, and stuff them in my mailbox. She went psycho. And now Monica doesn't want to be anywhere near me. She thinks the police are going to think we killed Kayla together, and it will ruin her career."

Again, everything he was saying matched what I had heard from Monica. There was just one problem. Who was telling the truth? Had Monica and Seth coordinated their stories? Or could Kayla have actually been making their lives miserable? Either way, it meant that both Seth and Monica had solid motives for killing her.

TWENTY-FOUR

Seth emptied his pitcher of beer and stood. "I'm getting a refill. You want anything?"

"No. I'm meeting a friend." Come to think of it, where was Pri? She should have been here a while ago. Dark thoughts invaded my mind. What if something happened to her? I immediately started to spiral into every worst-case scenario. I couldn't handle losing another best friend.

Don't go there, Annie.

My fingers were clammy and cold as I sent her a check-in text and finished my dinner.

She still hadn't shown up by the time I finished my burger and beer. Maybe Cryptic had gotten really slammed. I could swing by the coffee shop on my way to the next stop on the pub crawl. It wasn't like Pri to miss out on a chance for a pint and people-watching.

On my way out, I noticed Eli and Monica setting up his debut author display at the far end of the bar. I'd never seen so much effort for an author whose book didn't even have a release date yet. Monica propped up fold-out backdrops of life-size images of Eli and the cover art for *Of Hallows and Hauntings,* his forthcoming collection, in front of the bar. In the cutouts, Eli posed in his trademark black slacks, a black turtleneck, and a black beret with one hand on his chin in a pensive gaze. It was like a bad meme. If the goal was to have readers view him as arrogant and self-important, the artwork was a success. Monica had also set out bookmarks, stickers, hats, hoodies, and tons of other merch, along with a sign-up for Eli's newsletter.

How much money were they pouring into this release?

Monica stopped me as I passed by. "Great, Annie. I'm so glad you came. We have a huge surprise in store tonight, don't we, Eli?" She was wearing a sweatshirt with Eli's book cover that was so big it hit her just above the knees.

Eli brushed off his suit jacket and turtleneck as if he was tainting himself by just being inside State of Mind. I wondered how many turtlenecks he owned.

"I already made it clear that I won't be reading new passages from the book." He folded his arms over his chest and gave her a cold look that made the tiny hairs on my arms stand at attention.

"You already did a reading at the bookstore," I said, trying to lighten the mood.

"That was one small section to give readers a taste of what's to come," Monica answered for him. "Tonight, Eli is going to read a short story from the novel in its entirety."

"Your marketing method is backward," Eli countered. "If readers have already heard the material, what compels them to purchase the book when it comes out?" He threw a finger in the air. "Don't answer. That was a rhetorical question. Nothing. Nothing compels them to purchase a story they've already heard."

"Yes, they will, I promise. We're building your readership tonight. These are going to become your faithful fans." Monica pointed to a tablet resting on the bar. "I'll take care of pre-orders. Readers are going to be able to pre-order signed, personalized copies here tonight. It's a new approach in this ever-changing industry. They'll be able to say they met you, got an exclusive early look, and take a selfie. It creates buzz."

She handed me a promotional card with hashtags. "We're giving these to readers so they can share pics on social media and start hyping the book. Of course, all pre-orders will go through you. We want the Secret Bookcase to become our exclusive partner in direct sales. This is my first time implementing a promotional campaign like this, and if it works the way I think it will, it's going to become standard practice at the publishing house."

"It seems like a good idea." I had to admit that Monica was thinking out of the box when it came to book marketing. However, I couldn't help but wonder if Monica had an ulterior motive.

"Stick around for a minute," she said to me, motioning to the bartender. "I want you to hear the story we've selected for tonight. It's a spine-tingler."

I glanced at my watch. I needed to check on the other stops and find Pri. "I should really get going."

Monica took a microphone from the bartender and held up a finger for me to wait. "Please, it would mean the world to me if you stay to hear even part of his reading. I'd appreciate your professional opinion. This particular story is what sold me immediately on Eli. I knew I needed this book the minute I read it. It won't take long. It's a short story, after all."

"Um, well, when is he going to start?" I hesitated. One of my favorite thriller writers was due to start a demonstration on breaking down a crime scene soon. I really wanted to listen in on her talk.

"Right now." She held the microphone to her lips and announced that the reading was about to begin. "Please, stay, Annie. I could use some moral support and a friend right now.

Everything is riding on coming away from the festival with solid pre-orders," Monica whispered to me.

Her fixation with making him a bestseller left her oblivious to his flaws. How much of her job was riding on Eli's success? Was she in danger of being fired if his book flopped?

The bar quieted. It was going to be impossible for Monica to silence the frenetic energy, even with a room predominately occupied by readers. Eli was going to have to work hard to be heard over the sound of clinking glasses and conversations.

I was still hesitant about sticking around. I could read Eli's story when they sent an advance copy to the store, but I felt bad for Monica. Her desperation was palpable and Pri breezed into the pub at that moment. She caught my eye and waved frantically.

I exhaled relief and motioned her over. She weaved through the crowd toward us.

"I was starting to worry about you." I wrapped her in a giant hug, feeling my blood pressure coming down.

"Me too." Her cheeks were flushed with color.

I wanted to ask what she meant by that, but Monica began her introduction.

"I'll fill you in when this is done," Pri whispered. "I need a beer—now. Let's just say, it's been a day. Do you want one?"

I shook my head. "I'm good."

"Okay, back in a sec." She deftly maneuvered through the throng of readers, ordered a beer, and was back at my side before Eli took the mic.

His delivery was awful.

He slipped one hand in his pocket, taking long sideways glances at the bar while keeping his head still.

He kept pausing to clear his throat and check to see who was listening.

It was painful to watch.

He literally read from loose pages, his eyes never straying

from the paper, but his thoughts straying in a disorganized mess as he tried to figure out where he was in the story.

Many authors were shy, but Eli refused to make eye contact with the audience, making him appear disinterested. His voice remained in the same monotonous, neutral tone. There was no inflection or emphasis on a particular word or passage. His words were impersonal and unengaging. He seemed utterly unaware of the audience's reaction, unable to gauge that he was not captivating anyone's attention.

"He's bad at this," Pri said under her breath.

"Really bad."

How was Monica going to spin him as a household name if Eli had no charisma or ability to connect with an audience?

Could it be that he had a severe case of social anxiety? He came across as self-absorbed and distant, but I knew I shouldn't make assumptions. It was possible that public speaking was challenging for him, and he hated this part of the job. If that was the truth, I would have more empathy for him. Yet, it didn't explain his treatment of me earlier.

At least, from what I could hear, the writing was solid.

Monica hadn't oversold that. Eli's short story was a tightly plotted piece about a young student who slips away from an outdoor school camp and stumbles upon a murder in progress deep in the woods. In spite of his lackluster delivery, I was drawn into the tale that had not one but dozens of well-timed twists.

"The end," he said in the same deadpan tone as his story finished.

A smattering of applause broke out with the crowd. Monica looked at me with wild eyes, signaling me to do something. I wasn't here to be Eli's cheerleader. If she wanted to make him a big success, she was going to have to give him some coaching on how to do a reading or find another way for him to connect with readers.

Since I wasn't biting, she plastered on a smile and cheered and applauded wildly for her author. "Wasn't that incredible?" she said, taking the mic from Eli. "As mystery lovers, there's nothing better than a short collection of stories like these, is there? Tell me that's not a story to share around a crackling fire this winter. I'm taking pre-orders tonight, so come get in line for your copy. Eli will personalize the book for you, and the Secret Bookcase will mail it directly to you so that it arrives on or even before release day. We anticipate going into a second printing quickly with Eli's book, so I highly recommend pre-ordering to ensure that you don't miss out."

"She's desperate to create FOMO," Pri whispered. "Good luck on that."

"I agree. She has her work cut out for her."

Pri drank the last sip of her beer. "Should we ditch this place and get our pub crawl on?"

"Yes. I'm ready, and if I don't see Eli or Monica again for the rest of the weekend, that's fine by me."

Outside, the temperature had dropped with the setting sun. A refreshing breeze rattled the leaves in the eucalyptus trees. Pri and I crossed the town square, which was alive with infectious energy. Restaurants and shops beckoned readers in with open doors and inviting aromas.

"I feel like I know that story." Pri ripped off a piece of fragrant lavender from one of the terracotta pots. "There's something about that I can't quite put my finger on."

"What do you mean?" A group of musicians busked on the corner. Their dancing feet and upbeat melodies created an irresistible invitation for anyone passing by to join in.

"It's so familiar." Pri sighed and tapped the lavender to her chin. "It's on the tip of my brain."

"The girl wandering away from day camp and discovering a murder in progress?" I stole a peek into the Italian restaurant, which was aglow with hanging lanterns. Patrons filled every nook and cranny of the dining area, enjoying glasses of wine and spaghetti Bolognese.

"All of it. I must be having déjà vu."

"You weren't at his reading at the Secret Bookcase, were you?" I motioned to an open bench nearby and took a seat.

"Nope." She dragged the stalk of lavender beneath her nose as she sat next to me.

"It wouldn't have mattered anyway because Monica told me this was the first time he was reading that particular short story."

"It was good. He was terrible, but the story was good." She scooted closer to me as a woman stumbled by us, trying to catch up with her friends. "Terrifying in like a serial killer way, but I can't fault it."

"Good enough to make you buy the book?" I asked.

"Never." She pressed the lavender between her fingers. "He doesn't strike me as the celebrity author type, more like the 'he lives in his mom's basement and collects rare bones' type. I can't imagine any amount of training remedying that. He would need a complete personality change."

"It's so odd to me. I've worked with dozens upon dozens of wonderful authors over the years. It's such a gift to get to hear an author read their own work or talk about their writing process and how they create stories from seemingly thin air—it's like magic to hear how an author starts with a blank page and finishes with a full novel. That's the best part of my job, but Eli acts like talking about his book or writing is on par with getting a root canal. Monica told me that she's trying a new pre-publicity marketing strategy with Eli's book, which actually makes some sense, but I think she picked the wrong author." I winced.

"He doesn't give off a good vibe. He gives off an 'I'm sinking down to your pathetic level, and you should be happy that I'm gracing you with my presence' kind of vibe."

"Yeah, that sums it up."

"I don't envy Monica, but that story is bugging me. It's so familiar." She scrunched her cheeks.

I gasped, recalling what I had learned about Kayla and Monica's falling out in college. "What if Eli plagiarized it? Or it's based on a true story and he's stolen it? I wouldn't put that past him."

"That fits. I wonder how we can find out. Or if Monica knows." Pri brushed her hair out of her face.

"I'll have to think about it. What if Monica knows that he stole the story? She claimed that Kayla stole her college paper. Maybe it's the other way around. Maybe she stole Kayla's story and now is trying to publish it under Eli's name. That would explain why she's so desperate to make him a success."

"And give her a motive for murder if Kayla recognized her story at the reading!" Pri added, her eyebrows raised as the idea dawned on her.

My head felt like it was being swarmed by dozens of tiny insects. Could we have cracked the puzzle? Could Monica be the mastermind behind all of this?

"I can see that your head is about to explode, Annie, and I don't want to overwhelm you. How about I tell you about my evening because it's going to make things even fuzzier."

"Please do, I was worried about you." I pressed my hands to my cheeks and shook my head.

"I'm a modern woman. I don't spook easily, as you know." She ran her tattooed arm over her body and then gestured toward the shops. "Plus, we live in Redwood Grove. Nothing eventful ever happens here."

"Until now," I interrupted.

"Until now," she repeated with a nod. "That's why I was late. We had closed the shop. I was cleaning the espresso machine when I noticed that the bathroom door was locked. We usually do a sweep before we shut the garage doors and lock the front, but my coworker must have forgotten to check the bathrooms. I went and knocked twice. No one responded. I was worried that maybe someone had passed out in the stall. At that point, I was the only one left in the coffee shop. My coworkers had gone home. Now that I'm replaying this to you, I realize I probably should have called for help, just in case there was a crazed killer blockading themselves in the bathroom."

"Uh, yeah, you should have called for help," I scolded, feeling like Dr. Caldwell earlier.

Pri shrugged. "Well, I didn't do that. I took matters into my own hands, grabbed the key we keep at the counter, and unlocked the door."

My stomach tingled. Where was Pri going with this?

"You'll never guess who I found." She wiggled her fingers together and gave me a devilish grin.

"No, I won't. Put me out of my misery," I begged.

She raised her eyebrows twice. "Caroline."

"Caroline Miles?"

"Yep." She jumped to her feet and grabbed my arm. "Annie, she was huddled on the bathroom floor sobbing like a drunk sorority sister who got left behind at a party."

"What?"

"Seriously." Pri held out her hand like she was swearing an oath. "First of all, gross. I can think of a lot of other places to curl up for a good cry other than a coffee shop bathroom floor. Second of all, she seemed like she was on the brink of mental collapse. She barely registered my arrival. I asked her if she was okay or if I needed to call for help. I asked her if she heard our announcements and knew Cryptic was closed. She didn't respond. She just shook her head and kept crying."

"Did you call an ambulance? Was she hurt or sick?" Why did every new revelation lead to more questions?

Pri shook her head. "No. She was fine. She said she had done something terrible."

"Something terrible." I didn't like the sound of that. Something terrible sounded ominous. Was Caroline admitting she was the killer? I drew in a quick breath and tapped my finger against my lip waiting for Pri to say more.

"Annie, I couldn't console her. She managed to drag herself to her feet and stumble outside. I didn't get any more out of her, and honestly, I didn't try because I think she did it. She must have killed Kayla. Now reality has sunk in, and she can't deal with the guilt. It's the only explanation."

"Smart move not to engage with her." Moments ago, I was nearly convinced that Monica was the killer, but now Caroline was back on the top of my list. Her behavior spoke volumes. Why would she barricade herself inside the coffee shop if she wasn't guilty?

"I made sure the front door was securely deadbolted, then I called Dr. Caldwell. She said she would do a wellness check."

"That's good."

"And maybe while doing her wellness check, she's going to make an arrest because I never thought I would say this, but I think there's a chance Caroline could be the killer. After seeing her like that, I don't know, Annie, I'm worried that Caroline might have done something drastic."

TWENTY-FIVE

"Do you really think Caroline is capable of it?" I asked Pri as we headed to the next stop on the pub crawl—the Salsa Street Grill, which was featuring a variety of spicy drinks and a mariachi band. I had known Caroline since she moved to Redwood Grove to open Artifacts, and I knew Hal considered her a friend. Nothing about her previous behavior would have led me to consider her a top suspect. Caroline had gone out of her way to become an active member of the community from the moment she began renovations on the store. She donated to the school auction, volunteered for a variety of outreach programs, and had been extremely supportive of the festival. I couldn't fathom her snapping and resorting to murder.

"No, not exactly. But if we take away our personal feelings toward Caroline, she has a valid motive for wanting Kayla dead. Think about it for a minute. If Kayla stole your business, your clients, your vendors, and fleeced you out of money without delivering, wouldn't you be furious?"

"Yes, but I wouldn't kill her."

Pri agreed by waving her hand in a dismissive gesture. "Sure, but let's assume Caroline isn't as stable as you. She was desperate to bring in more money for Artifacts; she thought she had a new partner in Kayla but ended up betrayed. I'm not suggesting that she planned to murder Kayla. It was probably in the heat of the moment, and she snapped. Maybe she didn't even intend to hurt Kayla. Maybe they got into a scuffle in the bookshop, and she didn't realize her own strength?"

"It's a valid argument. Fletcher saw her in the bookstore before Kayla was killed. I'm not saying it isn't possible. It's just that Kayla's body was inside the secret bookcase. It took some muscles for the killer to drag Kayla's body behind the hidden door. Is Caroline that person? And how did she do it without being seen?"

"That is a question for Dr. Caldwell," Pri admitted. "I have no idea, especially since it wasn't like the bookstore was dead, right?" She grimaced. "Sorry. Poor word choice on my part."

"No, it's fine. And it's true that the store was busy, so I'm equally stumped about how the killer did it."

We were passing the Stag Head and Liam was chatting outside with a group of readers dressed in the trench coat costumes I'd seen earlier at the park. He caught my eye. "Hey, Annie, come over here."

Liam was the last person I wanted to talk to at the moment. What did he want now?

"Can you please make it clear to your book people that the Stag Head is not, I repeat *not*, participating in the pub crawl?" Liam glared at me.

The group of readers looked at me nervously. "Sorry, we read the map wrong and thought that since this is a pub, it would be one of the stops," a woman wearing a READ MORE BOOKS hoodie said with an apologetic smile.

"Let me show you where the next stop is." I pointed out the restaurant on the map. They thanked me and left while Liam's eyes felt like lasers burning a hole through my skull.

"Why aren't you one of the stops, Liam?" Pri asked pointedly.

It was good that she had jumped in because every muscle in my body tensed. I could feel the blood pumping through my veins and rising in my cheeks.

"As I explained to Annie, I don't have time to entertain these frivolous readers. Nothing against the event. It's just me and a couple of part-time staff. There's no way we can accommodate this many people." He shot his thumb behind him to the large six-paned windows. Paper stags' heads hung from each of the frames.

"You do historical trivia nights all the time," Pri protested.

"Yes." Liam tilted his head and gave her a superior gaze that made me want to punch him in the face. "If you'll recall, we require reservations for our trivia nights. They are refined, small events, not a drunken book crawl."

"Pub crawl," I corrected him. "And for the record, no one is drunk. The evening is a lowkey way for readers to meander between different restaurants and bars in town. These are readers who paid to travel here, not a frat party. Plus, they're spending money at all of your competitors' businesses."

"I don't have competitors." Liam gave me a challenging stare. "And that woman who died seemed fairly inebriated to me."

That was a low blow. Did he think that I had control over Kayla's behavior?

I opened my mouth to respond with a snarky retort but then thought better of it. "That was long before the pub crawl."

Liam shrugged. "Be that as it may, I'm not interested in a bunch of drunks hanging out in the pub."

"Your loss, man." Pri shook her head. "Cryptic had our best day ever. You should be thanking Annie for bringing this kind of business to town."

I gave her an appreciative smile for backing me up.

Liam started to say something but stopped himself. "I did acquiesce and add a drink special for the weekend—a brandy milk punch. Did you know that was Edgar Allan Poe's drink of choice? I felt like Poe's literary prowess is up to my standards. However, I'm not changing my mind about participating in the pub crawl."

Of course he was an Edgar Allan Poe fan. "It's too late anyway," I replied, reaching into my purse for a map. I held it for Liam to see. "The Stag Head is not listed, so I'd appreciate it if you would stop with the 'I'm too good for everyone' attitude and treating guests to our town the way you just did with those readers. If people happen to make the same mistake, you can simply point them in the right direction." I grabbed Pri's arm. "Let's go. There's nothing more to discuss here."

I yanked her away with Liam sputtering something I couldn't decipher behind us.

"I hate him so much, Pri." I clenched my teeth.

"I know. My wrist can feel that."

"Oh, sorry." I loosened my grip. "I swear it's his personal mission to make my life miserable. Why would he be rude to those readers? It makes no sense to me."

"I think that's his plan." Pri couldn't contain a sly smile. "He does that to get a reaction from you."

"I don't think that's true. I think Liam Donovan is a smug, pompous ass who only cares about himself." I had to unclench my teeth intentionally.

"But he got a reaction out of you." Pri tilted her head to the side and squinted at me.

"Because he was awful to those poor people. Come on, he doesn't have competitors. Everyone else in town is thrilled with Mystery Fest." I scrunched my nose and tightened my shoulders.

"They'll be fine. It's not a reflection on you, Annie. It's on him. I'm telling you there's a backstory there. You just have to chink away all of his armor, and if you don't want to do that, then my advice is to let it go and don't give him any attention. That's what he wants."

I ran my tongue along the inside of my cheek. "You're probably right."

"I'm always right." She changed the topic to what drink we should order at the next stop. "They're doing murderous mango margaritas at the Salsa Street Grill."

"I already had a beer." I hesitated.

"Come on, Annie." Pri grabbed my wrist. "Liam thinks everyone in town is a bunch of lushes. Let's not let him down."

A mango margarita did sound refreshing.

The grill was an outdoor food truck with a permanent spot across from the park. A converted refurbished VW, painted a vintage fire-engine red with white accents, served drinks and the best street tacos. Red, green, and white twinkle lights were strung from the shiny exterior, creating a canopy above a collection of matching bistro tables. A mariachi band strummed instruments and encouraged the crowd to clap along.

"This round's on me," Pri said, pointing to an empty table. "Grab us a seat, and I'll get our murderous margaritas."

When I sat down, I realized that Seth and Monica were huddled together a few tables away. They had pushed their chairs close together so their knees were touching, and they were studying something on Monica's phone.

How had they made it here before us? We hadn't stopped to talk to Liam for that long. Monica must have wrapped up Eli's talk quickly. Although that shouldn't surprise me; after his reading, I doubted there had been a long line for pre-orders.

I pretended to study the menu while observing them.

Their body language made me wonder if they were still dating. That, or they had conspired to kill Kayla together and were trying to make sure they hadn't left any evidence behind.

"A mango margarita for you," Pri announced, setting a giant

bowl-shaped glass in front of me. A ring of spicy sugar rimmed the glass, which looked like it could serve twelve. "They only had one size—huge. Drink up, my friend."

"I don't even know if I can lift this." I pretended to have to use both hands to raise my glass.

"What were you looking at?" Pri's gaze fell behind me.

"Monica and Seth. Casually glance over your left shoulder like you're looking for someone."

She popped a mango wedge in her mouth and then turned around. "They look pretty cozy if you ask me."

"I agree." I kept my voice down. I didn't think they could hear over the chatter of readers and the sound of the band. They hadn't looked away from Monica's screen yet, which meant they didn't know we were watching them. "Aren't they giving off couple's vibes?"

"His hand is halfway up her thigh," Pri said through clenched teeth.

"It is?"

Pri bobbed her head. "Lean a little to your side. You can't miss it."

I stole another glance at them, and sure enough, Seth was massaging the top of Monica's thigh. "Okay, get a room, but also, why would she lie about them being together? It must be because of Kayla."

She scrunched her eyebrows and twisted her lips together like she was swishing mouthwash. "Damn, Annie, you're going to ruin my Caroline theory."

"Let's think about this for a minute. If they are together, could they have killed Kayla because she wouldn't leave either of them alone? Maybe they'd had enough and joined forces. In some ways, two killers make the most sense. One of them could have stabbed her, while the other kept a lookout. Seth is certainly muscular enough to have been able to drag her body behind the bookcase."

"Yeah, that's a solid theory especially with this much PDA. Next time I look over, she's going to be on his lap." Pri stuck out her tongue and shifted to the side to get a better view of Monica and Seth. "If Kayla had been actively stalking them, why wouldn't they go to the police? They could back each other up. That would lend more proof that Kayla was harassing them, yeah?"

"Potentially, but Seth did say that Kayla took out a restraining order on him first. I don't know how truthful he was because he also admitted that he had been following her around in hopes of getting her back. If that's the case the court would likely side with her. But it's kind of a bold move if Seth's story is true. Kayla outwitted him and went to the police for help, even though she was the one who was violating Seth's personal space." I wasn't sure if I believed him, but he had seemed genuinely upset at my cottage.

"And Monica, too?" Pri sounded doubtful.

"Monica told me that Kayla followed her every move since college. She mentioned that Kayla had tracked her career and gone so far as to reach out to her employers to warn them about her."

"That is some dark, next-level stuff." Pri used the tip of a fancy toothpick to stab another slice of mango from her drink.

"Of course, we're taking their word for this, which could be lies, too, but if not, I can't imagine how stressful it must be to have someone stalking you for years." Just a few sips of the margarita were starting to go to my head. My shoulders swayed to the music. I pushed the drink away. I had to stay sharp tonight. Dr. Caldwell's warning replayed in my mind. She wouldn't have advised me to stay vigilant unless there was a real threat.

"Okay, so your theory does seem murder worthy." Pri held up a finger as she took a bite of the mango. "Maybe they had finally had enough. Didn't you say they were surprised that Kayla was in town?"

"Yeah. They must have thought that she was following them. Although, come to think of it, could that have been her plan all along?"

"Because of the festival?" Pri sounded skeptical.

"Well, if she were tracking Monica's career, she would have known that Monica was attending with Eli. It's been all over the publishing house's social media. They were great in helping us promote the festival. Or maybe there's a connection with Eli's short stories. If it was stolen, and let's say Kayla originally wrote it, she could have followed them here to confront them. She started to make a scene at his reading, but Seth swooped her out."

"My head feels like it's going to explode, and it's not from a few sips and a boozy mango slice." Pri massaged her temples. "So, let's go with this idea. Seth and Monica arrive for the festival because they are a couple, and one or both of them spots Kayla. They can't believe that she's followed them again, and they hatch a plan to put an end to her stalking for good."

I chewed on the side of my cheek. "It's possible. I still can't work out how they would have done, but like I said, having two killers seems easier in many ways. Maybe it wasn't premeditated either. When Kayla tried to interrupt Eli's reading, Monica was visibly angry. Maybe she realized that Kayla knew her work had been stolen. She could have confronted her, or Seth could have come to her defense."

"Yikes." Pri grimaced and dragged her teeth across her bottom lip.

"I know. I feel like we should tell Dr. Caldwell about this." I felt energized like every cell in my body was vibrating at the highest frequency. The pieces of the puzzle were beginning to fit together and fall into place. Dr. Caldwell used to talk about the drive and desire to resolve uncertainty and uncover the truth. She would say that hours flew by like seconds when an unexpected breakthrough would happen in a case and that there was nothing as satisfying as solving an investigation and bringing closure to the victims and their families. I had a taste of that now, and I was humming with a mixture of nerves and anticipation.

"Or follow them to see where they're going." Pri put her drink on the table. "Look, they're on the move. This is our chance. Let's go."

I hesitated. After my late run-in with Seth last night, I wasn't sure it was the best idea, but we were getting close. I could feel it. Plus, there were two of us and people out and about. Nothing bad could happen, could it?

TWENTY-SIX

Seth and Monica paid for their drinks. I watched them walk off hand in hand underneath the colorful twinkle lights strung above the patio. As they crossed the street and entered the park, their silhouettes faded into the shadows.

Pri and I followed from what I hoped was a safe distance. We didn't speak as we used the cover of darkness from the shady canopy of the trees in the park to shield us. I felt like the readers earlier, only this wasn't a made-up event based around a fake crime. We were actually tailing two potential murder suspects.

"Where are they going?" Pri whispered when we got to the edge of the park and they took a sharp turn in the direction of my cottage.

"Are they heading for my place?" I replied, matching her tone. Seth and Monica were far enough ahead of us that I didn't think they could hear us, but I wasn't going to take any chances. Not tonight. My restless legs and the tingling sensation spreading across my chest were a reminder that we couldn't let our guard down.

Pri's eyes glowed in the moonlight. "They're coming for

you, Annie. Oh my God, this is bad. We should call Dr. Caldwell."

"Why would they come for me?" I rooted myself to the sidewalk. Beads of sweat pooled on my lip. Were we in danger?

"Maybe they realized you're on to them?" Pri suggested, tightening her muscles like she was preparing to run. "You know too much, so now they have to silence you, too."

My stomach sank. It felt like I'd swallowed a rock. Could that be true?

I replayed my conversations with both of them. There was nothing I said that would have indicated that I suspected them, was there?

"Let's make sure that's where they're going before we involve Dr. Caldwell," I said, ungluing my feet from the pavement, feeling a surge of momentary bravery—or perhaps idiocy. I'd saved Dr. Caldwell's number in my contacts. If anything went wrong, I simply needed to place a call, and I knew she would be here in an instant.

"Fine, but if we see them banging on your front door, I'm calling the police." Pri squinted and pressed her lips together to show me she was serious.

"I won't stop you, but come on, we're losing them."

We skirted the edge of the park, ducking behind eucalyptus trees and trying not to make any sound. Sure enough, when we made it to my street, the lampposts illuminated Seth's and Monica's silhouettes, walking with a purpose to my cottage.

My heart was pounding and I realized I was holding my breath. It was like something from a bad dream. I gasped and covered my mouth with my hand. I focused my gaze to make sure I wasn't seeing things.

I wasn't.

To anyone passing by, they might have appeared to be a couple on their way home with their hands intertwined from a romantic date night. But to me, everything about their casually connected body language sent warning shivers in the form of tiny electrical shocks humming down my legs and arms.

"Do you need further proof?" Pri stopped at the end of the sidewalk and looked behind us to the rows of neatly trimmed roses lining the entrance to my complex.

"No. I'll call Dr. Caldwell now." I reached into my purse and pulled out my phone. The call went straight to voicemail. "She's not answering. What should I do?"

"Leave her a message." Pri's voice was unusually shrill.

Dr. Caldwell would probably think that I was delusional from my frantic, hushed message telling her that we were near my cottage where Seth and Monica had come to confront me and asking if could she please advise what we should do next.

I hung up. "Should I call 911?"

Pri kept her head tilted in the direction of my cottage, peering through the bushes with a slack jaw. "I don't know. They're knocking on your door. If you don't answer, they'll probably give up."

"Or try to break in." Professor Plum was inside. He'd never been an outdoor cat. If they let him out, I wasn't sure what he would do.

"I dare them." Pri motioned across the street. "Let's go stake out a spot behind those huge climbing rose bushes. We should be able to keep an eye on them without being seen."

We sprinted across the street like we were training at Quantico to be CIA agents. My limbs felt jerky as we ducked behind the thorny roses. The sweet fragrance of the early summer blooms didn't match the mood.

Seth and Monica knocked again and waited. Then Monica looked at her watch and shrugged. Maybe we were blowing this out of proportion. Monica and Seth could have stopped by to see if I wanted to join them for a drink.

But the minute I tried to rationalize their behavior, Seth

stepped away from Monica, left the porch, and went around the side of my cottage.

"What's he doing? I can't see." Pri used her pinkie to pry open a gnarly section of the rose vines.

I slapped a hand over my mouth. "He's peering into my kitchen window."

"Do you think he's looking for another way in?" Pri stood on her toes to try and get a better look.

"I can't tell. I hope I locked my windows." Living in a small town like Redwood Grove, especially next to neighbors who left casseroles and chocolate chip cookies on my front porch, meant that I often left my windows cracked open. I loved the cool misty breeze on summer evenings, and it wasn't like I had anything of value in my cottage, aside from Professor Plum. Unless you counted my first edition copy of *Evil Under the Sun* —it was worth nearly five hundred dollars and had been a gift from Hal for my eight-year anniversary working at the Secret Bookcase. I told him I didn't need anything, but he insisted and told me he had a second signed copy in his personal collection.

"Did you?" Pri asked in a hushed whisper.

"I think so. I was distracted this morning, so I can't remember. It wasn't very hot last night. I slept with my bedroom window cracked, but I think I shut it this morning. I hope I did. Professor Plum is inside."

"Where is Seth now?" Pri stood on her tiptoes to try and see through the roses.

I'd lost him. "I can't see him. He must have gone around to the back."

"That's not good." Pri twisted a prickly branch to try and get a better view. "Should we call 911 and report an attempted break-in?"

"Technically, they haven't broken in yet." I wished I was wearing something more practical than my bookish dress and the strappy sandals. I couldn't exactly confront or outrun them in my current outfit.

"What about trespassing?"

"Yeah." I reached for my phone again. "Seth has a restraining order against him. I bet that means the police will take him snooping around my cottage seriously."

"Call them." Pri's voice had a tinge of urgency that I wasn't used to.

I pressed the emergency button on my phone and was immediately connected to dispatch. "Hi, this is Annie Murray. My friend and I were just coming home, and we noticed two people on my property. They're looking into my windows, and it seems like they're trying to find a way inside." My breath burst in and out as I spoke, trying to stop the trembling in my knees.

The operator asked for my exact location and told us to stay where we were. They were sending a squad car that should be there in minutes.

Monica swiveled her head in our direction. I dropped my phone and yanked Pri down to the ground.

"Did she see us?" Pri made herself even smaller by crouching in a protective huddle.

Monica stiffened her back and used one hand to shield her eyes from the streetlights.

I could hear the operator's muted voice on the other end of the call but didn't dare move a muscle.

"Seth, Seth, is that you?" Monica called in a frantic whisper.

"I can't tell. Just stay down." A rolling sensation roared through my stomach, like we'd just parachuted out of an airplane. This was bad. We couldn't alert Monica or Seth to the fact that we were here, not until the police arrived.

"Seth, where are you?" Monica's voice carried an unmistakable intensity.

Had it been minutes already? Where were the police?

My phone continued to crackle.

Monica took a step toward us.

Pri let out a timid yelp.

I threw my finger to my lip. "Stay still. We're fine."

I wasn't sure that was true, but I had to be brave for her and for me.

Was staying put the best decision?

Should we make a break for the park while Monica and Seth were separated?

I tried to tap into my rational brain. There were two of us. Pri and I could take on Monica—unless she had a weapon.

My stomach dropped at the thought.

Why was danger following me around every turn?

Things like this didn't happen in my sweet, little Redwood Grove.

I considered our options just as I heard a police car slowly inching toward us.

The squad car had its lights and sirens off.

I guessed that was because they didn't want to scare away Seth and Monica.

Thank God.

Help had arrived.

Pri and I watched from the safety of the roses as another police car arrived on the scene. Since my cottage was situated on a dead-end street, there was no way out for Seth or Monica.

The first squad car barricaded the front of the street, and the second parked at an angle to block any attempt for them to flee through the park.

"This is like a movie." Pri sounded as incredulous as I felt.

"It doesn't feel real." What I didn't say out loud was that this wasn't the first time my life had taken a dark and surreal turn. Pri was right, it felt like the plot of a thriller, and I longed to go back to the slow, easy, albeit boring pace of normalcy and for Redwood Grove to feel like my own personal safe haven again.

The police were extremely professional as they exited their cars and fanned out to surround my cottage on every side. Not a single light came on in any of my neighbors' houses. The team worked in a silence so dense it felt like I could reach out and touch it.

Pri held back a gnarly section of the rose vines so that we could see.

There was no chance that Monica or Seth were aware they were about to be captured. I was impressed with how deftly the team worked, using hand signals and nods to direct their movements.

Once the police were within range, they turned on high-beam flashlights and held their tasers ready to shoot.

"Freeze," the lead officer commanded. "Turn around with your hands in the air."

Were we about to witness Kayla's killers being arrested?

TWENTY-SEVEN

Dr. Caldwell raced in on foot just as the first team of police officers approached Monica with their flashlights propped on their shoulders. Her heels clicked on the driveway as she sprinted past us with one hand adhered to the taser on her hip. She was surprisingly fast, especially for someone in slacks and heels.

"Turn around with your hands up. We don't want to use force, but we will if necessary," Dr. Caldwell warned as she reached the porch.

Monica slowly swiveled around. She held quaking arms high above her head. "I'm not doing anything. I don't have a weapon."

"There's another suspect around back," one of the officers announced, pointing to the side of my cottage.

Dr. Caldwell used two fingers to direct officers to head that way.

Pri and I emerged from the rose bush, watching the team fan out in every direction, flanking my cottage. My neighbors had finally awoken from the commotion. Lights popped on in the surrounding cottages, and my neighbors began to peer outside through partially drawn curtains.

"This is absolutely bonkers," Pri said, sounding as baffled as I felt. "Can you pinch me? Are we still in Redwood Grove?"

"The 911 dispatcher did say that they would be here in minutes." I was impressed at their lightning-fast response time.

"This is more action than the local police have had in their careers. What's a normal call? That someone's cat got lost? Or someone took more than two books from a little free library?"

I laughed. It felt good to break the tension for a minute.

Monica was trying to plead her case to the police. From our vantage point, she didn't look like she was succeeding. Her hands were like goalposts. "I was just coming to see Annie. I swear on my life."

Dr. Caldwell ignored her attempts to explain what they were doing and proceeded to handcuff her.

It took longer for the police squad to catch Seth. He must have found a hiding spot in one of my neighbors' patios. Each of our cottages had small four-foot-by-six-foot enclosed patios on the backside of the house. Mine had a porch swing, glowing paper lanterns, and potted birds of paradise. My neighbor to the left was a hummingbird whisperer. Dozens of enticing red feeders hung in every corner of her patio. There was rarely a minute when I was outside reading on the patio that I wasn't surrounded by the shimmery, iridescent birds flitting from one feeder to the next.

I hoped that Seth wasn't destroying anyone's property.

Fortunately, a few minutes later, he emerged from the far end of the complex with his hands cuffed behind his back. Two police officers escorted him down the dead-end street.

Dr. Caldwell motioned for me to come over. I wasn't even aware that she had seen us, but it shouldn't surprise me that nothing got past her. "Annie, would you like to press charges?"

I squared my shoulders and approached them with Pri at

my side. A couple of my neighbors stared at me wide-eyed with speculation. I gave them a sheepish shrug, knowing that I would be bombarded with questions and probably comfort food in the form of banana bread and blueberry muffins in the morning.

Monica blinked hard, like she had something stuck in her eye. "Annie, listen, you have to believe me, this isn't what it looks like."

"It looks like you were trying to break into my house." I motioned to my cozy cottage.

Monica and Seth spoke over one another.

Dr. Caldwell silenced them. "One at a time. You first." She nodded to Monica.

"It's not what it looks like. I swear on my life, we weren't trying to break in. We just wanted to talk to you, Annie. Seth and I realized something over drinks, and we had to come find you to see if you remember it, too." Monica tried to move her hands but realized they were cuffed behind her back. The motion made her lurch slightly forward.

Seth ignored Dr. Caldwell's orders and jumped in. "I get why you would think we were breaking in if you came home and saw us checking out your place. I went around the back to see if you were outside. That's all, Scout's honor." He bent his head in an apology.

"Looking for Annie, or anyone else for that matter, does not give you permission to so much as step foot on her property without permission," Dr. Caldwell said, giving them each a look that made me shudder.

I wouldn't want to be on her bad side.

"What did you remember at drinks?" I asked, ignoring Monica pleading "I'm sorry" under her breath.

"Do you remember the story Kayla told in our first-year English class?" Monica asked hopefully.

"I wasn't in your first-year English class." I wondered what her publishing house would say about her being arrested for murder.

"You weren't? No, you must have been. Are you sure?" Monica not believing me was like icing on the cake for the night.

"I'm positive. I didn't take first-year English because I took college-level English during my last two years of high school. So, yeah, I'm sure."

"Nice flex," Pri whispered, and bumped my hip.

"Damn." Monica shook her head and sighed. "I could have sworn you were in that class."

Then something occurred to me. "Are you remembering Scarlet?" Saying her name out loud in front of Dr. Caldwell and my former classmates made me suck in my breath. Scarlet used to complain about how disruptive Kayla was in that class. At least Scarlet would be proud of me now.

Pri must have noticed my reaction to Scarlet's name because she scooted closer and put her hand on my forearm in a show of solidarity.

"Scarlet." Monica threw her head back. "It was Scarlet. That doesn't help us at all," she wailed, directing her distress at Seth.

"Would you care to expand?" Dr. Caldwell asked, but it wasn't a suggestion.

Monica nodded. "Kayla was a, well, how can I say this kindly? A storyteller."

"She was a pathological liar," Seth interrupted.

"That too," Monica agreed. "It was hard to tell what was the truth and what was fantasy with Kayla. She was constantly reinventing herself, so you never really knew who you would get or what to believe. We had an assignment in our English class to write a short story about a life event that changed or altered our view of the world. We read our stories out loud, and students gave feedback on strengthening them."

"You must have had Professor Burke. That was always her first assignment," Dr. Caldwell said.

"Yes, she was great." Monica smiled nostalgically, and for a moment she reminded me of the girl I'd known from a distance at college, rather than the driven woman she seemed to have become. "Kayla's story was about an experience she'd had in middle school on a field trip to the forest. She said she got separated from the group because she heard a dog barking. She went to check it out because she wanted to pet the dog or, probably more likely, get out of the assignment. She wandered off in the direction of the barking and ended up deeper in the forest, where she spotted a man dressed in black huddled over the body, holding a bloody knife. Kayla freaked out and ran back to the group. She told her teacher, but when they returned to the site, there was nothing there. Her story was about not being believed. It's ironic because she exaggerated and told so many lies it was impossible to believe her. The story was good. It was powerful, but I don't think anyone in the class thought it was real. That is, until tonight."

"Eli's short story," Pri exclaimed, pointing at Eli's book cover plastered on Monica's sweatshirt and clutching my arm. "That's why it's familiar. I remember it from the news. The police found a body in the woods, but I don't think they ever identified the victim or the killer. I was in middle school then, too, and I remember we were all terrified to go to outdoor school because it was on the news for weeks."

Monica gulped. "How could I have missed it? It's so obvious now. It's like neon lights flashing in front of my face. I feel so dumb, but then I keep reminding myself, why would I make that connection? Kayla wrote a story about something similar that happened probably twenty years ago now. One thing I've learned in working in publishing is that there aren't many original ideas. Variations of that same plot have played out in hundreds of novels. The unique, individual spin, an author's voice, world-building, and characters make a story a story."

I agreed with her on that point but was still trying to put together what she was saying. "You think that Eli stole Kayla's story?" Pri asked.

"Yes and no," Seth answered before Monica could respond. "We think Kayla plucked that story from the news and used it in her paper."

"She probably saw it in the news, copied it, and changed just enough details to make it feel fresh and like it was her own story," Monica added, her words smashing together in a jumbled rush. "Eli must have also been aware of the body in the woods. This is so disappointing. I'm beginning to think that none of his work is original. He and Kayla had more in common than I realized. His entire collection of short stories is probably repurposed content."

Another thought began to form in my mind. A horrifying thought that made my blood run cold.

"That's why we wanted to find you, Annie," Monica said, looking at me with wide, pleading eyes. "I thought you were in the class. We weren't sure if you would believe us since we both had issues with Kayla," she said to Dr. Caldwell. "We figured that if Annie remembered it, too, she was a neutral party."

Dr. Caldwell hadn't said a word. She caught my eye, and waited expectantly.

"Or," I began timidly.

"Yes, continue," Dr. Caldwell encouraged, motioning her hand in a circle.

"Or," I repeated. "What if Kayla was telling the truth? What if she really did witness a murder in the woods that day? What if Eli was the killer? No one would know his story better. It's possible, and I think plausible, that Kayla saw him kill John Doe in the woods all those years ago. She must have put it together when she heard Eli speak. That's probably why she reacted the way she did at his reading." I stopped short of launching into the potential ways there could be a connection to Scarlet's murder. But were there? Nothing immediately connected, but I couldn't rule it out.

Dr. Caldwell pressed her lips together and nodded. "Your deductions are spot-on. My team has been combing through cell phone footage from every customer who was in the bookshop during the time that Kayla was killed, and we got a hit right before you called 911. Fifteen years ago, he might have been able to kill without leaving a trace, but that's nearly impossible today. It turns out that I was wrong about how the crime occurred. We have video evidence of Kayla entering the secret room and Eli following her minutes later. He either became too bold or desperate, but either way, we'll be making an arrest tonight."

The shock on Pri's face mirrored my emotions.

Eli had done it? A metallic taste filled my mouth, like I might get sick. I clasped my hand over my lips and swallowed hard.

He was the killer, and Dr. Caldwell had proof.

Monica hung her head and rocked back and forth, staring at her sweatshirt like it was suddenly toxic. "Oh my God, my star author. His mysteries are so compelling because he's had first-hand experience with *murder*. It makes sense. I'm such an idiot for not realizing it sooner. Eli was so weird about doing public signings. His whole vibe is very serial killer-ish. I thought it was part of him trying to create an author persona, but no, he's just a terrible person."

"Kayla told me the same story." Seth's shoulders curled over his chest. "I feel terrible for her now. Maybe her lies and need for attention were because of what she saw in middle school. That had to suck that no one believed her, including me."

Dr. Caldwell made a tiny motion with her head to one of the police officers standing nearby. It was as if they were speaking a coded language because the officer immediately began directing the team. Then she turned to me. "Annie, let me ask again, would you like to press charges?"

"No." I shook my head. "You can let them go."

Dr. Caldwell unlocked Monica's and Seth's handcuffs. "You're free to go. One of my team will need to take additional statements from each of you, and under no circumstances should you venture onto anyone else's property, understood?"

They nodded solemnly.

"Should I hear of any trespassing, you will both be placed into custody immediately."

"I understand," Monica said. "Thank you, Annie."

"Have either of you spoken with Eli?" Dr. Caldwell asked, narrowing her eyes at both of them.

"No," Seth answered first. "We literally were having a margarita, and a lightbulb went off. We started discussing it and realized we had to come here to find Annie."

"Good." She addressed all of us. "I'd like you to keep this under wraps. My team will take it from here. Do not interact with Eli. If you happen to see him, please do your best to act normally as if you have no understanding of his potential involvement in not one but two crimes."

"Do you know where he is?" Pri asked, glancing around us like she expected him to jump out from behind the rose bushes at any minute.

"He was fuming after no one bought any pre-orders at the last event. He took off in a huff, but I don't know where he went," Monica offered.

"I wonder where he might go or if he left town," I said, shuddering at the thought of how much interaction I'd had with Kayla's killer.

Monica sighed with remorse. "Honestly, I have no idea, but I'd like to find and tell him to his face that I'm not publishing his book now."

"I'll be in touch. Should any of you see Eli, contact me immediately or call 911, but do not engage." Dr. Caldwell gave us a curt nod and joined the waiting police team.

Her tone worried me. Eli had killed at least twice. He was more than a self-inflated writer. He was a killer. I refused to sit back and let him get away with murder. A newfound energy pulsed through my veins. Heat rose in my neck as I clutched my hands into balls for courage. This was my moment. This was my duty. I had studied for this and prepared for this. It was up to me to figure out where Eli was hiding, inform Dr. Caldwell, and see him brought to justice—immediately.

TWENTY-EIGHT

A palpable unease surged through my body as Pri and I cut through the park toward the Grand Hotel. The crisp night air and the adrenaline pulsing through my body made me shiver and rub my hands over my arms. My bookish dress wasn't exactly suspect-chasing attire.

A dew settled over the grass, making my feet damp. I could hear the sound of the mariachi band in the distance. The Grand Hotel was the last stop on the pub crawl, so I wasn't surprised to see a large group of readers gathered on the lawn. But I was surprised to see the hotel surrounded by dozens of police cars with flashing lights. Dr. Caldwell must have called in backup because I was fairly sure that Redwood Grove only had two police cars.

"This night just keeps getting more surreal," Pri said as we fell in with the crowds of people.

"Is this the grand finale for the weekend?" a reader standing nearby asked.

"I heard there's going to be a fireworks show," another replied.

"No, it's a sting operation. Just wait, rumor has it that

they're planning a shootout, but don't worry, it's all fake," yet another bystander said.

Pri and I shared a glance. If only that were true.

Police officers formed a barricade at the front of the hotel, holding anyone attempting to get in or out of the property.

Every cell in my body felt like it was on fire. I couldn't stop the strange pulsing sensation in my limbs. It was as if my feet weren't making contact with the pavement. Everything moved in a weird blur. I removed my glasses and tried to clean the lenses on my dress, but it didn't help.

"Do you think Eli's in there?" Pri whispered.

"I don't know. Something feels off. Why would Eli go to the most populated spot in town? The ending reception is happening tonight. There are probably a couple of hundred people inside. He's an introvert and a recluse. It doesn't make sense. I feel like he would seek seclusion, not a party." I couldn't believe the last night of the festival was ending like this. I laced my fingers together to try to stop them from quivering. The only thing that made me feel slightly better was that we finally knew who had killed Kayla. I had faith in Dr. Caldwell. Hopefully, this would all be over soon.

A gruff voice sounded behind me. I recognized the piney smell of Liam Donovan's aftershave. "What antics are you up to now, Annie?"

I turned to see him lumbering over me. It felt weirdly comforting to have his solid presence here just at this moment. Confusing, but also reassuring. There was something about the energy he exuded that brought a sense of calm, like even though we were always at odds, I knew he would step in to protect me at any cost. I nodded toward the scene. "This isn't me."

"Sure. That's what I've heard." Liam rolled his eyes. He moved so close to me that our shoulders brushed. "The Stag Head emptied as quickly as the air from a punctured balloon when news spread about a commotion here at the hotel. You could have warned us that you were pulling a stunt like this."

"This isn't a stunt," I repeated, hearing annoyance creep into my voice. "The police must be about to make an arrest." Even as I said it, I wasn't sure it was true. My interactions with Eli told me this was the last place he would go to try and make an escape.

"What?" Liam stared at me with disbelief, holding my gaze a second too long.

The intensity of his eyes made my stomach flutter.

Knock it off, Annie.

I pressed my hand over my belly button to try and stop the swarming feeling. It didn't work.

"Yes, they've got the hotel surrounded, and it looks like she called in support." I pointed out the obvious.

Liam let out a low whistle. "Who did it?"

"You mean, who's the killer?" Pri interjected.

"Yeah." Liam's voice was rough around the edges.

"We think it's Eli Ledger," I said, realization finally dawning on me. Eli wouldn't have come to the busy hotel; he would have gone to a place where he could hide out in a dark corner booth and not interact with anyone. A place like the Stag Head.

"The author?" Liam asked, his arm still touching mine. "I didn't like that guy from the minute I met him. Talk about arrogant."

That was rich coming from Liam, but my blood was pumping so hard I felt like my veins might burst. "Yeah, that Eli. Have you seen him?"

"What, did he kill over a bad review or something?" Liam moved closer to me as two police officers pushed past us. The heat from his body sent another wave of flutters through my stomach.

What was wrong with me?

"No, I'm serious. He's the killer." I looked at Pri for support.

"This is pure non-fiction, right up your alley," Pri said to Liam. "He killed Kayla for sure."

I couldn't tell if I was finding it hard to breathe because Liam's arm was touching mine, or if it was because I was fairly confident I knew where Eli was. The scent of Liam's aftershave lingered in the air. I was suddenly acutely aware of how I was holding my back perfectly straight and upright.

Why hadn't Liam moved away after the police passed us?

Was he trying to make me uncomfortable by invading my personal space? Why did part of me want to be scooped up in his burly arms and carried away?

Stop, Annie.

"Isn't that right, Annie?" Pri was asking me. "Annie."

"Huh, what?" I blinked twice.

"I was saying," Pri continued with a hint of a smile. "We think Eli realized Kayla was the student who saw him when he did the reading at the Secret Bookcase. Her reaction gave it away."

"Right." I had to focus. I couldn't let my inability to think coherently around Liam get in the way of finding Eli. "Have you seen him? Is he at the pub?"

"You guys are serious, aren't you?" Liam suddenly shifted. He pulled away from me and squared his shoulders. "Sorry, I thought you were theorizing." The urgency in his tone changed, too. "I did see him. He was at the pub earlier. He came in and ordered a whisky on the rocks. I was working the bar, so I didn't keep tabs on him."

I turned and started jogging toward the Stag Head. "He could still be there now—we have to go."

"What about the police?" Pri asked, running after me.

"Let's make sure he's there first," I huffed, trying to keep pace with Liam. "They could know something we don't. I don't want to pull them away on a wild goose chase if they have him surrounded."

We made it across the park in record time.

Liam stopped in front of the pub. "What now?"

My lungs burned from exertion. I gasped for air. It had been a long time since I'd sprinted that fast. "We can't barge in there and make it obvious that we know."

A bead of sweat trickled down Pri's forehead. "Why don't you two go in? I'll wait out here for the police, assuming you call them."

"That works for me." Liam held out his hand. "Annie, shall we?"

"We don't need to hold hands," I protested. My pulse thundered like a drum in my ears.

"It's our cover," Liam replied, keeping his hand extended.

I wiped my sweaty palms on my dress and took his hand.

"Act natural. We're getting a drink, right?"

"Sure." I managed to squeak out a response, but I didn't trust myself to say more.

His touch sent a surge of electricity through my body.

He reached for the door and squeezed my hand. "Ready?"

"Uh-huh," I lied.

Van Morrison played on the overhead speakers inside the pub. I scanned the room, noticing a handful of regulars at the bar and scattered throughout the high-top tables.

"Pretend like we're looking for an open booth. And look like you're enjoying yourself," Liam said with a forced, fake laugh.

I plastered on a smile and scanned the pub. All of the booths were occupied. I craned my neck, hoping that I looked like I was searching for a table. My gaze landed on the farthest booth where Eli sat nursing a drink.

He spotted me and lifted his glass of whisky to his lips, which thinned in a twisted smile that was so full of hatred, I whimpered. His nostrils flared as his eyes blazed, shooting a venomous glare in our direction.

The room fell into a frosty silence.

Has the music stopped?

Does everyone else feel the steely determination raging from Eli like a silent warning that his anger is boiling just beneath the surface?

"We're cool. We're cool," Liam whispered, gripping my hand tighter in a show of solidarity.

Eli refused to break eye contact.

I had to get in touch with Dr. Caldwell—now.

But how?

"Should I get us drinks?" Liam asked, intentionally speaking loud enough for Eli to hear as we moved toward an open table near Eli.

Whether he knew it or not, he opened the perfect opportunity for me. "Sure, let me text Pri and see what she wants." I felt like I was auditioning for a play, and I had no idea if Eli was buying my performance.

Liam pulled out the chair and gently ushered me into a seat. He stood guard, blocking my view of Eli while I grabbed my phone and texted Dr. Caldwell and Pri.

> Eli's at the Stag Head. Send help!!!

"Pri would like a sangria if you have it," I said pointedly to Liam, tapping my screen to signal that I'd sent the message.

Liam didn't budge. "What about you?"

I couldn't see Eli's face, but I didn't need to. I could feel his fury. It hung in the air, swirling and mixing, waiting for a final jolt before it exploded.

"Um, what do you recommend?" I studied the menu, wondering if our act was at all convincing.

"I think you might like our Bootleggers Secret. It's bourbon with honey, lemon, and a touch of bitters. I can make it cold or hot, whatever you prefer."

Is this how Liam would act on a real date?

He was so much kinder than normal. I knew he was stalling to give the authorities time to arrive, but it was hard not to imagine cozying up with a cocktail with him.

"That sounds good." I smiled up at Liam, batting my lashes like we were in a rom-com.

"Be back in a minute." He gave me a nod and strolled to the bar with casual confidence.

"You. You sabotaged my event. You wanted me to fail." Eli's words were laced with bitterness. He pushed to his feet and swayed like he might topple over.

I gripped the table.

Stay calm, Annie.

You've trained for this. You have the upper hand.

"I can assure you I want nothing but success for all of the authors participating in the festival this weekend," I replied with sincerity.

Eli swiped at the air like he was trying to catch an errant fly or warming up to take a swing at me.

I moved my body to the side.

"You're the cause of all of this." Spit sprayed from his mouth as he spoke. He shook a finger in my face. "You're not going to get away with ruining my career."

I held the table as tightly as I could. If necessary, I could knock it over to block him.

Where are the police?

They should be here by now.

"What do you know? What do you know?" Eli's eyes narrowed into fiery slits.

His blistering anger felt dangerous. He was unhinged.

I wasn't sure he could be reasoned with. The pent-up

energy quivering in his body made me convinced that he was about to implode.

"Annie, you never told me if you wanted your drink hot or cold." Liam appeared like a gift from the heavens, placing his body between me and Eli like a barricade.

"I'd love it hot." I let out a deep, audible sigh. Never before had I been so grateful for Liam's presence.

Eli huffed and darted his eyes in every direction. I could tell that he realized he was no match for Liam and was trying to calculate his escape plan. In a flash, he made a break for the front door.

My heart dropped.

He couldn't get away. Not now. We were so close.

I didn't hesitate. Neither did Liam.

We raced for the door and were immediately blinded by flashing lights.

Sirens wailed, and a team of police officers stood at the ready.

Liam held me back. I watched in awe as the officers tackled Eli to the ground and read him his rights.

Pri snuck up next to us. "Good work, team. I think we deserve a fist bump."

"Or something much stronger." Liam bumped her fist.

"I'm so relieved the police were here. I didn't hear the sirens inside, so I was worried he was going to get away."

Pri doubled her fists and softly hit them against mine. "I had your back. I called Dr. Caldwell right away when I got your text. They were here in seconds and set up a perimeter. The other cars arrived right when you came outside."

My eyes drifted to Eli.

I wasn't in any danger now. Two officers flanked his sides and his hands were cuffed behind his back, but his beady eyes landed on me momentarily. I felt the hairs on my arms stand at attention when he directed all of his anger at me. If looks could kill, I might be on the ground at this very moment.

Law enforcement secured him in the back of one of the waiting squad cars.

A crowd had begun to gather, spilling onto the sidewalk and street in either direction.

"I wonder if Eli is the reason Kayla drank so heavily," I pondered out loud. "Especially this weekend. If she put it together and realized that Eli was who she saw in the woods all those years ago, it had to bring up so much trauma. No one believed her before. Who would believe her now? That would make me want to seek solace in a bottle of wine. It also makes me feel even sorrier for her."

"You couldn't have known that, though," Pri said reassuringly.

"I know, but I could have shown her more grace. She came across as so narcissistic, but now I have more empathy for where that came from." Why hadn't I been more kind to her? I felt terrible that Kayla had suffered alone.

Liam cleared his throat and placed a warm hand on my shoulder. "It's not your fault, Annie."

Who is this version of Liam Donovan?

And why do I feel like a teenager around him?

I didn't have time to dwell on my confusing feelings about my nemesis because Dr. Caldwell arrived in another squad car and took command of the scene. "Folks, sorry about the disruption. We appreciate your cooperation. The pub has been secured. You're free to return to your normal activities."

She instructed her team to let people pass. Then she approached us. "Is it safe to assume you're all doing okay?"

We nodded in unison.

"Thank you for alerting us to Eli's whereabouts. We're taking him to the station now. My team will need to follow up with each of you for an official statement. I'm heading to the hotel to relieve the rest of my team. You can either speak with one of the officers here or find me at the hotel."

"Well, I stand corrected, Annie," Liam said once Dr. Caldwell was out of earshot. "You may not have planned Eli's arrest as a stunt, but people are going to be talking about this for years to come."

"The weekend was already a success. Now it's going to be legendary." Pri snapped her fingers at Liam. "You know what this means?"

"What?" He tried to cover a smile.

"Annie's Mystery Fest will put Redwood Grove on the map. You're going to have to get on board, Mr. Donovan." She shook her index finger like she was scolding him.

Liam shook his head. "Over my dead body." Then he winked and strolled off to give his statement to a police officer waiting nearby.

"He's so into you." Pri threw her head back and laughed. "Can he be more obvious?"

I could feel my cheeks flushing and didn't trust myself to reply, so I gestured toward the park and said, "Should we go to the Grand Hotel and catch everyone up on what happened?" I didn't want to admit that Liam's physical proximity had been throwing me off balance.

"I thought you'd never ask." She grinned and laced her hand through mine.

TWENTY-NINE

As expected, the ballroom at the Grand Hotel was a flurry of activity. Word of Eli's arrest had already begun to spread.

"I can't believe how awesome this weekend has been." A reader grabbed my arm to stop me. "You're in charge, right?"

I smiled. "Not exactly in charge, but I did help organize the festival," I replied, feeling a surge of happiness and relief that the weekend had surpassed my wildest expectations despite the drama that had shaken my sweet hometown of Redwood for the last few days. It meant the world to me to know that the festival had resonated so deeply.

"When's the next one? Because I'm telling all of my friends, and I'm ready to book my tickets and hotel right now."

"Honestly, I hadn't thought that far ahead. We're just glad readers showed up."

"Oh, we'll show up and keep showing up. You should do them monthly. I'll come every month and bring dozens of friends." She made an X over her heart. "I promise. I'm ready to book my hotel for next month now."

"Monthly?" I winced. That might be a lot.

"Okay, how about once a quarter?" She wasn't giving up.

"You could do a Halloween event, a dark winter night weekend, and then something in the spring."

I had to admit that sounded pretty fun and I could feel my imagination sparking with ideas already. "I'll have to talk it through with everyone in town, but that's a great suggestion, and I'm so thrilled that you've enjoyed yourself."

"Enjoyed myself? It's the best weekend of my life." She took me by surprise and wrapped me in a tight hug. "Thank you for making my book dreams come true. I've met the most wonderful people who are going to be friends for life. I hope you understand what you've created here. You've created a community for readers to connect. That's huge."

When she finally released me, I felt my eyes misting. "Wow, thank you, that means a lot."

"It's true."

"You have a fan club," Pri teased when the reader let me go and headed off toward her friends. "Look at what you've created!" She swept her hand across the packed ballroom.

A swell of pride made me straighten my shoulders. "It is pretty amazing. I'm touched that readers had a good experience and want more."

"Oh, there are going to be more. Many, many more if I have anything to say about it," Pri replied with confidence. "Love the Halloween concept, by the way. We should get on that right away. I'm thinking a pumpkin and peril pour-over coffee for starters."

"You know I love Halloween, but maybe we should take a couple of days to regroup before we go all in for the next event."

"No way, we are 'gourd' to go here. You just pulled off a super successful event; we have to strike while the iron is hot, as they say. There's no time to waste."

"Oh no, not the puns." I clasped my face and hung my head, grinning from ear to ear. "Once the puns come out, I can't win."

"This is why you love me." She made a heart with her index

fingers and thumbs and then glanced at the bar. "Another drink while we brainstorm a total world domination with your next mystery event?"

"Okay, but only if it's coffee."

"I'll see what I can do, but I refuse to let you drink bitter hotel coffee that's been sitting in a pot for hours."

"Fair enough. I'll find a spot for us to sit." I suddenly felt exhausted and needed to get off my feet.

I found a cozy couch near the back shrouded by planted palms and plopped down, claiming my territory. I rested my head against the plush edge and took in the scene in the ballroom. Dr. Caldwell was talking with Monica and Seth near the front doors. Fletcher and Hal were deep in conversation with Caroline over by the drinks table.

I couldn't believe that I had considered Caroline a suspect not that long ago. I was relieved that she hadn't done it. I felt a sense of camaraderie with her and had a feeling that she would throw her support to future festivals. I could use Caroline on my side. And was it just my imagination, or did it seem like Hal agreed?

Hal caught my eye and waved. Then he said something to Caroline. The two of them got up from their table and headed my way. I noticed Hal's hand brush Caroline's. She looked at him with bright eyes, a hint of blush inching across her cheeks. He gazed at her with such tender adoration that it nearly took my breath away.

Hal was a bit older than Caroline, but still age appropriate. How cute. I made a mental note to use my investigative skills and find some subtle or maybe not-so-subtle ways to bring up Caroline's name at the bookshop.

"What a turn of events," Hal said with a shake of his head. "I didn't anticipate such a public arrest. Hercule himself would be proud of Dr. Caldwell's swift ability to close the case. And I know that you played no small part in tracking him down,

Annie. I always knew you were a star sleuth in the making." He gave me a warm smile and winked.

"I'm so relieved." Caroline placed her hand over her heart. "I was quite worried that she would arrest me. In fact, Hal came to my rescue. I had a panic attack earlier, and he helped calm me down."

So that was why she'd been crying in the Cryptic bathroom?

"What made you think Dr. Caldwell would arrest you?" I suspected I knew the answer but wanted to hear it from her.

"Circumstantial evidence." Caroline frowned, making her wrinkles more pronounced. "The police were very aware of what had happened between Kayla and me, and I would venture a guess that I had the most likely motive out of anyone in town."

"Except for Eli," Hal said, patting her arm in a show of support.

"There were plenty of other suspects, too." I told them about how, at different points throughout the weekend, I had convinced myself that Monica, Seth, and Justin had all done it. "Do you know why Kayla targeted you? Justin made it sound like she forced him to connect the two of you."

Caroline ran a manicured nail over her lips in contemplation. "I've wondered that as well. I think it was likely due to the nature of Artifacts. It's a relatively easy business model to replicate, and she probably realized she could easily take advantage of my lack of digital knowledge."

"That makes sense," I replied. "It doesn't make what she did to you any better, but it does explain her motive."

Caroline waved her hand in front of her face to stop herself from crying. "I do feel terrible for the things I said about her. I was angry, but I certainly didn't want her to die."

"None of us did." I was relieved that Caroline hadn't been involved in Kayla's death, and I understood how she felt. Kayla had made some serious mistakes, but none of them justified murder.

"I'm thankful for the authorities restoring our little town to order again. I'd happily keep murder between the pages," Hal said, reaching for Caroline's hand. "And I'm thankful for you, Annie."

Caroline leaned into him and smiled broadly. "I'll second that. All of Redwood Grove is grateful for everything you've done for our community."

I grinned and felt another surge of pride. As Hal and Caroline were called over to another conversation, I took a minute to let everything sink in. Now that I knew Kayla's killer had been caught, a huge weight fell off me. The weekend had saved the bookstore. For that, I was forever grateful. I had a job. I had a purpose, and it sounded like I had some future mystery festivals to plan.

Tomorrow, there were still a handful of author talks. Everything would wrap up by noon to allow readers time to travel home. I had intentionally scheduled a very light morning. It was quite fortuitous now. I couldn't imagine another full day of events. As soon as we sent the last of the readers home, I had a feeling I was going to take a well-earned break and cuddle up on my couch with Professor Plum and one of Pri's steaming pourovers. And maybe a little stash of mysteries that had been lingering on my TBR pile to keep my brain ticking over, just in case the urge to solve a crime stayed with me.

"Annie, do you mind if I join you?" Dr. Caldwell appeared out of nowhere, cradling a cup of tea.

"Sure."

She sat next to me, carefully balancing the steaming mug. "How are you holding up?"

"Pretty good, all things considered."

"Eli confessed, which should make the DA's case easier. My team is completing the interview and the mountains of paperwork that go with any arrest. Surely, you'll remember our discussions in class about the importance of proper documentation when filing reports. Paperwork might not be glamorous, but it's a necessity, especially in building a solid case for the prosecution." She crossed one leg over the other and sat back against the couch. "He admitted that he realized Kayla recognized him. After his reading at the Secret Bookcase, they happened to bump into each other. He claims that she wanted to talk to him. He believed she was going to blackmail him to keep quiet about his past. He found her passed out and seized the opportunity. Now it will be up to a judge and jury to decide his fate."

Poor Kayla. If only she had gone to Dr. Caldwell and the authorities, she would be alive now. "I guess it's good that he confessed."

"It is." She pressed her lips on the edge of her tea but didn't take a drink.

"Is there something wrong?"

She kept her eyes focused on the crowd. "Seeing you again, Annie, has brought some things back to the surface for me. I'm guessing the same is true for you?"

I nodded but couldn't say more.

She turned to me briefly to gauge my response. "This is going to be painful. Let me begin with an apology."

"Why would you need to apologize?" Painful? I didn't like the sound of that.

"Because there are some things about Scarlet's murder that I never shared with you." She plunged the tea packet into the hot water like she was buying time. I was used to Dr. Caldwell being direct and to the point. I didn't like this more cautious version of her. It had to mean that she knew something—or things—I wasn't going to like.

I thought I might throw up. I swallowed hard to force the mango margarita from earlier to stay down. "I don't understand."

"No, you wouldn't. Kayla's murder and Eli's confession have given me insight into how you operate. You've been a huge asset to this investigation. I can't thank you enough for that and I've realized that your unique skill set could be just what we need to finally get a break in Scarlet's unsolved case, even with you being so close to her. I think it's worth the risk, but I want to be completely transparent." She closed her eyes briefly and drank air in through her nose, deliberately buying herself a minute before continuing. "There are some things you need to know about Scarlet's death—things that I haven't been able to share. However, I need to warn you that if we go down this path, there's no turning back. Can you handle that?"

"Absolutely." I sat up. My heart thudded so hard against my chest that I thought I might crack a rib.

"Annie, this is serious," Dr. Caldwell said with a slight smile.

I felt a surge of determination. If there was a chance to find out who killed my friend and see justice delivered, then I was all ears. "I'm serious, too. Whatever you know about Scarlet's murder, I want in. All in. I don't care about the risks. I've spent almost ten years consumed by her death. I need answers."

Dr. Caldwell sighed and blew on her tea. "I can't guarantee that I can give you answers."

"What can you give me?"

"More information."

"I'm ready." I folded my hands together and squeezed them tight.

She gave me a small, pained smile that didn't reach her eyes. "I suspect you are. But there's no urgency. Do me a favor and sleep on it. Going down this path might eventually lead to answers, but I can't promise it will. You need to be sure, and there's going to be work ahead for both of us, together. We should start after a good night's sleep. Let's talk tomorrow."

I watched, wide-eyed, as she stood and walked away.

I wanted to run after her. I was ready. I was ready now.

If Dr. Caldwell had information, I wanted it. I didn't need a restful sleep to decide. Far from being exhausted by the events of this weekend, I felt energized. My mind was already made up.

Tomorrow.

Tomorrow, I would wake up and go straight to Dr. Caldwell's office.

Tomorrow, I would have my first breakthrough in Scarlet's cold case in years. There was no chance I was sleeping tonight. I took a deep breath and let my gaze roam around the busy ballroom, full of happy new customers and familiar faces I knew and loved, enjoying the celebration.

This was where I belonged. Where my future was. And tomorrow a new adventure was about to begin.

A LETTER FROM THE AUTHOR

I can't thank you enough for reading *The Body in the Bookstore*. I hope you enjoyed Annie's first foray into hosting a mystery festival. If you want to hear all about my upcoming books, what's next for Annie, bonus content, and more, sign up for my newsletter.

www.stormpublishing.co/ellie-alexander

If you enjoyed the book and could spare a few moments to leave an honest review, I would be forever grateful. Reviews really do help. Even a short review can make all the difference in encouraging a reader to discover my books for the first time. Thank you so much!

Thanks again for being part of this amazing journey with me, and I hope you'll stay in touch—I have so many more stories and projects in the works.

Happy reading,

Ellie

KEEP IN TOUCH WITH THE AUTHOR

www.elliealexander.co

facebook.com/elliealexanderauthor

instagram.com/ellie_alexander

tiktok.com/@elliealexanderauthor

ACKNOWLEDGMENTS

This book and series started long before I opened a blank document or typed a single word. I can trace its origins to the summer I turned thirteen and decided to read every Agatha Christie book shelved at my local library. I was convinced that librarians were illusionists who could extract my favorite reads from thin air. *The Body in the Bookstore*, or some version of it, has existed in my mind ever since. Over the years, I've spent countless hours lingering in libraries and bookshops, large and small, which have served as inspiration for creating Annie's world. By the way, adulthood has only solidified the fact that librarians are actually book sorcerers.

A big thanks to my reading crew on Patreon for early feedback, name suggestions, title ideas, and so much more. To Flo Cho, Courtny Drydale, Lily Gill, and Kat Webb, huge gratitude for our Zoom chats and discussions that helped me really start to flesh out Redwood Grove and the story.

I can't gush enough about the team at Storm, especially my editor, Vicky Blunden. It's been incredible to have a partner in building out this series. Thank you for the tea and brainstorming sessions, your enthusiasm for Annie and the cast of characters, and your insight into making this book the best possible version it could be. I'm so thrilled to be working with the innovative team and Storm, and I'm absolutely awed by your vision for the future of publishing and the way you build community with authors.

A special shoutout to Gordy and Luke for being my hype

team. Thanks for the book road trips, dinner chats, merch, Mystery Fest planning, and always being up for any book adventure. I love that writing is a family affair, and am so glad you're my family.

Last but not least, to you. Thanks for making the world a better place just by the sheer acting of reading—reading anything!

Made in the USA
Middletown, DE
03 July 2024